WHISPERING PINES SERIES

Everything I Long For

MELODY CARLSON

HARVEST HOUSE PUBLISHERS
Eugene, Oregon 97402

Cover by David Uttley Design, Sisters, Oregon

Map illustration by Jan Cieloha, Springfield, Oregon

EVERYTHING I LONG FOR
Copyright © 2000 by Melody Carlson
Published by Harvest House Publishers
Eugene, OR 97402

ISBN 0-7394-0908-5

*I lovingly dedicate this book to my sweet husband;
for he is, without a doubt, the single earthly
representation of everything I long for.
This one's for you, Christopher!*

*All my love,
Melody*

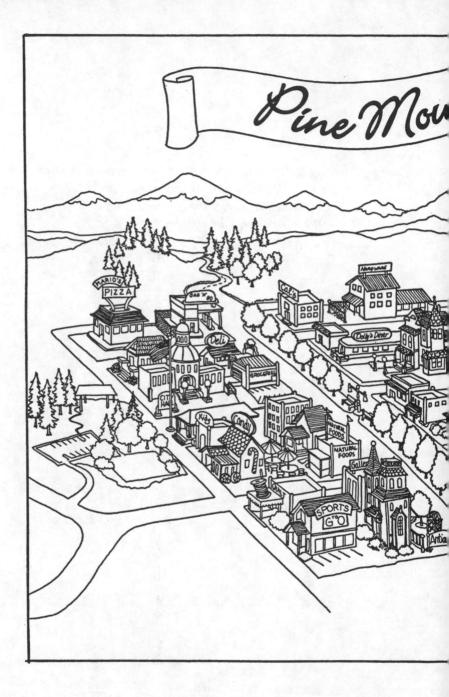

One

*L*aying down the weekly paper, she reached across her cluttered desk to answer the phone. "Maggie Carpenter," she said automatically as she circled an overlooked typo with bright red ink.

"Mom?" Spencer's voice sounded urgent.

Her pen stopped. "What is it, Spence?"

"I found a girl!"

"What do you mean you 'found a girl'?" She smiled to herself then added, "Does Sierra know about this new development?"

"Mom, be serious. I found *this* girl out in the woods."

"Was she lost?"

"Not exactly."

"Well, does she live around here then?"

"I don't think so."

Maggie's voice grew firm. "Spencer, could you deal me a few facts here?"

"Well, I took Bart to the woods like I always do, and I found this girl wrapped up in an old army blanket, lying underneath a tree. At first I thought she was dead or something 'cause it seemed pretty weird to be lying out there all by herself. When I realized she was just asleep, I thought she might have something to do with those drug guys, but then

I saw she was all alone and all she had was a backpack with her..."

"Where is she now?"

"In the kitchen."

"You brought her home?"

"Yeah. I couldn't leave her out there like that."

Maggie frowned. "How old is she? Do you know her name?"

"She won't talk to me. But I think she's about my age. Maybe older. Grandma's trying to get her to eat something. She's awfully skinny."

"Will you please put your grandmother on the phone, Spence?"

Maggie drummed her fingers on her desk as she waited. Who could this strange girl be, and what should she do about her? Notify the authorities?

"Hello, Maggie," said her mother cheerfully. "I told Spence he should call and let you know that he brought home a girl."

"You make it sound as if he'd simply brought home another stray dog."

Audrey chuckled. "Well, it's sort of like that."

Maggie groaned. "Hopefully he doesn't want to keep her too. I wonder if I should call the sheriff."

"Maybe not just yet." Her mother lowered her voice. "She looks pretty down and out. I feel real sorry for her."

"I think I'll come home and see for myself exactly what's going on there." She hung up and began loading her briefcase.

"I've got to go home early today," she called to Abigail.

Abigail looked up from her filing. "Anything wrong?"

"No. It just seems Spencer has brought home another stray."

"He sure loves animals, doesn't he?"

Maggie smiled, not ready to divulge the nature of this particular stray. "Yes, he has always had a big heart. He's a lot like his dad in that way."

Abigail wagged a finger at her. "Not *just* his dad, Maggie."

⌒

When she got home, the three of them were sitting silently around the table. Maggie did a quick study of the strange girl sitting in her kitchen. Being a reporter had helped her become fairly adept at processing a lot of details simultaneously. The girl was probably in her late teens, which would make her older than Spencer. She was petite and very thin with long brunette hair and large brown eyes that were smudged underneath with dark circles. Sad eyes, as if they had seen too much too soon. She glanced at the girl's bare arms to search for needle tracks but thankfully found them clean. The girl was somewhat attractive in a waif-like way, but her face was extremely pale—especially for this time of summer when most kids sported a tan. And her ragged clothing was in dire need of a good wash. Maggie sat down next to her, resting her arms on the pine kitchen table, the one Jed Whitewater's hands had carefully crafted and finished.

"I'm Maggie," she began gently, looking straight into the girl's blank face. The girl said nothing, just sat there with her arms hanging limply at her sides, so still it almost seemed she wasn't breathing. Maggie glanced over at Spencer and her mother as they looked on with interest. Then she cleared her throat. "It appears that you may be in some kind of trouble," she spoke more firmly this time, hoping to capture the girl's attention. "We'd like to help you, but if you can't tell us what's going on we'll be forced to call the sheriff and have him handle this."

The girl's eyelashes flickered ever so slightly and Maggie grew hopeful.

"Now, are you able to speak?" she asked.

The girl nodded by barely dipping her chin, then sighed.

"Would you like for us to help you?"

"No one can help me," said the girl in a raspy voice just above a whisper.

Maggie blinked in surprise, and Audrey reached over to take the girl's hand as she spoke. "We can only help you if you let us, honey."

Silent tears began to trickle down the girl's smooth cheeks, and Maggie felt her heart go out to this poor, stray girl that her son had found sleeping in the woods. "Has she eaten anything?" she asked, glancing at her mother. She sadly shook her head.

Maggie picked up a spoon from the bowl of chicken soup still on the table and held it before the girl. "First you must eat something, and then you'll have some rest. After that we'll talk. Okay?"

The girl nodded again, then took the spoon. After a couple of hesitant bites she began to eat more hungrily. Audrey nudged Spencer with her elbow. "You see," she explained with a wink, "it's never wise to discuss important matters on an empty stomach."

Before long, the girl had finished most of the soup and a full glass of milk, and then Maggie led her to an upstairs bedroom. Maggie quickly rummaged through her own dresser until she found a clean oversized T-shirt for the girl to rest in. After posting Spencer downstairs, Maggie took the girl's dirty clothing along with a ratty-looking backpack to the laundry.

"Are you really going to wash those awful rags?" asked Audrey. "I think I'd just burn them."

"And how would that make her feel?"

"I suppose you're right." Audrey perused through the backpack. "There are a few more bits of clothing in here, but they look almost as bad as what she had on. Better throw them in too. This girl is traveling awfully light. There's a little loose change, a watch, and a necklace in the bottom, but that's about all she has."

"She seems to be down on her luck," said Maggie as she poured in a generous amount of soap and turned on the washer.

"Sad, isn't it?"

Maggie nodded. "It wasn't unusual to see homeless kids and runaways down in the L.A. area, but I thought I'd gotten away from all that up here."

"No escape, is there?"

"I guess not." She sighed sadly. "What'll we do with her, Mom?"

"That's mostly up to her. But first off we need to find out exactly what her situation is—whether she's a runaway or a throwaway."

"Neither scenario sounds very good to me." Maggie pulled a load of towels from the dryer and began to fold them. "You know, Mom, I nearly ran away a time or two."

Audrey picked up a towel and gave it a shake. "I'm not surprised, dear. There were times when I wondered why we all didn't just run away."

Maggie stopped folding and stared at her incredulously. It was the first time her mother had ever openly acknowledged that a problem had existed within their family's home. "And all this time, I thought it was just me."

Her mother shook her head and smoothed the towel. "No, it wasn't just you, honey. I know it must've seemed as if your father's anger was directed solely at you, but we all got a fair share of it from time to time. And after you left home for college, your father focused his acrimonious attentions onto Barry."

"Poor Barry. He never told me."

"He probably thought it was simply his turn to take what you'd been getting all those previous years." Audrey shook her head sadly.

"And besides, we never really talked about *it*."

"It. Like some dreadful disease that we had to keep secret lest the neighbors find out."

"Exactly." Maggie placed another towel on the quickly growing stack. "If we could pretend that *it* wasn't there, then we could continue to live our normal little lives hoping that no one was the wiser."

"Except that you kids rarely brought your friends home."

"Too risky. We never knew for sure when Dad would go into one of his tirades and begin yelling about one thing or another…"

"Like leaving your bike in the yard…"

Maggie nodded grimly. "Or forgetting to turn off a light in the living room…"

"Or not having dinner ready on time…" Audrey's voice caught and Maggie noticed that her eyes had grown misty.

"I'm sorry, Mom," she said, placing a hand on her mother's arm. "I didn't mean to dig up old wounds like this."

"It's okay, honey." Audrey blotted her tears with a hand towel. "You know, I've always wanted to talk with you about this, but it was just so hard to bring it up."

"I know. And after Dad died, I figured that was the end of the whole thing anyway. I thought if we didn't talk about it, it would slowly go away of its own accord. But I guess it never completely left any of us."

Audrey looked at her compassionately. "Yes, even though your father's dead, our memories are still very much alive. And sometimes memories can be cruel. How many, many times I've wanted to tell you how sorry I was for what you kids went through during those years. Sometimes I look back in retrospect and wonder why I didn't just leave him, but you kids were so little and I felt trapped financially. If only I'd known about counseling back then. I didn't realize how things could've gone so differently. And I know your dad was frustrated, parenting just like his father before him, doing the very things he'd vowed not to do. And despite his problem with anger, your father always was a good provider. I guess I just kept hoping that things would get better as you kids got older. I mean, everyone loses their patience with little kids from time to time. And then you remember how he was always so sorry and contrite after one of his ridiculous outbursts."

"I remember. But I think it would've been easier and less confusing if he'd just been mean all the time." She paused and closed her eyes for a moment, then said, "You know, sometimes I truly felt like Dad loved me, but at other times I was equally certain that he hated me."

"What do you think now, Maggie?" Audrey studied her daughter's face.

"I actually believe that he loved me—that he loved all of us. But I also think he had a very real problem with anger."

Audrey nodded. "That's what I believe too. After he died and I went back to college to get my counseling degree, it occurred to me that I should've done something back at the very beginning, gotten help when I first began to see a pattern emerging. Just 20-20 hindsight, I suppose. Even now I don't know if I can ever completely forgive myself for not doing something."

"But you didn't know any of that counseling stuff back when we were kids, Mom. You did the best you could. And look, Barry and I turned out just fine—at least I hope we did."

Her mother smiled. "Of course you did! Although I do wish Barry would find a nice girl and settle down. But you know how proud I am of both of you."

"And you know, Mom, I do believe that God can use these hard things in our lives. Somehow he manages to bring good out of evil."

Audrey pressed her lips together. "I'd like to believe that too. But the truth is, most of the time I just don't allow myself to think about that part of my life very much. It's too painful."

"But what if our pain can help us to understand someone else's troubles? Doesn't it almost seem worth the price?"

Her mother looked thoughtful. "You mean like our little stray upstairs?"

"Yes. When I looked into her eyes, I saw her sadness and it reminded me of my own teen years. I felt a real empathy for her. And although I suspect her story is probably a lot worse than mine—most of them are nowadays—at least maybe I can relate to her just a little because of what I went through."

"I hope so, dear. The poor girl certainly seems to be in need. The question is, will she allow anyone to help her?"

"All we can do is try." Maggie placed the last towel on top. "And pray."

Audrey's brows lifted. "You seem to put a lot of stock into prayer these days. Is that something new or just something I was never fully aware of before?"

Maggie thought for a moment. She had never shared much about her faith with her mother, and she wasn't even sure where to begin now. "I suppose I first started depending on prayer after losing Phil, then even more so after moving up here to Pine Mountain. And the amazing thing is how God actually answers my prayers."

"You know I believe in God, Maggie." Her mother frowned slightly. "But I guess I never figured that he actually takes time to listen to our prayers. I suppose I think that praying is more for us than anything."

"Sort of like therapy?"

"Yes. I always encouraged my patients to address a higher power if that was important to them. But I must confess I considered it to be purely therapeutic."

"Maybe," said Maggie as she picked up the laundry basket. "But the difference to me is that besides simply the benefit of feeling better, and there's certainly nothing wrong with that, I find when I pray that I see real things happen. And that's what I call the God factor."

Her mother grinned skeptically. "'The God factor'? Sounds like the title of some sci-fi novel. What exactly do you mean?"

Maggie laughed. "It's sort of hard to describe, but I've seen real life circumstances change and suddenly improve for no explainable reason, and I credit that to God's intervention. When it happens you can't miss it."

Two

"You've done an amazing job with these flower beds, Mom," said Maggie as she stepped out onto the deck, balancing a large platter as she closed the glass door behind her. "The colors are just gorgeous." She opened the barbecue and placed a large whole salmon on the hot grill, watching with satisfaction as it began to sizzle.

"A lot of these plants were already here; they just needed a little fertilizer, some tilling, and a lot of encouragement." Audrey smoothed a bright madras plaid cloth over the picnic table. "I'm glad we're eating outside. Abigail mentioned just last week how we all had better enjoy every sunny day from here on out because fall's right around the corner."

"I know, but I still find it hard to believe. It seems impossible that it's already the end of August. Although I must admit, I'm looking forward to seeing some real seasons."

"Do you think you'll really like all that snow and ice in the wintertime?" Audrey shuddered as if the mere thought of it made her cold.

"I hope so. I don't have much choice, do I?"

"Well, if things don't work out, you and Spence can always come live with me in San Jose."

"Thanks, but who knows, Mom, you may decide you like it year-round here after all. You might even want to sell your house in San Jose and relocate here permanently."

Her mother neatly arranged the last place setting. "I suppose stranger things have happened. But I just can't imagine me enjoying a cold, icy winter very much, especially at my age when arthritis is probably right around the corner."

Maggie glanced over her mother's shoulder to see Spencer motioning to her from the dining room doorway. "I bet our stray girl is awake," she whispered. "I'll go check. Can you keep an eye on the salmon?"

She found the girl standing in the upstairs hallway with a dazed expression, almost as if she couldn't quite remember where she was. "Hello there," said Maggie tentatively. "You've had a nice, long sleep. You must have been exhausted." She pointed to the bathroom. "I put some clothes and bath things in there for you. Go ahead and get cleaned up and then come downstairs. We're eating outside this evening."

"Thanks," the girl muttered without lifting her eyes to meet Maggie's.

"Dinner will be ready pretty soon. The salmon's already cooking."

Maggie met Spencer at the foot of the stairs. "Try and make her feel comfortable, Spence. Maybe see if you can find out her name."

In the kitchen she began making a salad, but her mind was on the girl. Even though she felt it was the right thing to help her, she wondered if it was crazy to take a stranger in like this. Who knew what problems the girl might have? What if she was wanted for some sort of crime?

"Hey there!"

Maggie jumped in surprise, causing her knife to clatter to the floor. She quickly turned to see Buckie Porterfield coming through the doorway with a large, flat package in his hands.

"Sorry, Maggie. Didn't mean to startle you."

She picked up the knife and rinsed it in the sink. "That's okay." She glanced at the clock. "But what are you doing here, Buckie? Just in time for dinner too."

He grinned sheepishly. "I guess I hadn't noticed the time. But I come bearing gifts." He laid the package on the table and removed the brown paper to reveal a beautifully framed photo.

"My barn!" she exclaimed, eagerly wiping her hands on a kitchen towel. "And there's Spencer and Bart. Oh, Buckie, it's wonderful! Do I really get to keep it?"

He grinned. "You bet. Remember when I took it?"

"Was it that day when you first came here to take photos for the magazine?"

"Yep. I still remember you storming out, all irritated because I was snooping around…"

"I suppose I was a little grumpy that morning." She held up the photo to admire. "I know just where I'll hang this. Thank you, Buckie. And now, it would only be right for me to properly invite you for dinner."

He rubbed his hands together. "I saw the salmon on the barbecue when I said hello to Audrey. It smelled mighty good."

"And we have another guest too." She lowered her voice. "Spencer found a girl in the woods, probably a runaway. We're trying to help her."

His brows raised. "I'd be careful if I were you. Kids like that usually come with a lot of problems. Could be drugs—or even worse. And you never know, she might just be casing your house so she can steal…"

"Shh," she hissed. "I hear someone."

"And to finish our tour, here we are back in the kitchen," Spencer announced formally as he led the girl into the room. He looked over and saw Buckie, then turned to the girl. "Leah, I'd like you to meet Buckie Porterfield." He nodded to Buckie. "This is Leah."

Maggie smiled at her son's unusually good manners, then noticed the transformation of the girl—*Leah*. Her hair, still wet from her shower, was neatly parted and combed; her ragged jeans were now clean with a fresh white T-shirt tucked in—one that Maggie had donated from her own closet. "I hope you're hungry, Leah. I fixed enough to feed an army."

"Well then, it's a good thing I stopped by," said Buckie as he popped a radish into his mouth. "Is that corn on the cob in that pot?"

"Yes, and it's time for everyone to help out." She assigned tasks, even asking Leah to fill a pitcher with ice water. Soon everything was ready and they were all seated at the picnic table outside.

"Spencer, will you say grace?" asked Maggie.

Spencer glanced at Leah, then bowed his head and said their regular blessing. He added, "And help us so we can help Leah, and make her feel at home here. Amen."

Food began to be passed around and small talk was made, but Leah remained silent, just watching and listening with wide dark eyes. Maggie hoped the girl was feeling a little more comfortable, and thankfully noted that she was eating.

"So, Leah," began Buckie, "where are you from?"

The table grew quiet. Leah laid down her fork and looked at him, then exhaled slowly as if calculating how best to answer. Finally she said, "Lots of places, I guess."

"Lucky for you," said Maggie quickly. "I'd only lived in California before we moved up here. But I'm sure enjoying the change." She glanced at Spencer. "And Spencer had only lived in the Los Angeles area."

"Yeah. And when I heard we were moving out to the boonies of Oregon I didn't want to come."

Audrey laughed. "But you sure came around. So, Spence, have you missed your old home very much?"

His brow creased. "Yeah, at first. I guess I missed my friends most of all. But I do still sort of miss our old house and neighborhood too sometimes."

"Are you sorry we came then?" asked Maggie, unsure of what his answer would be or if it was even smart to ask.

He shrugged. "Nope. I like it here. I mean it's sort of boring sometimes, but in some ways there's more stuff to do—outdoor stuff. And I've made some good friends."

"And school will be starting before long," added Audrey optimistically. "That'll keep you busy."

"And then there will be snowboarding," said Buckie with enthusiasm.

"Yeah!" agreed Spencer. "That's something I'm really looking forward to."

The conversation began to flow more easily again, and thankfully Buckie didn't try to extract any more information from Leah.

"How's business in your gallery, Buckie?" asked Maggie as she refilled his water glass.

"It's great. In fact, I think I'll have to hire some help soon. Especially now that I have a photo shoot in Alaska coming up before the cold weather sets in. At first, I thought I'd just keep the gallery open while I'm in town, but business is going so well with our fair-weather tourists that I hate to close up shop and lose any customers."

"It shouldn't be hard to find someone to help out," said Maggie. "You should ask Rosa, she'll probably know of someone looking for work."

"Or Elizabeth," suggested Audrey. "She just hired another girl for the Window Seat." She smiled at Leah. "That's a bookstore and coffee shop, dear. You'd probably like it. The young folks seem to spend a lot of time there."

"Don't you like it, Grandma?" asked Spencer.

She set down her glass. "Well, it's a nice business and all, but you know I always did enjoy going to the public library. That's something this town could use."

"That's a great idea," said Buckie. "Why don't you start one?"

Audrey laughed. "Oh, I wouldn't know the first thing about starting a library."

"You could learn, Grandma. Aren't you the one who's always telling me that nothing's impossible?"

She grew thoughtful for a moment. "I suppose I could do some research and find out what it takes..." She glanced at Maggie. "Say, you got all that grant money for the town and the road repairs, do you suppose there's any more funding available for something like this?"

"Could be, Mom. Why don't you have Spencer show you how to access the Internet and do some research online?"

"I might just do that."

While Spencer and Leah cleared the table, Maggie dished up ice cream topped with fresh raspberries in the kitchen.

"Thank you for dinner, Mrs. Carpenter," said Leah quietly as she watched her spoon red, juicy berries onto the ice cream.

She turned to the girl, slightly surprised by her formal manner. "You're very welcome, Leah. But you can call me Maggie."

Leah nodded solemnly. "Shall I take these out now?"

"Sure, let's each grab a couple dishes. Like Mom always says, 'many hands make light work.'"

After dessert, Spencer showed Leah around the outside property and then they threw a tennis ball for Bart to chase. Meanwhile, Maggie, Buckie, and Audrey relaxed with coffee in the long evening shadows on the front porch. A gentle breeze whispered through the leaves of the nearby aspens, and the few wispy clouds took on a peachy-pink hue in a pleasing contrast to the dusky periwinkle sky. In the west, the sharp outline of the mountains was softened by a curtain of hazy smoke—the remnant of a small forest fire twenty miles south and now under control. A perfect August evening.

"How completely bucolic." Maggie leaned back into the wicker rocker, allowing the peace of the evening to wash over her like a warm, gentle shower.

"That's such a strange-sounding word to describe this lovely setting," said Buckie. "Somehow, the word bucolic always makes me think of a sick cow."

"A *sick cow*?" Maggie frowned over at Buckie.

Audrey chuckled. "You mean like *bovine colic?*"

"That must be it!" said Buckie.

"You're both crazy," said Maggie, then she sighed with satisfaction. "But look at that sky. Isn't it absolutely blissful out here?"

Buckie frowned. "Well you know what they say, ignorance can be blissful too."

Maggie stopped rocking and glanced sharply at him. "Are you just being difficult, or do you have a specific point here?"

He nodded towards the two teenagers now tossing a stick for Bart. "Like I said earlier, you'd better be careful about taking in strangers like that."

She bristled. "What would you suggest I do, call the sheriff?"

"Maybe."

"But if Leah ran away, she might have some very good reasons."

"Or she might be running from the law," suggested Buckie.

Audrey leaned forward to join in the conversation. "She doesn't exactly strike me as a dangerous criminal, Buckie."

"You never really know," he replied. "Until it's too late, that is."

Maggie leaned back into her rocker and closed her eyes. "Well, I'm not worried. Besides, if I called the sheriff she might just run away again."

"Then it would be her problem, not yours."

Maggie threw up her hands and looked to her mother for support. "Do you think I should call the sheriff, Mom? After all, you're the counselor—you should have all the answers, right?"

Audrey sighed. "If only it were so simple. But I happen to agree with you, Maggie. I don't see how calling the sheriff can help. I think we need to get to know Leah and see if there's anything we can do to help her. She's obviously in some kind of trouble…"

"See," said Buckie, pointing to Maggie. "That's what I'm trying to say…"

"I *said* she's in some kind of trouble," interrupted Audrey sharply, "but not necessarily of her own making. It's quite possible that she has been a victim of some sort."

"Oh…." At least that seemed to quiet him. And perhaps it gave him something to think about too.

Maggie leaned back into her chair again. "I know you're just thinking of our welfare, Buckie. But we're not complete fools. If we see some sort of warning signs, we'll certainly be careful. But for now, we just need to earn her trust." She looked out across the steadily darkening horizon in time to see the shadow of a nighthawk streaking down from the sky to the nearby grass field, probably snatching up some unfortunate mouse that had ventured out too early for his evening meal.

ᴖ

Later that evening, just before bedtime, Maggie looked through her closet to find a few more items of clothing to add to Leah's meager and raggedy wardrobe. Then she knocked gently on the spare bedroom door.

"Come in."

Maggie opened the door tentatively. "Here are some things I don't need, Leah," she held the small stack before her. "They might be a little big on you, but that seems to be the style nowadays anyway."

"Why are you being so nice to me?"

Maggie blinked in surprise at the blunt question, then sat down in the rocking chair across from the narrow single bed. She studied Leah for a moment, the large eyes set into the small pale face reminded her of the wide-eyed moppet prints that her mother used to have hanging on their bathroom wall. Once again, Leah wore the oversized T-shirt as a nightgown, and she sat cross-legged on the bed with a book in her lap. "Because we like you, Leah," Maggie finally answered in a quiet voice.

"How can you like me?" Leah frowned down at the unopened paperback. "You don't even know me."

Maggie thought for a moment, then pointed to the book resting in Leah's lap. "I know they say you can't judge a book by its cover, but what made you pick that particular book up?"

The girl shrugged. "It just seemed interesting."

Maggie smiled. "It is. And it happens to be one of my favorites. Madeleine L'Engle is a brilliant author. I think you'll like her too."

Leah studied Maggie, then finally spoke. "Are you saying that, like this book, you've somehow judged me by my cover?"

"You seem to be a very perceptive young woman," said Maggie. "And I suppose you're partially right. But I'd like to say it's more than just your *cover,* because the truth is, when we first met you your *cover* was a little misleading."

Leah nodded sadly. "I must've looked pretty bad."

"But even so, we could see something beneath that. And whatever it is, we happen to like it. And we want to help you—if you want our help, that is."

"At first, I didn't want anyone's help. I just wanted to be left alone under that tree to..." She bit her lip and then exhaled slowly. "But now I guess I'm not so sure what I want anymore."

"Well, you don't have to make up your mind tonight. Get a good night's rest, and we'll talk again in the morning."

Leah frowned, averting her eyes from Maggie's gaze. Then Maggie noticed Leah's backpack, neatly packed and leaning next to the bed as if she were planning to make a quick escape.

"I guess I'm assuming that you'll still be here in the morning, Leah."

The girl didn't answer.

Maggie stood now, setting the small pile of clothes on the chair. "What you do with your life is up to you. If we can be of any help, we're more than willing, but we won't keep you here against your will." She sighed. "If you choose to keep running it seems that your life will only get more difficult."

Leah still didn't look up, and Maggie moved towards the door.

"Thanks, Maggie," she said quietly.

"You're very welcome. And just for the record, I really do hope you'll stay. I like you, Leah, and I'd like to get to know you better. We may have more in common than you realize. Good night."

She closed the door and walked to her own room. Was this the last she'd see of the girl? Should she have said something more? Been more forceful with her? More convincing? Or, like Buckie suggested, should she have simply called the sheriff? No clear answers came. And so, once again, she prayed for wisdom, and then finally just placed Leah in God's hands. There seemed nothing more to do.

Three

The next morning, Leah was gone.

Maggie tried to shake off the gloomy cloud that now seemed to hang over their house as she gathered her things for work. Why should she have expected anything else of her in the first place? And why should it even matter? Less than twenty-four hours ago she hadn't even known the girl existed.

"I just don't see why she didn't stay," said Spencer as he dejectedly poked his spoon around a bowl of soggy-looking cereal. Up much earlier than usual, he'd been the one to make the initial discovery that Leah had slipped away without so much as leaving a note. And to Maggie's dismay even the donated clothing had been left behind. A shame when the girl had so little to begin with.

"I don't know either, Spence. I really did try to make her feel welcome."

"What do you think she'll do now, Mom?"

Maggie shrugged and picked up her briefcase. "Hopefully, she'll go back home or get some help. All we can do now is pray for her safety."

"At least we tried," said Audrey as she poured a second cup of coffee.

"I'll see you two this afternoon," said Maggie, trying to sound cheerful.

As she drove to work, she found herself looking to the left and right, searching for Leah. With virtually no money and no mode of transportation, how would this poor girl ever get to where she needed to be? And where exactly was that anyway? Once again, she prayed that God would intervene and help the lost girl. There seemed little else to do.

"Good morning," chirped Abigail as Maggie stepped into the newspaper office. "Everything turn out okay at home yesterday?"

Maggie forced a smile. "Yes. Everyone's just fine. Anything new here?"

"Well, old Mrs. Bowerman called this morning with another one of her 'newsworthy' stories."

Maggie smiled as Scott stuck his head around the corner and called out, "What is it this time—a porcupine stuck in a garbage pail?"

"No. But it seems that a family of skunks have made themselves right at home underneath her back porch steps— a mother and three little ones."

Maggie shook her head. "That poor woman has more problems with animals..."

"It might help if she had her garbage picked up," said Scott. "She leaves trash all over the place, and every animal this side of the Cascades thinks she runs the local wildlife diner. I'm surprised it wasn't a black bear this time. Now *that* might be a good story."

"And then she has all those animal feeders," reminded Abigail. "I'm sure she spends more money on wild animal food than she does for her own groceries."

"I think she's just lonely," said Maggie. "The animals seem to be her only friends." She thought for a moment. "Maybe we should do a feature on her, Scott. How about something like: She Talks to the Animals."

"Well, there isn't much in this week's paper," he said. "I suppose it wouldn't hurt to throw in a human interest piece. I could spice it up a little. Might be fun."

"Why don't you go out there this morning and get some photos and see if you can make a story out of it? If nothing else she'd love the company."

"Just watch out for those skunks," warned Abigail. "My husband, God bless him, had a run-in with a skunk once and it took *weeks* to get rid of that horrible smell. I even gave him a bath in tomato juice, but there was nothing left to do but burn his clothes. But I must admit I didn't mind seeing his nasty old hunting jacket going up in flames."

Scott winked at her. "I'll be real careful, Abigail."

Maggie worked most of the day on a story explaining how the new grant funds would be used for various town improvements, and barely took time for lunch. Finally it was almost four and she was ready to call it a day.

"Excuse me, Maggie," said Abigail on the intercom. "Someone to see you."

Maggie pushed the button. "Who is it?"

"A young woman." Then her voice quieted. "She says her name is Leah Hill. Do you want to see her or…"

"Send her right in, Abigail." Maggie saved her story, then turned her full attention to the door which was opening slowly.

"I'm sorry to bother you," began Leah as her pale face peeked inside. "I know you're busy. Spencer told me how you run this newspaper and everything…"

"No bother," said Maggie. "Come on in, Leah. Sit down."

Leah dropped her backpack onto the floor with a thud, then sank wearily into the chair opposite the desk. "I'm sorry I left without saying goodbye."

Maggie smiled at her. "A goodbye would have been nice."

"I really wanted to stay, but I…I just didn't want to be a…I don't know…" Leah's chin dropped to her chest and little sobs began to shake her shoulders.

Maggie rose from her chair and went over to place a hand on her hunched-over back. "It's okay, honey. You're still welcome to stay with us if you'd like. We really do want to help you."

She looked up with dark, watery eyes. "Really?"

Maggie nodded as she handed her a tissue. "But if we're going to help you, you'll have to be honest with us. Can you do that?"

"I think so."

"Good." Maggie stepped back and leaned against her desk. "For starters, what brings you to Pine Mountain—or were you just on your way to someplace else?"

"I was on my way to Pine Mountain."

"Why?"

She shrugged. "It's a long story."

"I've got time." Maggie moved back around her desk, seating herself comfortably in her chair as she studied the dark shadows beneath the girl's hollow eyes. "Have you had anything to eat today?"

Leah shook her head and Maggie pushed the intercom button. "Abigail, would you bring in some juice, please? And see if that box of crackers is still around—and is there any cheese in the fridge?"

Within moments, Abigail brought in two bottles of apple juice and a nicely arranged plate of cheese and crackers. Glancing curiously at the girl, she set them on the desk and then left without saying a word. Maggie waited as Leah ate, distracting herself by casually proofing a freelance story about the school's new computers that had just arrived that week. Finally she looked up and noticed that the cheese and crackers were completely gone and Leah was just finishing her juice. "Now," began Maggie, "you were going to tell me what brings you to Pine Mountain."

"I came here from...from Arizona," began Leah, as if to catch herself from repeating a specific name of a town. "My mother has some...uh, some problems. She has a pretty hard time just getting by, if you know what I mean. But she does her best, and I always tried to help her as much as I could. But when she married this last guy, at least I think they're married...Well, anyway, he is just such a lowlife...And finally I just couldn't stand him anymore. So, I got a job at a café and saved up almost every penny, including tips, for a whole month just so I could come up here."

Maggie nodded as she absently drummed a pencil on her desk. "But that still doesn't tell me *why* you came up here."

Leah looked directly into her eyes. "Can I trust you?"

Maggie blinked. "Of course you can."

"Will you promise not to repeat this to anyone?"

She considered this for a moment. "Well, it depends. If it concerns anything dangerous or illegal..."

"No. It's not anything like that. It's just personal."

"Then you can trust me, Leah."

"Well, a long time ago my mom told me about my real father. She doesn't even remember because she was sort of out of it. You see, she got pregnant with me when she was about my age..."

"And that would be?"

"I'm eighteen. Anyway, this one time I needed some money for a school choir trip and she was pretty drunk or high or both, not to mention broke, and she told me I should just go on up to Pine Mountain, Oregon and ask my dad since he was the one with all the money. I was only about thirteen then, but I wrote down the name of the town and hid it. Later on, I even looked it up on a road map. And for the next few years, especially when things got really bad, I'd tell myself I was going to Pine Mountain to find my dad."

"And did you find him?"

Leah sighed and shook her head. "I've looked in the phone book and even asked around town, but no one seems to have ever heard of him."

"Do you mind telling me your father's name?"

"That might be the problem. My mom told me my dad's name was Jerry Jones. But there's no such name in the phone book, and I asked several people who say they've lived here all their lives and no one has even heard of him or that name."

"Are you sure your father was from Pine Mountain?"

"Well, one time when I mentioned Pine Mountain to my mom, she got all shook up and wondered how I'd found out about it. It seemed like I'd hit the nail on the head."

Maggie considered this. "Then perhaps you've gotten your father's name wrong."

Leah nodded. "I think that could be. My mom might've told me that name just to throw me off track. I heard her mention to a friend once about how she got some big chunk of money from my birth father just because she agreed never to contact him."

"I see." Suddenly Maggie began to consider all the men she knew who'd lived in town long enough, and were old enough, to be Leah's father. And the list wasn't short. But for some reason there was one name that stood out in her mind—Gavin Barnes. It seemed just the sort of thing he might've been mixed up in. Besides that, even if he had nothing to show for it now, everyone knew that Gavin came from money.

"Do you have any ideas who he might be?" Leah looked at her hopefully.

Maggie pressed her lips together. "No doubt there are a number of possibilities. But I don't know where you'd even begin, Leah. It's not as if most men would own up to fathering a child so long ago. Especially if he went to such trouble to pay off your mother to keep quiet."

"I know." Leah shook her head. "It's hopeless. That's why I finally just gave up yesterday and went into the woods to..." Her voice choked.

"...to be found by my son," finished Maggie triumphantly, then glanced at her watch. "It's time to go home now. Do you want to come?"

"Are you sure it's really okay?"

"Of course. We were all sad to learn that you'd left this morning. My mom and Spencer were both eager to help you. They'll be glad to see you're back."

"You won't tell them about my dad, will you, Maggie?"

"It can be our secret. And if you like, I'll try to do a little undercover work myself to see if I can learn anything about your father. But you know, Leah, you may need to just let it go. It might be easier to get on with your life without him anyway."

"I suppose...But I've always had this dream that my father was really *somebody*. Somebody good and smart and maybe even rich—not that *that* matters so much. Best of all, I imagined that he'd be really glad to see me. And that he would help me and..." her voice trailed off. "I know it's totally stupid. Just a fairy-tale dream."

"No, it's not stupid." Maggie thought about Gavin again. "But it might not be wise to set all your hopes on one person like that."

᪲

Audrey and Spencer warmly welcomed Leah back with no questions. During dinner she seemed much more open than the previous night, and by the time she and Spencer were cleaning up in the kitchen, she almost seemed like one of the family.

"Have you learned much about her, Maggie?" whispered Audrey as the two sipped iced tea on the front porch.

"A little. Mostly that she comes from a pretty messed-up home. Her mother may have some addiction problems, plus a series of husbands or boyfriends. Leah describes the current one as a real creep."

"That's a lot for a young girl to put up with."

Maggie nodded. "But despite the runaway part, she seems mature and even somewhat sensible."

"That often happens when kids are forced to grow up fast. But what in the world brought her to Pine Mountain of all places?"

Maggie thought for a moment. She hated to keep things from her mom, but at the same time felt compelled to keep her promise to Leah. "I'm not at liberty to say just yet."

"I see….Well, that's perfectly all right. Confidentiality is critical to good counseling. Do you know how old she is or if she plans to stay here?"

"She's eighteen. And I don't think she knows what her plans are. I told her she could stay with us as long as she needs to. As you know, she's flat broke right now. She worked in a café just long enough to make travel money to get here."

"Say, wasn't Buckie wanting someone to work in his gallery?"

"Yes. But don't you remember how he acted about her? Like she was going to steal the family silver or maybe even murder us in our beds?"

"Oh, I think he just needs to get to know her better."

"Maybe. But I'm afraid I wouldn't have the patience to convince him of that. I like Buckie, but sometimes I want to just knock him across the side of the head."

"Well, maybe I should lend a hand," said Audrey, then laughed. "Not knocking him in the head, of course. But maybe I can encourage him to give Leah a shot. Maybe I could sweeten the pot a little by offering to volunteer at his shop too, just until the girl gets up to snuff."

"That would be so great, Mom. I don't know how Buckie could refuse you. I just wonder if Leah will be willing."

That evening Maggie took a few moments to send her friend in L.A. an email.

RB

Well, I always wanted a daughter…And right now we have an eighteen-year-old runaway girl living with us. Crazy? Maybe. But as silly as it seems, somehow it feels right. I don't know how long she'll stay, but I really want to help her if I can. Mom and Spence are just as enthused. She comes from a tough home, but she seems to be a good, solid person. And I like her. I wish I could say more (especially to get some free legal advice) but I've promised confidentiality. I'll keep you posted on how it goes. I assume you're back from Atlanta now, and knowing you, you won your case. Sometimes I envy you, still doing the big city thing, rubbing elbows with the power people. . . then I look out my window and see the pink sun setting against the snowcapped mountains . . . and I'm just fine. I still love it here! Come visit.

mc

Four

A s she parked her car in front of the house, Maggie noticed the aspens were starting to turn a warm golden shade. She paused for a moment to admire the sun coming from behind the trees, illuminating the green and yellow leaves almost like a stained glass window. Soon all the leaves would begin to fall. Just another sign that summer was on its way out. And although she'd recently noticed the nights growing steadily colder, she felt relief that the days remained sunny and warm. Just today, Clyde said the Farmer's Almanac had predicted an extended summer this year, followed by a colder than usual winter. As she went up the porch steps, she heard a vehicle pull up and turned to see a familiar red truck.

"Hey there, Magpie," called Jed as he climbed out and walked toward the house. She smiled to herself. The only other person to dare call her Magpie was her younger brother Barry when they were children. And she hadn't liked it then. But somehow it sounded better with Jed saying it.

"What brings you out here?" She asked as she set down her bag of groceries on the table next to the front door.

"Spencer called and said he needs to borrow my jig saw."

"Your jig saw? What—is he making a puzzle?"

Jed laughed. "No, he's cutting some outlet openings for the..."

She waved her hand. "That's okay. Don't bother trying to explain it. My knowledge of tools and household repairs is limited at best. And that's exactly how I intend to keep it."

"I'm sure you have plenty of other important things to occupy your mind." Jed gestured back to his truck. "Shall I put the saw in the barn or does he want it in the house..."

"Hey, Jed," called Spencer as he jogged around the side of the house with Bart at his heels. "I thought I heard your pick-up. I'm working around back."

Maggie smiled at the two of them as they began to discuss the project at hand with Spencer asking questions about how to fit crown molding, then she turned her attention back to getting the groceries inside the house. She loved that Spencer continued his interest in restoring the old house, and that Jed always seemed available and glad to help. But sometimes she envied their relationship—they always had something to talk about. And often she felt the intruder as they went on about the right type of wood to replace a broken spindle, or what kind of caulking went on who knew what. She had considered getting more involved in understanding the renovation processes, but then that seemed to be Spencer's territory, and she didn't want to do anything to discourage him. Still, she thought as she walked through the quiet house, she couldn't remember having had one single, solitary conversation with Jed in the past two weeks. In fact, the last time she'd had him all to herself had been on the dance floor at the Pine Mountain Days dance. And of course it was ridiculous that she even gave it any thought now. Especially when everyone in town assumed that there was more to Jed and Kate's relationship than just pure business.

She exhaled loudly as she flopped the bags onto the pine table in the kitchen. She began to unload groceries and wondered where her mother and Leah had gone. She'd expected to find them at home, but had noticed her mother's car missing from the driveway. Actually she found it rather sweet the way her sixty-four-year-old mother had taken Leah right under her motherly wing. Only yesterday Audrey had convinced Buckie to take on the two of them to help out in his gallery when he went up to Alaska in September. And after much coaxing he finally agreed to give them a try starting on Saturday morning, which would be tomorrow. Leah had been so heartened at the prospect of a real job that her dark eyes had lit up and given her pale little face a whole new look. Maggie just hoped that no one would be disappointed in all this—most of all Leah. But her mother had promised to handle any fallout if for some reason things didn't work out, and she told Maggie not to give the matter a second thought, which was exactly what Maggie intended to do.

"Hello in there," called Jed from the hallway.

"I'm in the kitchen," yelled Maggie as she shoved a package of frozen vegetables into the freezer. Her mother had convinced her to get an upright freezer to set alongside an identical upright refrigerator in order to create what now looked like an enormous side-by-side. "It'll be perfect for your bed and breakfast someday," Audrey had said with a sly smile. Sometimes her mother seemed more enthralled about the prospects of running a B & B than Maggie.

"Spencer said I might find something cool to drink in here." Jed said from the shadows of the doorway.

"Sure. I just saw a pitcher of lemonade and I think Mom made some fresh tea this morning…"

"Iced tea sounds perfect." Jed ran his hand over the pine table. "Nice piece of furniture you got here."

"Thanks, a friend of mine made it." She poured him a tall glass of tea and stuck a fat lemon wedge on the side, thinking how pleasant it felt to refer to Jed as her friend.

"You better hang on to it, might be an heirloom someday." He grinned smugly.

"So, how's the woodworking business doing these days? Buckie says he's been real busy in the gallery." She handed him the tea, noticing how his eyes changed ever so slightly when she mentioned Buckie's name. Or was it her imagination?

He took a swig then nodded. "Business has been excellent. I've had a record month. I thought I had enough stock to last a year or two, but I might actually have to start making furniture again to replace my inventory before too long."

"That's great, Jed." She poured herself a glass of tea, then glanced over the groceries making sure that nothing cold still remained to be put away. "Want to sit out on the porch, or do you have to run?"

"I've got all the time in the world." He led the way to the front of the house. "Kate's closing the shop tonight."

Maggie sat down in a wicker rocker and kicked off her loafers. "Are you still staying open until eight on Fridays and Saturdays like some of the other shops are doing?"

"Yeah. Trying to make hay while the sun shines."

She took another long sip. "Do you think the tourist traffic will really slow down when the weather cools and autumn comes?"

He nodded as he leaned back in the chair. "That's the way it's always been. But that's okay. It'll be a relief to have some catching-up time. And I'd still like to build up my stock to the point where I can consider selling to some bigger stores around the country someday."

"I'm sure you could sell your furniture anywhere, Jed. I know people in L.A. who'd pay top dollar for the quality of your work."

"Thanks. But I go back and forth on the idea of expanding. Sometimes, like lately when everything's going so well, I think it's time to grow. But then just talk to me in the middle of winter...I'm sure I'll be singing a different song by then."

"But this winter could be different. The highway ought to be finished by October. And what with all the promotion and publicity we've been getting lately...and of course, there's always the ski season to bring 'em in."

"I hope you're right. It'd be good to have a steady winter for a change." Jed jiggled the ice in his glass. "Say, I saw your mother in town with a strange girl. Is she a relative?"

"No. Just a friend. She's going to be working for Buckie starting tomorrow. Actually, both she and my mother will be working at the Blue Moose while Buckie's in Alaska."

"What's Buckie going to do in Alaska?"

"Shoot photos for a travel magazine."

He sighed. "Ah, yes. That must be nice."

"Have you been there?"

"No. I just meant it must be nice to travel around like that and have someone else foot the bill." He looked out over to the mountains still wearing small caps of snow on top. "Not that I don't like it here. In fact, I remember a time when I promised myself if I ever made it back home that I'd never leave again."

"Where were you?"

"Nam." The word came out flat, void of emotion or intonation.

"You were in *Viet Nam*? I didn't think you were that old."

He gave a little forced laugh. "Actually, I enlisted when I was only seventeen—was sent to Nam in the summer of '73. My old man had a fit. He was certain I'd be killed— either by the enemy or some red-necked boy who didn't like fighting alongside an injun."

"I wouldn't think race would be much of an issue with a serious war going on all around you."

Jed looked thoughtful for a moment. "Actually it wasn't. In fact, it was one of the best times of my life in that regard. Sure there were guys who didn't like me, but they were usually right up front about it. No games. But for the most part divisions were minor, we were all in the same boat, watching out for each other, and just fighting to stay alive..."

"It must've been horrible."

He didn't say anything.

"I'll bet your dad was relieved to see you return in one piece."

"I wouldn't describe my return quite like that."

"Were you injured?"

"Not in body. But my mind and spirit were a mess. I didn't come straight home. I didn't want my dad to see what I'd become." He looked down at his feet. "You see, I got mixed up with drugs over there. Sometimes getting high seemed like the only way you could survive. I know how stupid that rationale sounds now, but at the time..."

Maggie nodded with understanding. "That happened to a lot of guys. It's so sad. But at least you got your life back together."

"But not in time to patch it up with my dad." He took a sip of tea. "I wasted some precious years, a lot of time that can never be replaced."

"How do you know it was such a waste, Jed? Maybe you were on a journey that took you places you had to go in order to get to the place where you needed to be."

He smiled slightly. "Maybe *you* should give this week's sermon, Magpie."

She looked down at her lap. "Sorry, I didn't mean to preach."

"No, it's not that. You weren't preaching—you just seemed to have unearthed a real nugget of wisdom there."

She glanced at him in surprise. Was he teasing her? She studied the serious expression of his smooth, even features, and his intense dark eyes returned her gaze. "Why, thank you, Mr. Whitewater."

"No. *Thank you.*" He stood up and stretched lazily. "And now I'm suddenly reminded that I haven't prepared a single word for Sunday's sermon. Mind if I mull over what you said and see where that takes me?"

"Not at all." She grinned. "I grant you permission to use whatever you please—just don't quote me."

He squinted toward the road. "And I think I see your mother's car approaching. It's probably getting close to dinnertime."

"You're welcome to stay, Jed." She looked up at him hopefully. "If you'd like."

He seemed to think about it, then said, "Thanks. Maybe some other time. I'm afraid if I don't get Sunday's message down, I'll get too busy and forget it altogether. Tell Spence I'll pick up that saw next week."

Jed drove out as Audrey drove in, and Maggie spied Leah in the passenger's seat talking to her mother with animated features. How nice to see Leah so happy!

"Sorry we're late," called Audrey as she climbed from the car. "Was that Jed Whitewater? You should've asked him to stay for dinner. I've got a huge bunch of ribs marinating in the fridge right this moment."

"I did ask him, but he said another time. Where've you two been?"

Leah had an armload of bags. "Your mother took me shopping in Byron for some working clothes. But I'm going to pay her back for everything—right out of my first paycheck."

"Well, we'll discuss that later," said Audrey. "I think I should pay for a couple of those things that I insisted upon."

"But you were right…"

"Enough arguing," said Maggie as she held the door open. "Just get yourselves inside and let me see what you've got!"

Leah excitedly opened the bags to display a nice selection of sensible clothes, slightly casual but completely appropriate for the Blue Moose. With enthusiasm, she explained how they found each one. "And these jeans were on sale for *half-price*…then Audrey found this shirt for only $9.99! Can you believe it? It was regularly about fifty dollars." She smiled at Audrey. "You're a really good shopper."

Maggie laughed. "Yes, I always told Mom that if she had wanted to give up her counseling career she could've easily become a personal shopper for those of us who are too busy to take the time."

Audrey waved her hand at her. "You know how I enjoy getting out once in a while to look around. I used to call going to the mall my own personal therapy time." She glanced at her watch. "Oh, Maggie, did you remember that Elizabeth is having that author do a reading at the Window Seat tonight at seven?"

"I completely forgot," said Maggie.

"Well, let's get dinner started if we want to make it on time." Audrey began moving toward the kitchen. "Buckie would never forgive us for missing this. He's been going on and on about this guy—he's some special friend of his from the Seattle area."

"I know," said Maggie. "And actually I've been looking forward to meeting him."

"I'll run this stuff upstairs and be right back down to help," called Leah. "Do you mind if I come to the reading too?"

"I was hoping you'd want to, Leah. And would you please remind Spence about it? He'll probably need to clean up some."

They quickly fixed and ate dinner, then headed off to the Window Seat. Elizabeth was just having people seat themselves in the tightly packed rows of folding chairs when they walked in.

"Come on, you latecomers," she scolded good-naturedly. "You'll have to sit in the back now." Lowering her voice, she said, "Haven't we got a nice little crowd here?"

Maggie listened with interest as the novelist told what had inspired his book and how long it had taken him to complete it while working full-time as a commercial pilot. Then she sat spellbound while he read from a particularly moving section at the beginning. It was the kind of writing that communicated right to the center of her, utilizing words and descriptions that she might herself use if she ever got more serious about writing her own novel. The strange thing was, something about his writing actually made her want to get serious.

Afterwards Buckie proudly introduced her to his friend. "Conrad, I'd like you to meet my dear friend Maggie Carpenter, who's also a writer."

She blushed. "Actually I'm more of a journalist, and I run the weekly paper in town—it's called the *Pine Cone* and that's about how big it is."

Buckie made a face. "Oh, she's just playing it down, Conrad. She used to report for the *L.A. Times*, and I happen to know that she's received some fairly prestigious awards for her writing."

"That's great," said Conrad as he signed a book for her. "We writers need to stick together—it's a tough world out there."

She smiled. "I have to admit that hearing you tonight has ignited an old desire in me to write—something more than articles and editorials, I mean. I have this old novel that I started a long time ago, and now I'm thinking that maybe it needs another look."

"Better get it out then." He handed her the signed book. "And stick with it. Like I told the group, it took me thirteen years to finish this, but it's been well worth it. And now I'm nearly half done with my second novel."

"So, when are you quitting your day job?" teased Buckie.

Conrad punched him playfully in the arm. "We're not all as lucky as you, Buck. Somehow you always manage to get the best of both worlds—running your own gallery and still doing freelance photography!"

Buckie grinned. "Hey, don't let what looks like my quick success fool you. It took me years of planning and preparation to get here. And I still don't know if I'll make it through the winter without going broke."

Conrad looked around the room crowded with townsfolk. "Well, I couldn't think of a nicer bunch of people to go broke with, or a prettier town to do it in."

"What a pleasant way to think of it," said Maggie.

Buckie frowned. "I don't know how nice everyone would be if we were all going belly up together. Don't forget how all those nice people acted aboard the *Titanic* when it was going under."

Maggie shook her head at the horrible imagery. "Bite your tongue, Buckie Porterfield!"

Five

$\mathcal{M}$aggie stopped by the Blue Moose on Saturday to see how her mother and Leah were doing at their new jobs. Leah seemed a little tense around the edges, but she looked professional in her neat white shirt, topped by a khaki jumper and matching tights. Such a different girl than the one Spencer had found sleeping in the woods! And it was plain to see that Audrey was having a great time playing shopkeeper in the pleasant little gallery. Maggie pretended to browse as her mother wrote up a purchase with Leah looking on over her shoulder. Then Leah carefully wrapped the framed photo in craft-paper, taking time to fold and tape each edge with perfection.

"I told Buckie he should consider consigning some other types of art in here too," said Audrey as the customer left. She pointed to an open area in the front of the shop. "Can't you just imagine a big table there, with an attractive arrangement of pottery and sculpture displayed, and then perhaps some metal over…"

"Oh no, I see she's still going at it," said Buckie sarcastically. "Whatever possessed me to hire someone who acts and talks and thinks just like my very own mother is beyond me!"

Maggie laughed. "Well, at least you can ignore *her* advice. Now just think if she were your own mother…"

Buckie threw an arm around Maggie's shoulders. "Did you come to rescue me? Won't you please get me out of here and let me take you to lunch?"

She glanced around the gallery for Leah, finally spying her in the back by the framing table. It looked like she was cleaning up scraps from some matting and framing projects just completed. Maggie turned back to Buckie. "Okay, I'll go to lunch with you. But it's really just a mission of mercy because I'm sure these two ladies need a break from *you!*" She waved at Leah and walked out the door with Buckie.

"Before lunch, do you have time to help me look for something over at Whitewater Works?" asked Buckie as he led her across the street.

"Sure," she said breezily, although she really didn't relish the idea of seeing Jed while she was with Buckie. Of course, it wasn't even likely that Jed would be in. And besides, what difference should it make anyway? They were all simply good friends.

"I want to look for a table," said Buckie as he opened the door for her.

"What sort of table?"

"Something to use in the gallery..."

"You mean like to display consigned sculptures upon?" she said accusingly.

He grinned sheepishly. "Well, I never said your mother didn't have good ideas. I only said she reminds me of my mother."

She laughed. "Maybe we all need a little mothering from time to time."

"Hi there," called Kate from the back of the store. "What are you two up to?"

"We're here to look around," said Buckie, already eyeing a sturdily built pine table. He ran his hand over the smooth, golden top. "This is a handsome piece."

"Jed does such incredible work," said Maggie with admiration.

"What are you looking for?" asked Kate, directing a bright smile toward Buckie.

"I need a good-sized table for my gallery. This one might work, but maybe I should look around a little to be sure."

Maggie wandered back into the shop until she came across a table she hadn't seen before. It was even-grained fir with a dark, chestnut-colored stain, built in a classic but simple style. "Hey, Buckie, come look at this one."

He joined her, leaning down to more closely examine the table. "You've got a good eye for quality, Maggie. This is beautiful." He looked at the tag. "And not a bad price…"

"Hey there," said Jed. "Guess I walked in at just the right moment. Too late to bicker on the price now, I already heard you say it's not bad."

Buckie stood up and shook Jed's hand. "Well, now don't be too hasty. I was actually thinking you might like to throw in a little discount in exchange for some free advertising." He quickly explained how he planned to use the table to show off some consigned art, and on the table he would post a little placard advertising Jed's shop right across the street. But the whole time Buckie was speaking, Maggie sensed Jed's eyes upon her—as if to question why she was out shopping tables with him. But then again, maybe she was just blowing the whole thing out of proportion. What was wrong with helping a friend pick out a piece of furniture?

Soon they came to an agreement, and Maggie continued to browse while Kate wrote up Buckie's purchase. She finally stopped before a large wardrobe. Like the fir table, this piece was also a bit different from Jed's usual rustic style.

"Like it?" asked Jed from behind.

Without turning she said, "Yes. It's beautiful."

"It's an Arts and Crafts era reproduction, like that table you picked out for Buckie."

"Is this that new style you were telling me about before?"

"I wouldn't call it a new style, it's been around for nearly a hundred years, but I only started doing these pieces several months ago. The Arts and Crafts period was sort of the fine craftsman's rebellion against all the frivolous Victorian furnishings that were being mass-produced on the assembly line around the turn of the last century."

"I see. Well, I really like this style. I think it would go quite well in my house. Don't you?" She turned around to see him smiling as if pleased.

"Actually, I do. And even though your house isn't a craftsman design, it's built in the right era for this style. And that's not just the salesman in me talking, Maggie. When I was building this piece I imagined it in your..."

"Hey, Maggie," called Buckie. "You ready to go to lunch now? I'm starved."

"Coming," she called, then turned back to Jed. "Will you hold this piece for me?"

"Sure."

She said goodbye then joined Buckie, and the two headed down Main Street to Galloway's Deli. "It'll be a shame when the frost comes and wipes out these beautiful flowers," she said as they passed a luxuriantly filled oak barrel spilling out over the edges with pansies, phlox, and columbines.

"Oh, that won't be for a while yet," reassured Buckie.

"Don't count on it. Abigail said the first freeze could come at anytime now."

"But it's only the end of August."

Straight ahead was the Pine Mountain Hotel, now under serious renovation. "It will be so great when the Jordans finish up this place," said Maggie as they paused on the sidewalk to view the latest progress. "Cindy is really getting into it. Last week she showed me the decorator boards with color and cloth samples for the rooms. They are going to be gorgeous!"

"Does it make you want to pursue your bed and breakfast dream?" asked Buckie.

She sighed. "There's just so much going on in my life right now. But I do feel that when the time is right, I'll start moving in that direction."

Buckie examined a stack of new, wood-framed windows leaning against the building and whistled. "Boy, it must cost a fortune to restore a place like this—and I happen to know they aren't sparing any expenses."

"I know. I saw the kitchen last week and the upgrades were amazing, yet they're not compromising the historical integrity at all. And I'm so glad that they're keeping the dining room like it was originally…"

"Speaking of dining rooms, I'm starved!" He nudged her elbow and they hurried to the deli where he eagerly opened the door, taking a loud sniff. "Smells like Rosa's got some good soup on today."

The deli's interior was filled to capacity and a number of people were sitting outside as well. "Hi there," said Rosa from behind the counter. "Hey, Maggie, I've been meaning to call and invite you out to the lake for our annual Labor Day picnic." She glanced at Buckie. "You come too, Buckie."

"Sounds good to me," said Buckie as he eyed the menu posted behind the counter.

"Speaking of Labor Day," said Maggie. "Have you heard if the new lampposts are here yet?"

"They should be here by next week," said Rosa. "And Sam said the lamppost committee plans to get them all installed before the Harvest Festival in October." Then she leaned her face close toward Maggie's and lowered her voice. "Now when are you going to tell me all about this girl you've taken in? Sierra's told me a little, but even she doesn't seem to know too much."

Suddenly Maggie remembered the Pine Mountain paternity list she'd made up in her mind, and how even Sam's name was on it, although he seemed one of the least likely candidates. "We'll get together soon," she promised, glancing over her shoulder to see more customers flocking into the deli behind them. "We better order now."

"That's right," said Buckie, and he quickly placed his order for pastrami on rye and a bowl of lentil soup. Maggie ordered the veggie sandwich and they went outside to find a picnic table in the shade.

"So, how do you think it's going at the gallery?" she asked as they sipped their sodas. "With Leah and Mom, I mean."

He shrugged. "It's kind of soon to tell. But it'll probably be fine. Audrey is a sharp lady. I expect her to keep Leah in line."

Her brows lifted. "You really mean to say that you think Leah needs to be kept in line?"

"I don't know, Maggie. She's still an unknown factor to me. And the truth is I just don't trust her quite the way you do."

"Well, at least you're honest about it." She forced a smile. "And under those circumstances, I think it's kind of you to give her a chance like this."

"Hopefully it will all work out in the end. And if it doesn't I can just say I told you so."

She frowned. "I never realized you were such a pessimist."

"Usually I'm not. It's just that I had a bad experience once." He explained how several years ago he'd taken on an intern while working for a magazine in Seattle, and somehow the careless girl had managed to mess up three rolls of irreplaceable negatives from a very important photo shoot, and had nearly cost him his job. "So, you see..." He laid a tip on the table and rose to leave. "Once burned..."

She picked up her purse and stood. "I suppose that does makes sense. But I'm hoping you'll find that Leah is different."

ᴕ

After lunch Maggie stopped by the newspaper office to check the answering machine. The staff took turns keeping track of possible leads to stories that came in during the weekends. But as usual, nothing earthshaking had occurred since yesterday, not even a quirky animal story from old

Mrs. Bowerman. But then again, perhaps the visit from Scott had satisfied her need for attention—at least for the time being. Maggie was still pleased at the way Scott managed to extract a touching story from the whole thing. It would be nice if his special interest feature brought a few more visitors of the human kind into Mrs. Bowerman's isolated little world. Maggie absently thumbed through the small pile of mail that she'd picked up at the front door. Nothing exceptional—until she came across what looked like a personal letter addressed to her but minus a return address. The postmark was from Tustin, a town in the L.A. area, but she could recall no one she knew who lived there. With mild curiosity, she sat down at her desk and slit it open, flipping straight to the end to see who it was from—and it was from none other than Gavin Barnes!

Dear Maggie,

I'm sure you're surprised to hear from me. I'm a little surprised myself to be writing, but I feel compelled to communicate with someone in Pine Mountain. I tried to call Greg not long after that big drug bust in town (I saw the whole thing on TV in Portland) but he was so angry and accusatory. He said that rumor had it that I was involved and possibly the instigator of the whole stupid mess, and that he no longer cared to speak to me, and then he hung up! So much for lifelong friendships—or "innocent until proven guilty." But I'm not writing to whine—okay, maybe just a little. But the truth is, Maggie, you seem like the only one in town who might possibly give me the time of day right now. At one time you seemed to honestly care about me. So I just wanted you to know that I had nothing to do with that drug business in Pine Mountain.

Yes, it's true I've had a checkered past. Everyone knows I've made more than my share of mistakes—I'm sure Uncle Clyde has told you all about them by now. And I suppose it's possible that I unwittingly invited the initial drug traffic into Pine Mountain. But I swear to you, after I left that was the end of it for me. I have no connections with those people. I'd go into a more detailed explanation, but I don't

*think it's wise to put too much into writing. Not that I don't trust
you, because I do. What I'm wondering is whether or not I can
call you sometime. I'd like to talk to you and see if you could help
to clear my name. It's funny. I used to care very little about Pine
Mountain, but now that it seems like the door has been slammed
in my face, I find myself thinking about the old hometown and
actually longing to be there. I hope that someday I'll be able to
come home and walk down Main Street without feeling like a
common criminal.*

*I'll call you at home sometime. If you don't care to talk to me, just
hang up. And I promise never to bother you again.*

*By the way, I borrowed some money from my mom and put
myself into a rehab treatment center down here. Maybe your
prayers made a difference after all. Thanks for being a friend,
Maggie.*

Sincerely,
Gavin Barnes

Maggie laid down the letter and shook her head in
amazement. Could it be true? Was it possible that Gavin had
nothing to do with the drug bust that had brought Pine
Mountain all that publicity—both good and bad? He was
right about the rumors. They'd begun to circulate right on
Main Street during Pine Mountain Days. Poor Clyde, he'd
managed to keep a low profile in the following days, taking
an extended fishing excursion until things simmered down.
But when he returned, Maggie noticed the hurt in the old
man's eyes. He never spoke specifically of Gavin to her
again, but she felt certain he still suspected his nephew to be
the cause of the whole unfortunate episode. Now she realized how even Greg Snider had turned against Gavin. That
was news to her. But for some reason it actually made her
think better of the ill-tempered postmaster. Maybe not in
regard to his loyalty to old friends, but it did seem to prove,
once and for all, that he wasn't, and never had been, involved
in the whole thing. She folded the letter and returned it to
the envelope. Of course she'd be willing to talk to Gavin.

Eager even. And it would give her the chance to question him about any possible paternal relationship to Leah.

"Hello?" hailed a familiar gruff voice from the office.

"Is that you, Clyde?" called Maggie as she rose from her desk, slipping the letter into her purse to read again later in private.

"Yep. I was in town and thought I'd check the phone messages." Clyde leaned over Abigail's desk to peer at the answering machine. "But looks like you beat me to it. Anything up?"

She shook her head. "No, nothing new."

"So how does your young lady like her new job?"

Maggie smiled, cheered by his interest. She'd told everyone in the office about Leah, careful to give the story a positive spin. "I think it's going to be okay. Although she seemed a little jittery this morning."

"To be expected. But I still say she's a brave little thing to up and move to a completely new town like she did. Gotta hand it to her." He rubbed his bristly chin as he glanced over the headlines of the latest *L.A. Times* lying on the stack of mail.

After Buckie's negative reaction to Leah, Maggie had decided not to tell anyone else in town the details of how Leah had been discovered in the woods behind her property. Even though Maggie had only lived in Pine Mountain for a few months, she fully understood the impact of the town's sometimes vicious rumor mill. Fortunately, most folks simply assumed Leah to be a friend of the family. But with sudden clarity it occurred to Maggie that Clyde Barnes might actually be Leah's great uncle! And the mere possibility that this dear, goodhearted, benevolent man could be related to Leah filled her with fresh hope. What a happy surprise it could be for Clyde (and Leah too!) to discover an honest-to-goodness living relative! And suddenly, despite her promise of confidentiality to the girl, she knew she needed to ask Clyde some questions in order to determine if her suspicions about Gavin might be accurate. Besides, who knew when

Gavin might actually call her? And even if he did, he might not be willing to confess to fathering a child he had paid good money to cover up. Plus if she raised this paternity issue, she might simply scare him off altogether. And what good could possibly come from that?

"Clyde?" she ventured cautiously.

"Uh-huh?" He laid down the thick newspaper and studied her with kind, yet faded, blue eyes.

"Have you got a minute to talk?"

"Why sure. It's too hot to fish until evening anyhow. Is something wrong, Maggie?" His shaggy gray brows knit together with concern.

"No, no.... Everything's fine. But I do want to talk to you about something important. And I need you to promise that our conversation will be completely confidential. Can you agree to that?"

"You know you can trust me."

She smiled. "I know. But I guess I just needed to say that for my own sake. Want to come in my office?"

After they were comfortably seated, she began tentatively. "It's sort of about Gavin..."

"Have you heard from the scoundrel?" His tone reminded her of an old grizzly bear.

She thought for a moment. Perhaps it was best to lay all her cards on the table. "Actually, I did get a letter. Gavin wants to clear his name..."

"I'll bet he does!" Clyde's hands turned into tightly gnarled fists.

"He says that he had nothing to do with that drug operation in town."

Clyde grunted skeptically.

"And he plans to call me and fill me in on the details."

Clyde exhaled loudly. "If that's all it is, why are you so worried about confidentiality, Maggie? Surely you didn't think I'd go shooting off my mouth about Gavin. Good grief, I'd cross to the other side of the street just to avoid the subject altogether."

"I know you would. And that's not why I needed you to promise. You see, it concerns Leah."

His face grew puzzled. "Leah?"

She nodded. "You see, she came here because she believes her father—a man she's never met—lives in Pine Mountain. Or perhaps *used* to live in Pine Mountain."

Clyde chuckled. "You don't mean to say you think that I might be…"

"No, no!" Maggie waved her hand, laughing. "That's not it at all."

He made a show of mock relief. "Well, then who do you suppose it might be?"

"Do you happen to know what Gavin was up to about nineteen years ago?" she asked timidly.

"Gavin!" He slapped his hand on his forehead. "Of course, it would just stand to reason, wouldn't it!"

"Now, we don't know anything for sure yet, Clyde. But Leah told me that she heard her mother mention to someone that the birth-father was well off, and she knew he came from Pine Mountain."

"Well, I sure as heck wouldn't put it past that rogue nephew of mine to father a child and then leave the poor mother in the lurch like that. It's just like the dirty scoundrel!" He shook his head sadly. "You know, sometimes I'm thankful my poor brother never lived to see all this. It would've just plain broken his heart, I tell you."

Maggie looked down at her desk, saddened to consider how one person's selfish actions could so painfully affect so many innocent bystanders.

Then suddenly he sat up straight in his chair. "Well, now I'll be! It just occured to me that if Leah is Gavin's daughter, that would make her my great niece!"

She brightened. "That's right. And that's exactly why I decided to bring it up with you. She's such a dear girl, but her life's been hard and her mother is pretty messed up. Leah has virtually nothing, and no one—besides us, that is. And

I'm more than willing to continue helping her, but for some reason she feels it's important for her to find her father."

Clyde stood now and began pacing across the old wooden floor of her office as he spoke. "But if we were to find out that she truly is Gavin's child, I'd be *real* happy to help her out too. I've always been loyal to my kin—not that I've had much kin to speak of."

"I know you care about family, Clyde. And I know you'd do right by Leah too. But the fact is we don't know anything for sure…"

"But you say she believes her dad's from Pine Mountain and that he came from a family with money?"

She nodded. "Her mother tried to keep those things from Leah because apparently the father paid her a nice sum to leave him out of the whole thing and never contact him again."

"*That* sounds like Gavin!"

"The mother lives in Arizona…"

"Phoenix?" exclaimed Clyde suddenly. He stopped pacing and looked at her eagerly.

"I don't know exactly what town…"

"Gavin *lived* in Phoenix! It was after he'd dropped out of college. I remember calling up his mother once to check on him, and she said he was out there working for some real estate developer—he was only there about a year or so, but it seems to me it was in the early eighties—because it was another case of bad timing on his part. The recession was just hitting that area, and the development plan turned out to be a wash. But…" His face screwed up as if he was figuring a math problem. "That was about nineteen or twenty years ago!"

Maggie took in a deep breath. "It seems the puzzle pieces are beginning to fit."

"This is the best news!"

"Do you truly think so?"

He waved his hand in dismissal. "Oh, naturally, I'm real ashamed of Gavin—nothing new there. But wouldn't it be

wonderful to have a relative right here in town. Leah *Barnes!*
Imagine it, Maggie. Why I'll send her to the best college
and..."

"Hold on there, Clyde. We don't know anything for
absolute certain. And even if we find out she is Gavin's
daughter, you'll still need to allow her to make her own decisions."

"Oh, I know, I know. I'm just getting such a kick out of
this." His cheeks were flushed pink with excitement now.

She smiled. "It's understandable. Kind of like when you
find out you're going to have a child—only this one's delivered to you all grown up. But what will we do about
Gavin?"

He rubbed his chin again. "Did he give you his phone
number?"

"No. I don't even have a return address. He's down in
southern California. And, oh, I left out something really
important. He's put himself into an alcohol rehab center."

"You don't say?" He sat back down in the chair, and it
seemed as if his whole body relaxed now. For the first time
in weeks, his countenance reminded her of the old Clyde that
she'd first met last May. "You say Gavin is going to call you?"

"Yes. He said he wants to clear up any suspicions about
this drug business."

"Well, somehow you need to find out, without revealing
your hand, whether it's even possible that he's actually
Leah's father. You'll have to be like an undercover detective,
Maggie. Ask him about dates and whereabouts and those
kinds of things without making him suspect anything's up.
We don't want him to run."

"So, you're saying I shouldn't come right out and ask
him up front?"

"Of course not. He'd probably just lie about it anyway.
The same way he's probably lying about not being part of
that drug business now."

She frowned. "So you still believe he was involved."

"I know it."

She nodded sadly. "Well, okay. I can understand how you might think that. But just the same I'd like to give him a chance."

Clyde leaned over and whacked her desk loudly, causing her to sit up straight in her chair. "That low-down swindler's had plenty of chances, Maggie! I say it's about time we give this little Leah girl a chance!"

She blinked. "Well, I certainly don't have a problem with giving Leah a chance. But if you don't mind, I'm not ready to write off Gavin just yet."

"Fine." He stood and shoved his fishing hat back onto his head. "But if you don't mind, I, for one, don't care to hear another word about Gavin's stories of innocence. What I *do* want to hear about is whether or not this young Leah is really a Barnes. Now that's a piece of news that I'd be plum tickled to hear about. Can you get to the bottom of this, Maggie Carpenter?"

She stood and made a mock salute. "Yes, sir. I'll do my best, sir."

He grinned. "Now that's a good foot-soldier. You keep me posted on any new developments. And if I come up with anything—any letters or documentations, I'll be sure to let you know. In the meantime, do you s'pose you might bring that young lady around here so we can all get a little better acquainted?" His eyes twinkled hopefully.

"You bet. She's only working part-time for Buckie right now. Maybe I can stir up an odd job or two around here for her."

"That'd be just swell." He gently slapped her on the back. "You've made my day, young lady. I tell you, this was better than hooking a prize bass! Now you go ahead and be on your way, and I'll lock up for you."

Six

MC

How's your little runaway doing? I must admit, being a savvy city girl, I felt somewhat alarmed to learn you'd taken in a stranger like that. Of course, I'm sure you've considered things like drugs, criminal tendencies, possible diseases like HIV, or even serious psychological problems. You certainly wouldn't want to expose Spencer to some disturbed young woman like that... Okay, okay, enough said. But do be careful, Mag. Now as a lawyer I am curious about what kind of information you might be seeking, and need I remind you about the attorney-and-client confidentiality privilege? You could tell me absolutely anything, and you know I'd never repeat a word. On another note, I'm seriously considering a ski holiday this winter. Perhaps I should come to Pine Mountain. Is it very difficult to get there? I know I can fly into Portland, but I'm not too sure what comes after that. And I really don't like to drive on snow or ice. Let me know what you think. And now I'm off to see if I can land a great, big, fat settlement for (name withheld due to client confidentiality). Later, dear one.

RB |

Maggie read Rebecca's email and exited without responding. She found her friend's concerns about Leah slightly offensive. Of course she knew Rebecca only meant well, but why did some people feel the need to be so judgmental? What if Jesus had reacted that way with some of the people he'd come across? What if he'd shied away from the leper, afraid to be exposed to that disfiguring disease? Or suppose he'd refused to speak to the tax collector because everyone else considered him to be lower than a worm? And yet, she knew she wasn't Jesus. And in some ways she supposed Rebecca's concerns about any negative influence upon Spencer seemed justified. Of course, Maggie didn't want to expose him to anything harmful. Yet she had a peace about the whole thing, and so far Leah seemed to be settling in so well. Far better than Maggie ever would've expected based on that first day when Spencer had found her. Even Buckie couldn't complain after a full week of Leah training and working in the gallery. He'd even decided to teach her how to cut mats to frame photos, and just yesterday he'd mentioned how Leah had a natural ability for careful and precise work—whispering that she was actually much better at matting and framing than Maggie's mother.

Maggie had hoped and halfway expected that Gavin would phone during the past week. She had even made a point to remain at home every evening, but for nothing. He never called. On Friday, she'd invited Leah to stop by the newspaper office for a little tour, taking time to introduce her to Clyde in private. Leah had been quite taken with the old man, listening with keen interest while he explained the intricate processes of the old printing press, and the cutting and folding machines he used to produce the weekly paper. On the drive home, Leah told Maggie how Clyde had even mentioned the possibility of some part-time work at the paper. "He's so nice," she'd said with bright eyes. "He really seemed interested in me as a person. I have a grandpa on my mom's side, but he just married his third or fourth wife and is really into his own life. Plus it doesn't help that he can't stand my mom, so we've never really gotten along that well. But if I could pick out a grandpa, he'd be someone just like Clyde." Maggie could hardly keep silent about the possibility of Leah being related to him. But it had seemed premature and even cruel to get the girl's hopes up without any concrete evidence.

And now she glared at the phone as if it were the culprit in all this. Oh, if only Gavin would pick up the phone and call!

"Hey, you guys, it's almost three. Are you ready for the Labor Day picnic?" called Audrey from the kitchen. "I could use some extra hands in here to load this stuff into the car."

"Coming, Mom," said Maggie as she snapped her laptop closed.

Everyone carried things to the car and Spencer let down the tailgate while Bart jumped in back, and they were off.

"Are you looking forward to school starting up, Spencer?" asked Leah in the back-seat. Maggie watched Spencer's face from the rearview mirror as she waited to hear his answer.

He shrugged. "Sort of."

"I always liked school," continued Leah. "I actually cried when I graduated last spring."

Spencer made a face. "You sound like Sierra. She likes school too. I think it's just a girl thing."

Leah laughed. "You make it sound like a sickness or something."

"What about the ski team, Spence?" asked Audrey from the front. "Aren't you looking forward to that?"

"Yeah, that might be fun…that is if I can get on," said Spencer. "But I hope they decide to add snowboarding."

"When's your snowboard going to get here?" asked Maggie.

"Clint at the Alpine Shop said it'll be here by the end of September—I guess the company was backordered."

"If I'm still around, I think it would be fun to learn," said Leah wistfully.

"You mean you're thinking about leaving?" asked Spencer with surprise.

"I don't really know what I'm going to do. I'd like to stay, but I guess I don't really know for sure..."

"Maybe you should just try to live one day at a time," suggested Maggie. "You know, like Jed said in church yesterday."

ᴑ

Cars and RVs filled the campground and parking lots around Silver Lake, forcing Maggie to park near the highway. But everyone helped pack baskets and coolers as they trudged like a small army of ants down toward the lake. Fortunately the Galloways had arrived early enough to secure a lakeside picnic site, and it appeared that Scott and Chloe had been left to hold down the fort. But as Maggie approached them, she noticed the serious expressions upon their faces as they talked.

"Hey there," she called, as if in warning. They looked up and waved to the group. "Where is everyone else?" she asked, setting the picnic basket on the table.

"Dad's down at the dock, and Mom and Sierra had to stay at the deli until three," said Scott. "They should be here any minute now—that is, if Mom can stand to leave and let Elaine close up."

Maggie smiled. "It's kind of like leaving your child with a baby-sitter."

Spencer and Leah plunked down the cooler next to the picnic table. "I'm going to go find Sam," said Spencer as he headed off toward the dock. Chloe invited Leah to walk over to the store with her for another bag of ice, and Audrey and Maggie sat down with Scott.

"Everything okay, Scott?" asked Maggie with concern.

He shook his head. "Not really. It's Chloe."

"Oh...." She appreciated Scott's candid answer, but had no desire to get caught in the middle of a lovers' quarrel.

"Her old boyfriend from Portland is coming to town this week."

"I thought Chloe said he was just an 'old friend,'" said Maggie lightly.

Scott frowned. "What's the difference? They used to go out, and her family thinks Aaron Jackson is just about the greatest."

"But what does Chloe think?" asked Audrey in her counselor's voice.

Scott sighed. "Well, she *says* she considers him to be nothing more than a good friend."

"There," said Maggie. "You see."

"But if he's only a friend, why's he coming to visit for a whole week? And why is she looking forward to seeing him?"

Audrey chuckled. "Haven't you ever spent a week with a friend, Scott?"

"Not a *girl* friend!"

Maggie nodded. "I think I can see why you and Chloe are having a problem with this..." Scott just groaned and leaned his head into his hands. Maggie glanced over at her mother who only winked knowingly. Just then Maggie noticed that Rosa and Sierra were quickly approaching with Buckie right on their heels.

"I forgot Buckie was coming," said Maggie.

"You sound disappointed," noted Audrey, and Scott looked up with mild interest.

"It's just that..." She didn't quite know how to explain it.

"Is Buckie boy getting a little too interested?" asked Scott with a raised brow.

"Shh," hissed Maggie as the trio approached.

Soon they had all reconvened to enjoy a good picnic supper, then Sam took everyone out on the boat except Maggie, Audrey, and Rosa. The three women opted for the shore side, arranging comfortable lawn chairs near the edge of the lake. Together they visited over a thermos of hazelnut coffee that Rosa had brought from the deli. Maggie glanced across the lake, busy with boats and enthusiasts enjoying the last hurrah of the season. By next week it would be quiet.

"I can feel the nip of fall in the air," commented Maggie as she took a sip.

"My flower beds are starting to fade," said Rosa sadly. "But this year I'm going to try putting in some ornamental cabbages and chrysanthemums to brighten it during the autumn. Abigail started a bunch earlier this summer to put into the town's flower boxes and she offered me some for my own garden."

"You should start a garden club," suggested Audrey. "Then everyone could help out with the town's planters. I know Elizabeth is interested in gardening, and of course, I am too."

Rosa studied Audrey. "Isn't there some way we can all talk you into moving here permanently? You're always so full of ideas, and it seems like you'd actually have time to help carry them out."

Audrey smiled. "I need to go back home and take care of things. But who knows…"

Maggie patted her mother's arm. "It's not that I haven't tried to convince her to relocate here. But I think maybe she's just a California girl at heart."

Rosa laughed. "So was I once. But it didn't take too long to acclimate and now I couldn't imagine living anywhere else." She turned to Maggie. "I can't contain my curiosity much longer, Maggie. When are you going to tell me a little something about Leah?" Maggie thought for a moment. She knew she could trust Rosa, but how much was it really necessary for her to know?

"Sierra has already told me a little," confided Rosa. "I would never repeat any of it, and I warned Sierra to keep her mouth closed—and I'm sure she will—but she told me that Spencer actually found the girl in the woods and that she looked pretty hard up at the time."

Maggie sighed. "That's true. And I don't think it would help Leah for the whole town to know that."

"That's for sure. But what I'm just curious about is why she came to Pine Mountain in the first place. I mean, we're not exactly a convenient stop along the beaten path."

Audrey chuckled. "That's putting it mildly."

"Leah has her reasons for picking Pine Mountain," said Maggie carefully. "Right now I can't reveal exactly what those reasons are. I promised her to keep it confidential. But when the time is right, I'll let you know more."

Audrey nodded. "Don't feel bad, Rosa. Maggie hasn't even told me yet."

"Does she have any family around here?" asked Rosa.

Maggie pressed her lips together, then said, "Maybe…"

Rosa nodded. "Okay. I won't pry. She seems like a real nice girl to me. Sierra likes her too. And if there's anything we can do to help out, just let us know."

"Thanks. I think one of the best things is to make her feel welcome. I think she's made a great adjustment to Pine Mountain so far. But I know she's a little concerned about her future. And I doubt that she'll want to work for Buckie forever. Although it's good experience right now, it doesn't seem like a great future career."

"Well, you never know," said Rosa philosophically. "I mean, look at Kate Murray. She seems perfectly content to keep working for Jed. And if you ask me, there's no great future career in that job either."

"But Kate really enjoys the recreational lifestyle here," said Maggie, then to her surprise added, "not to mention her present and future relationship with Jed."

Rosa shook her head. "There's no future there."

Maggie studied her carefully. "What do you mean?"

"I mean, Kate Murray, after three and a half years, should know that Jed isn't interested in anything beyond friendship and a working relationship with her."

Maggie didn't know how to respond. "But I thought everyone in town just assumed that they were a couple…"

"It depends on whom you talk to. Folks who know Kate might think so. But the few of us who are close to Jed know different."

"That's sad," said Audrey. "Kate is such a nice young woman, and certainly quite attractive too. It's sad to think she's hanging onto something that might never be. Why doesn't Jed just tell her outright that he's not interested?"

"That's a mystery," said Rosa. "Sometimes I almost think that he might actually be interested—you see them together so often and all. But then I'll hear him say something that totally convinces me otherwise. Personally, I just don't think it will ever happen."

"Poor Kate," said Maggie.

"What brought her to Pine Mountain originally?" asked Audrey.

"She moved here from Byron to work for a dentist— she's really a dental hygienist. But only a couple years after she came, Dr. Lindall decided there wasn't enough business to keep him here and he relocated back to Byron. He offered Kate the same position there, but she turned him down. By then she was clearly infatuated with Jed, and she convinced him to let her work for him. Poor Jed was having a hard time keeping his shop going and making furniture at the same time—it seemed that something was always being neglected. So Kate offered to run the shop and work for him on a straight sales commission. Well, Jed could hardly pass that up. And she's very good with the customers and an excellent salesperson—not to mention gorgeous. Anyway, it's proved a winning combination. Even in the leanest of years, Kate has helped Jed to stay afloat. And for that reason alone, I'm sure that he feels somewhat indebted to her."

"Wow," said Maggie. "I had no idea. Now I feel even more sorry for her."

"Well, you can never tell," said Audrey. "Jed might simply be one of those slow movers, you know, a late bloomer. If they have a good solid relationship, and they work so well together, maybe there will be a wedding in the future for them after all. And you must admit they make a strikingly handsome couple."

Right then and there, Maggie wanted to smack her mother—well, not actually. But somehow, as foolish as it seemed, her mother's words felt like a personal betrayal. "Just because they look well together doesn't mean they should get married," said Maggie, instantly regretting her tone. Then more softly, "You of all people should know that, Mother. Remember how everyone said you and Dad made such a handsome pair."

Audrey nodded thoughtfully. "I guess that was a pretty shallow observation on my part. But you have to remember my generation, Maggie. Raised in front of the silver screen, our values can be somewhat superficial at times." She chuckled.

Rosa laughed. "It's not only *your* generation, Audrey. Sometimes I just think it's our whole American culture in general. I swear, I think this country would vote Mel Gibson into office as president based solely upon his looks."

"Hmm," said Maggie, pretending to be thoughtful. "Mel would make an awfully handsome president."

◦꒰─

That night, Maggie pulled on a warm sweater and slipped out of the house a little later than normal for her usual evening walk. Her mother often joined her, but tonight had discovered a TV movie she wanted to watch instead. Besides, Maggie sensed she was fatigued from her day at the lake, a reminder that her mother wasn't as young as she used to be. But after the people-filled day, Maggie relished the solitude of a quiet walk by herself. Overhead the stars burned brightly against an obsidian sky, and a half-moon lit the night with its cool, blue light. She walked briskly across the meadow and then alongside the road, following her familiar route, and always keeping the homestead in sight. It amazed her when she recalled that this was only her fourth month of living here. And yet, she felt so completely at home. How could any other place ever have been home? Unexpectedly, she remembered her life with Phil, realizing with a mixture of relief and guilt how it had probably been weeks since she'd last thought of her departed husband. Certainly a good sign that she was moving on. But a little scary too. How was it possible to love someone with your entire heart, lose him, and then barely think of him after only two and a half years? Her mother would describe it as healthy, normal, the final phase of the grieving process.... But just the same, Maggie wasn't entirely sure she wanted that process to end. As incongruous as it seemed, there was a very real comfort in grieving—a familiar sort of grounding. Somehow it made that missing part of her life seem closer. The thought of completely letting go of her grief was unsettling. Yet at the same time, she eagerly looked forward to what lay ahead for her—something she never would've dreamed possible even a year ago. Now it almost seemed as if her life had been dissected into two neat sections. *Before* losing Phil and *after*. And she now lived solidly and even contentedly in the *after*. She paused and looked up to the brilliantly lit sky. "Thank you, God," she said out loud. "You have brought me such a long, long way, and I thank you!"

Seven

"Did you get your boy off to school okay this morning?" asked Abigail when Maggie walked into the newspaper office.

"Yes. It was so sweet to stand in the house and watch him waiting by the road for the bus," she said as she flipped through her small pile of mail. "It was all I could do not to run out with the camera and take a snapshot like I did on his very first day of school when he was only six."

Scott grunted from his office. "Good thing you exercised some self-control there, Maggie. That's just the sort of thing that can scar a boy for life."

"I think someone's in a bad mood this morning," teased Abigail.

Maggie held a forefinger to her lips in a signal, then whispered, "It's a little bit of love trouble."

"I heard that!" snapped Scott, emerging from his office with a dark scowl.

"Sorry," said Maggie, "but it's not as if you were keeping it secret. How's it going anyway? Did the 'friend' make it here okay?"

He rolled his eyes. "Unfortunately, Aaron arrived last night. I was hoping he might have a wreck, or at least a flat tire, coming over the pass."

She shook her head. "That's not very sportsmanlike of you, Scotty."

"Yeah, Mom says I'm acting pretty childish. But she actually wants to invite the two of them over for dinner this week!"

"I think that's a good idea…"

"*You women!*" exploded Scott dramatically. "You all think alike!" He stomped back to his office, solidly shutting the door behind him.

Abigail and Maggie both laughed over this, then Maggie went into her office and started to look over the layout for that week's paper. By noon she felt blurry-eyed, but continued to work while nibbling at a bagel and apple. Finally she stopped, leaning back into her chair for a long stretch. Why was she pushing herself so hard? There was no real urgency to get this finished today. In the past she'd often worked compulsively like this as a distraction—to keep her mind from dwelling on other matters. She thought for a moment. Was there something she was trying to avoid? Sure enough, there was something gnawing away at her.

As much as she'd unconsciously tried to suppress it, it hadn't gone away. And now she wondered once again, *why hadn't Gavin called her yet?* She picked up a pencil and began to thump it rhythmically upon her desk, trying to think if there might be some way she could contact him, something she had overlooked. Or, she thought suddenly, could it be she was experiencing a huge blind-spot by simply assuming that Gavin was the only possible candidate for Leah's birth-father? Sure, it all seemed to add up and make perfect sense. But what if it was only circumstantial evidence? And if so, how much time might she have already wasted on a wild goose chase? Not to mention how Gavin himself had written how it was wrong to judge a person guilty until proven so. Perhaps she'd simply been too eager to link Clyde with Leah, allowing the potential of a storybook ending to obscure her judgment. As she continued to drum her pencil, her eyes fell across a rough advertisement for the Eagle. She absently read the type. It seemed Richard was bringing back happy hour to his bar, complete with complimentary nachos. Now she'd heard more than once that Richard had a reputation for being something of a ladies' man, and although she wouldn't describe him as wealthy, he lived comfortably enough. Why had she so easily dismissed *him?* Or anyone else for that matter? As a good reporter, she'd been trained to examine and research all the resources and possibilities before coming to a conclusion. Why had she so easily stopped her investigation at Gavin?

Suddenly she began to write out a list of the men in town who could feasibly be Leah's father, starting with Gavin and working her way through every single possibility. In fact, about the only name she left off was Clyde Barnes and that was because she'd already spoken to him. The list was fairly long, and she decided to prioritize it numerically with a one to five rating, based on the information given to her by Leah. She gave many of the men, like Lou Henderson, a five because it seemed so inconceivable. She also placed a five by Sam Galloway's name, remembering how he and Rosa had still been in California at the time Leah was conceived. But even as she studied the list, it was still Gavin's name that stood out like a neon light. She shook her head. No, she must keep an open mind, and there were several others who still bore a one rating, including Richard's. Glancing back at the ad for the Eagle, she searched her mind for a reason, a legitimate one, to call him about it. Finally she dialed his number, waiting until she heard his deep voice answer.

"Hi, Richard. Sorry to bother you, but I was just looking at your ad for this week's paper and noticed you didn't have any prices listed. Is that how you wanted it? I was thinking that happy hour usually included a reduced price for beverages."

"Hmm. I suppose so." He quickly rattled off some prices, which she wrote down. "Thanks for picking up on that, Maggie. I'd say that's pretty good service."

"No problem." She paused. "Say, Richard, I was just wondering—did you ever live in Phoenix?"

"Phoenix? Why? You thinking about moving?"

She laughed. "No. Just curious is all."

"Nope. Never lived in Phoenix."

"Ever visit?"

"Well, yes. I've been there several times. I've got a buddy who lives down there."

She strained to think of an innocuous way to question him further. "What time of year do you usually visit him?"

"Winter, of course. Mostly late January to early February—you know, the time of year when the sight of snow makes you nearly crazy, and you want a warm spot to take the chill out of your bones. Why? Are you thinking about taking a trip this winter? I'd be glad to help you plan one. My buddy has this great place..."

"Thanks, Richard. That's so nice of you. But I'm looking forward to my first winter here." A creative escape to this conversation occurred to her. "But I'm not so sure about my mom. You see, she's considered living up here, but I think the winters would be hard on her. I wanted to keep some other places in mind where she might go to get away too."

"Well, Phoenix is as good as any for a winter break."

"Thanks, Richard. I appreciate the information."

She hung up. She knew Leah's birthday was in May which, if her math was correct, meant she would've been conceived toward the end of the previous summer. She lowered Richard from a one to a five, then changed it to a four just in case he wasn't being honest. Greg Snider's was the next name with a one beside it. She glanced at her watch—not too late for a quick workout. Everyone from the office was still at lunch, so she left a note on Abigail's desk saying she'd be back before two, then walked over to Cherise's fitness center.

"Hey there, you!" said Cherise. "You don't usually come on Tuesdays."

"Well, since yesterday was a holiday—"

"Of course! Well then hurry up and get dressed down and I'll schedule you for the stepper machine while no one's using it."

Maggie quickly tugged on her gym clothes, formulating in her mind how she would broach the subject with Cherise, then hurried out to the exercise area.

Cherise, always eager to chat, hung about while Maggie plodded away on the stair-stepper. Cherise reminded her of a tropical bird fluttering about to build its nest. She kept herself busy cleaning and polishing the nearby weight machines, chattering all the while.

"I think I know how you stay in such terrific shape," commented Maggie. "It's because you never stop moving."

Cherise giggled. "That's exactly what Greg says. He's always telling me to sit down and shut up for a change. But I can't. I think it's just the way I'm made."

"How long have you and Greg been married?" asked Maggie, suddenly realizing that Cherise could possibly be unaware of Greg's whereabouts nineteen years ago.

"It'll be our seventh anniversary in December." She paused for a moment. "Do you think that means we'll get the seven-year itch?"

Maggie shook her head as she continued to step. "I don't think it really exists, I know I never had it with my husband. So how did you guys meet?"

Cherise waved her hand. "Oh, we've known each other for—well, forever. Of course, I was just a flat-chested junior-high girl when Greg was in high school. But I always admired him from a distance. He and Gavin Barnes were high-school jocks, if you know what I mean. They played all the sports."

Maggie grabbed a towel to wipe her face. "Did you both always live in Pine Mountain then?"

"Except for when Greg was away at college up in Washington state." She looked down at the spray bottle of cleaner in her hand. "I never did go to college. And about the time I graduated from high school, Greg came back to town with his new wife…"

"His wife? But I thought…"

Cherise laughed. "I mean his *first* wife. I guess you never heard about her. They met in college. I was totally crushed when I learned that Greg Snider had gotten himself married off. But I held my head high, and I was still friendly to him. He'd gotten himself a CPA degree and started up a tax accountant business in one of those offices over on Ponderosa Street. After about a year, he hired me on as his receptionist. I'd taken some business classes in high school and had been doing receptionist work for Glenda's Glamour Shop back behind the grocery store."

"I see," puffed Maggie.

"You can probably guess what happened after that. Some people say I broke up their marriage. But the truth is their marriage was already a mess, and I just tried to be real nice and understanding to Greg. And besides, Janice, his first wife, absolutely hated Pine Mountain. She was always pushing him to move away from here."

The timer went off on the stair-stepper and Maggie climbed down, obediently following Cherise to the next piece of equipment, listening as she went.

"I guess it was about twelve years ago that Greg's marriage fell completely apart, and back then the economy wasn't so hot; and what with the highway problems and all, well, he just lost his whole business. He was really depressed for a while. But lucky for him, the postmaster job came up, and I guess it somehow helped that he belongs to the National Guard. Anyway, I just stuck with him like glue through all those hard times, and then one day I finally said to him, 'Greg Snider, it's about time you made an honest woman out of me.' And he said, 'okay.' So we drove on over to Reno that same weekend and tied the knot." Cherise's brow creased. "I suppose that's not a very romantic story."

Maggie gave a final pull on the weights then stopped. "I think what matters most is that you both love each other."

Cherise frowned. "I guess so." She moved Maggie to the next machine. "Okay now, let's work those abdominals." She proudly patted her tiny waist. "Not having babies has helped keep me in perfect shape."

Maggie groaned as she performed a crunch, then gasped, "I wouldn't trade my son for a perfect waistline any day."

"Yeah," Cherise's voice sounded sad. "Between you and me and the lamppost, I'd trade mine in for a baby too."

Maggie blinked up at her. "Then why don't you?"

"Greg." As if that explained everything, and Maggie supposed it did.

Finally she finished her workout, then showered and dressed quickly. She felt fairly certain that Greg was an unlikely candidate for Leah's father and mentally moved him to a five rating as she told Cherise goodbye, pausing to give her a hug. Poor Cherise. Such a sweet and benign personality, yet she'd made some poor life choices and now had to live with them. Although she had to hand it to the woman, she always seemed to persevere as the perennial optimist, which was no small thing being married to a man like Greg. And it hardly surprised Maggie that his first wife hadn't lasted—how many women could? Cherise was one in a million, and Greg Snider ought to thank his lucky stars for her!

As Maggie walked back to the office, a new thought occurred to her regarding Leah's parentage mystery. Was it possible that her mother might have come to Pine Mountain for a visit nineteen years ago? She'd have to run that scenario by Leah tonight. As she began to cross the street, she noticed a flash of long red hair in time to spy Chloe and a tall young man going in the door of the newspaper office. That must be Scott's rival, Aaron Jackson, with her. Maggie braced herself for fireworks as she entered the reception area, but to her amusement Scott was greeting them both like a perfect gentlemen. She winked at him from behind, then waited until he introduced her to Chloe's old friend.

"Pleased to meet you, Ms. Carpenter," said Aaron. "I've seen your little newspaper on the Internet, and find it quite amusing."

"Did you see Scott's story about Mrs. Bowerman's skunks last week?" asked Abigail brightly.

Aaron laughed. "I sure did. I even told a coworker about it, and we both had a good laugh."

Maggie noticed Scott's smile fade. "Well, that was exactly the purpose of the story," she said quickly. "Nothing wrong with some lighthearted entertainment. You city dwellers could use a little more, I'd imagine."

"That's for sure," said Aaron. "Our news just seems to get more dismal and disgusting every time you turn around."

Scott gave Aaron the two-bit tour, even taking him back to see the old-fashioned machinery, while Chloe chatted with Maggie. "I don't understand why Scott is taking Aaron's visit so seriously," she said quietly.

"You *don't?*"

Chloe rolled her eyes. "Well, I guess I do. But he shouldn't feel so threatened."

"He's very fond of you. And I suppose Aaron's visit makes him feel a little insecure."

Chloe smiled mischievously. "Maybe that's a good thing. You know how Scott can be so self-assured sometimes. I mean, he can even come across as kind of cocky if you're not used to him."

Maggie nodded knowingly. "Now that you mention it, I suppose this little experience might be good for him after all."

"Just the same, I'll try to reassure him a bit more," said Chloe kindly. "I suppose I haven't made it very easy on him. Although...I must admit that I have enjoyed watching him squirm."

"You kids," she said, sounding to herself like an old woman, yet at the same time not actually feeling that much older. She went into her office and noticed her scrawled list of the local men who might be Leah's father. She folded the list and tucked it into her pocket. It might not be good to leave a list like that lying around. She laughed. Someone might actually think she was composing and ranking a group of local men—and to what purpose?

⟶

It was the end of the first week at school, and so far Spencer had nothing good to say about anything. Each day he seemed more quiet and glum than the day before. Maggie knew adjusting took time, but felt certain that everything would soon fall into place. And at least he had Sierra to help ease his way. Being such an outgoing girl, she surely had plenty of friends to share with him. On Friday Maggie pulled into her driveway after work to spot Spencer sitting on the front porch steps, Bart by his side with head tilted up and tail thumping happily. She called out a hello and Bart darted down the path to greet her. Perhaps this was a good sign.

"How was school, Spence?" she asked tentatively as she stroked Bart's head and braced herself for her son's answer.

"Okay, I guess."

She looked up in surprise. "So, are things improving then?"

"Yeah, I guess so."

"That's good." She set her briefcase on the steps. "Meet any new kids?"

Looking at her as if she were demented, he answered with sarcasm, "Yeah, Mom. I've met about three hundred or so this week."

"Oh, I know. But have you made any new friends yet, or perhaps some potential friends?"

He brightened a little. "Actually, there's this guy in my art class who seems okay. His name's Ed and he lives on a farm a few miles out of town. He snowboards, and he plays bass guitar and wants to start up a real band."

"Sounds interesting."

"He saw me drumming with my drawing pencils while the teacher was droning on and on in art class, and he told me he thinks I might make a good drummer."

She suppressed the smile that threatened to undermine what she suspected should remain a serious conversation. "A drummer?"

"Yeah. Ed thinks I should get a drum set and start practicing right away."

She nodded solemnly. "Aren't drum sets pretty spendy?"

"I've still got money left over from my summer jobs, and I could keep working on the house after school if you want."

"Sure, if it's that important to you. But wouldn't it be smart to take a drumming class or something first just to make sure you really like drums before you plunk down all that money for a set?"

"Maybe. I'll think about it. Are you saying it's okay, Mom?"

"I don't see why not. It sounds like fun."

"Great, 'cause you know that wherever the drummer lives is where we have to practice."

Maggie considered that. The idea of a beginning rock band's music blasting through the house every night didn't seem terribly conducive to working on her novel. She'd been envisioning getting a really good start on it during the long winter evenings. "Uh, do you think maybe you could practice your music in the barn? We could probably find some way to heat out there."

"Cool. I can't wait to tell Ed."

At the dinner table, Audrey asked Maggie if she'd been upstairs.

"Actually, I haven't had a chance." She looked up from her roast beef with concern. "Is something wrong? Plumbing problems?"

"No, not at all. I was going to wait until you saw it for yourself, but I might as well tell you—Jed brought that wardrobe by today."

"Oh, that's great!" she exclaimed. "I almost forgot. And I didn't tell you where I wanted it—"

"Jed thought it was for your bedroom."

"But I never even told him."

"Was that where you wanted it?" asked Leah as she passed Spencer the potatoes.

"Yes. But I don't know how he knew."

"He's a smart one, that Jed Whitewater. And you should have seen him and Kate maneuvering that big thing up the stairs and around the corner on the landing. They make quite a team, those two." She glanced at Maggie. "And no matter what Rosa says, I think there's something there."

"Kate is so beautiful," said Leah. "I think she could be a fashion model if she wanted—except that she's probably too old."

"Too old?" Audrey laughed. "I doubt that Kate is even thirty."

Maggie shook her head and stabbed her fork into the meat. "Well, now it'll be hard to sit here and eat. I can hardly wait to see how it looks."

After dinner, she went up to inspect the wardrobe. It was placed against the very wall she'd had in mind. And although she'd imagined it more to the center she had to admit it looked perfect set just off to the right. And it looked great in her room, almost as if specially designed to go there. The only problem now was that her existing bedroom furniture suddenly appeared small and mousy compared to this masterpiece. Well, perhaps in time she could replace her things with pieces specially made by Jed as she saved up for them.

On her way back down, she met Leah going up. "I need to talk with you privately," she said. "Can you meet me in the library in a few minutes?"

She continued downstairs, then opened the large glass-panel double-doors into the seldom-used room. Although they'd begun calling the wood-paneled room "the library," not a single book graced its barren and dark shelves as of yet. Spencer and Jed had convinced her that all the woodwork in there needed to have the ancient, darkened varnish removed in order to reveal the beautiful luster of the old mahogany beneath. Perhaps that would be the perfect project for Spencer to begin after school to earn money for his drums. She cracked open a window to reduce the musty smell, then sank into the old leather couch that she had found tucked in the back of Cal's secondhand store last month. Buried beneath a pile of moth-eaten blankets, she'd discovered what she'd been certain was a prize. Then she and her mother worked long and hard to clean and restore the burgundy leather. And the reward was the soft lustrous patina of aged leather. In Maggie's opinion, a new couch couldn't compare to this one. Plus it looked just right in "the library." Now she hoped to find a big, old desk to go in this room. She'd already searched Cal's store to no avail, but at the same time had spotted a few other treasures worth salvaging. "You've got some good stuff mixed in here with all these things," she'd told him. His eyes lit up. "Why don't you show me some of it," he'd said, eagerly rubbing his hands together. But she'd just laughed, saying, "Are you kidding—then you might raise the price. But don't worry, I'll be back and I promise not to steal you blind." She ran her hand over the arm of the couch, fingering the brass tacks hobnailed along the edges as she studied the old mantle in front of her. Nearly black with age, its design was classic. She looked forward to seeing the grain of the wood revealed again. She could imagine it glowing warmly as the old fireplace crackled on a cold winter's night, and here she would sit as she reworked and finished the old novel she had begun so many years ago.

"What's up?" asked Leah, closing the doors behind her.

Maggie patted the sofa. "I just wanted to ask some questions about your mom. And to let you know a little about how my search..."

"Did you find him?" Leah's face brightened.

She shook her head. "I don't think it'll be that simple. But I do have some leads. What I want to know is whether you think it's possible that your mother ever came up here to Pine Mountain?"

"I asked her that once. At first she acted like she didn't know what I was talking about. But after I made it clear that I knew about this place, she said she'd never laid eyes on it, but from what she'd heard it was 'some fancy resort town where rich people went to play.'"

Maggie laughed. "Well, I'd say that very nearly proves that she's never been here."

Leah looked surprised. "But it is sort of a resort town, isn't it?"

"That's what it's trying to be. But I wouldn't call it 'fancy' or a place where 'rich people go to play.'"

"I guess not." Then Leah held her chin out. "But I do think it's an awfully nice place for a little town."

Maggie smiled. She could just imagine Clyde taking that same defensive position about his hometown. Sometimes it seemed so obvious to her that Leah had to be a Barnes! But still she must watch herself. No sense in getting Leah's hopes up prematurely. "Well, then," she continued, "has your mother always lived in Phoenix?"

Leah thought. "When I was in second grade, Mom married Jeff and we moved to Albuquerque for about three years. I kind of liked it there, and Jeff wasn't too terrible, but then he just took off and disappeared one day, so we went straight back to Phoenix. My mom's parents both lived there, in separate houses of course, but I think my mom sort of liked being near Grandma, although she never said so. Then my grandma died a few years back. But just the same my mom seems pretty much stuck in Phoenix. I guess she likes it. And that's where I was born."

"And you're sure your mom was living in Phoenix the year before you were born?"

"You mean, like did she go someplace else to get pregnant?" asked Leah bluntly.

"Well, yes. It is possible. Like say, she might have taken a trip to—Las Vegas or perhaps some other place..."

"I don't really know how. She was only seventeen when she got pregnant. She was about to be a senior in high school, but she never graduated. At the time she became pregnant, she was working at a convenience store, and my grandma told me once that she was already using back then. Guess I'm lucky to be normal."

"Were you close to your grandma?"

"Not really. She tried to help me sometimes. But mostly it just seemed like she wanted to turn me against my mom. And I felt sorry for my mom. A lot of the time she didn't have anyone at all. I felt like she needed me." Leah looked down at her lap. "I still worry about her."

"I'm sure you do." Maggie reached over and placed a hand on her arm. "But your mom made her own decisions to live life in a certain way. Now it's your turn to make your decisions and to live your life however you feel is best. It's okay to leave her, Leah. She's a grown-up."

"I know." Leah nodded. "And I sure don't want to end up like her. I just wish I could help her somehow."

"You *are* helping her."

Leah looked at her with curiosity. "How?"

"Mothers love their children more than anything. And mothers want the very best for their children. But your mother was unable to give you the best. So I think the fact that you're working toward a better life should make her extremely happy and proud."

Leah brightened. "It should."

"But, you know, I do think it'd be thoughtful to let your mother know you're okay. As a mom, I'm ashamed that I didn't consider this sooner."

"But I don't want her to know that I'm here."

"I realize that, but how about if you write a letter, and we can have it sent from someplace else. I could send it to my friend in L.A. and have her forward it from there."

"Really? That would be perfect. I'll explain to my mom that I'm not really in L.A.—I'm sure that'd be a relief—but that for the time being I don't want her to know where I am. Do you think that's fair?"

"Some kids wouldn't even bother to do that much. I think that's very thoughtful. You write the letter and I'll send it. We can trust my friend, who also happens to be an attorney, to send it right off."

Leah reached over and gave her a gentle hug. "Thanks so much. I know I've told you thanks over and over. But honestly, I don't know where I'd be without you guys right now. Sometimes I think it might not even matter if I ever find my real dad or not, because you guys have been like family to me. But then at other times, I feel like such a misfit. Like what am I doing here? Everyone else has a reason to be in Pine Mountain, but what right do I have to hang around like this?"

"You have every right, honey. Don't you forget, I'm a newcomer too. So is Buckie and Chloe and Elizabeth Rodgers—just to mention a few. This town is certainly big enough to take in a few strays like us. And, believe me, I think it will be the better for it."

Eight

*I*t didn't take long for Spencer to locate a used set of drums in the classified section. During the past couple weeks, he'd diligently researched a number of music equipment sources on the Internet as well as questioned his band teacher at school until he felt he had a basic understanding of what was best to look for in a trap set, and to Maggie's amusement this information was shared nightly at the dinner table until she almost felt like an expert herself. He was convinced that this set in the ad was a reputable name for a very decent price. After all the time and work he'd put into stripping and refinishing the library woodwork, Maggie had no desire to question his judgment. She'd already told him it was his decision and his hard-earned money. And she was pleased to drive him over to Byron after school to see how the drum set sounded.

"You're a natural, man," said the drummer after watching Spencer play around for a few minutes. "These are really good drums, but I just got me a new Zjion set. My band's starting to make some bucks and play in some good places, and it was time for an upgrade."

Spencer happily paid the guy, and somehow the three of them got everything loaded into the back of Maggie's Volvo. As she drove toward home, she listened as Spencer talked with excitement about how Ed had found this really talented guitar player, and now that he had his drums they could start practicing right away.

"We're hoping we'll be ready to play something in time for the Homecoming Bonfire," said Spencer as he drummed the drumsticks upon his knees.

"What's that all about?"

"Ed says they have this huge bonfire before homecoming and some of the local bands play—kind of like a concert. It'd be so cool if we could do a song too."

Maggie hated to squelch his enthusiasm, especially after his first gloomy weeks of starting out at a new school, but she knew that homecoming was only a few weeks away and honestly wondered how their barely begun band could possibly be ready to play in public so soon. Just the same, she kept these thoughts to herself.

Sure enough, the next day when she got home from work, she could hear loud screeching sounds—not exactly music—coming from the direction of the barn. An old orange VW bug plastered with bumper stickers, somewhat remnant of the hippie era, was parked in the driveway. Though tempted to go take a peek, she decided to respect her son's space, hoping he would bring his new friends by the house later. But she didn't actually meet them for a couple of days, and then only when she literally ran right into a strange, tall, longhaired young man coming out of her kitchen with a can of soda in his hand. "Hello?" she said with wide eyes.

"Hey." He tipped the soda to his lips then said, "I'm Daniel."

"Are you a friend of Spencer's?" she asked, trying not to stare at the dark tattoo on his forearm. She couldn't tell exactly what it was and wondered if she'd rather not know.

"Yeah. I play guitar." He tossed his head to get a strand of hair out of his eyes.

"Well, I'm Maggie, Spencer's mom." She extended her hand.

"Yeah, sure, whatever." He shook it limply, and it was then she noticed the pair of silver studs protruding from his lower lip. He released her hand and said, "Spencer said I could get something to drink in here."

"Sure, that's fine. Say, do you happen to know where my son is?"

He jutted his thumb over his shoulder. "He and Ed are out in the barn."

Of course, she'd seen boys like this before. In L.A. you could see almost anything. But somehow the idea that someone like this had befriended her son and was now playing in his band disturbed her more than she cared to admit.

"Oh, there you are, Maggie," said Audrey, coming around the corner. She paused with raised brows as Daniel continued toward the front door. "That a friend of yours?" she asked after the door closed behind him.

"No. He's in Spencer's band," she answered flatly.

"Is he the same age as Spence?"

"I don't know, Mom. I take it you haven't met these boys either."

Audrey shook her head. "I see that little orange car come and go after school, but that's the first time I saw one of the boys up close. Goodness, I hope Spencer doesn't decide to pierce something now."

"Actually, I thought body piercing was on its way out."

"Maybe they're a little backwards up here, dear."

She wanted to see the humor in her mother's comment, but at the moment she just couldn't. Instead she searched her mother's eyes. "What do I do, Mom? I know it's stupid, but suddenly I feel really scared. It's as if my little boy's life is flashing before my eyes, and he's speeding down the wrong road."

Her mother smiled. "Not to worry, dear. You've done a good job raising him. No need to think that some thug with earrings in his lip will corrupt our boy. Well, at least not yet."

"Not yet?"

"Well, I'm sure you realize how influential peer pressure *can* be. Let's not fool ourselves on that account, Maggie. We all know it's usually kids who lead kids astray."

"I know, I know. What can I do to prevent it?"

"Oh, the age-old question. If I knew the answer to that, I would write a book and make a million."

"Mom, be serious. You're a family counselor, you're supposed to have the answers about things like this."

Audrey thought for a moment. "In that case, I'd first of all recommend you keep those communication doors open with Spence. Maybe even gently voice your concerns about his new friends, but in a non-threatening way. You certainly don't want to make a big deal about the way his friends look…"

"That's easier said than done."

"Oh, honey, don't you remember how it was when you were that age? Teenagers just want to look different, they're searching for their identity. The real irony is that at the same time they want to look strange, they all have this desperate need to be accepted just as they are. So, I would pick my battles carefully. Of course, you may need to remind Spence of the house rules or limits or whatever you call them these days. And then you need to be prepared to dole out some consequences if necessary. But most of all, you just need to keep on loving him through thick and thin."

"I was considering going out to meet his friends," said Maggie cautiously. "Do you think that's a bad idea?"

"Not at all. This is your home and Spencer is your son. Go ahead."

With her mother's encouragement to bolster her spirits, Maggie traipsed out toward the source of the cacophony of electrically amplified sound (not music!) reverberating through the air. Thank goodness she had no close neighbors to complain! She glanced at the beat-up VW parked by the barn. It looked like graffiti on wheels from all the weird bumper stickers splayed across it; and the car's interior looked like a large, mobile waste receptacle—oh, the things to look forward to. She cautiously cracked open the door to the barn and was instantly met by the acrid smell of cigarette smoke. Now she angrily shoved the door fully open and stepped inside to see the barn full of smoke! She actually felt her nostrils flare with rage as she stared at the would-be musicians and equipment that had taken over the barn.

"Mom?" Spencer stopped drumming as a look of surprise—and perhaps fear—washed over his face.

"What is going on in here?" she demanded loudly.

"We're playing music," said Spencer, drawing his head down to his shoulders like a startled tortoise.

"I mean this *smoke!*"

Another young man, the one she hadn't yet met, stepped forward. His hair was blond and shaggy, but he seemed void of any tattoos or body-piercing—at least nothing she could see. "Hi, I'm Ed Tanner," he said politely. "And I guess I'm the one you should be mad at. I didn't realize you didn't want anyone to smoke out here."

She blinked, somewhat surprised by his manners, but still irked at the nerve of these kids. "This is an old barn," she declared. "And as you can see, there is still very dry hay in here. Have you no idea how easily this place could all go up in flames?"

Ed nodded. "I see your point. I just wasn't thinking. I promise it'll never happen again."

"How old are you?" she demanded.

"Uh, eighteen," he stammered.

"Oh. But aren't you in art class with Spence..."

"*Mom,*" pleaded Spencer, but Ed stopped him.

"It's okay, I don't mind explaining. I'm the only senior in that class, but it's 'cause I never took art before and I needed another elective to graduate."

"Oh." She pressed her lips together. His candid demeanor and politeness had managed to disarm her a little.

"Can we get back to practicing now?" asked Spencer in an irritated voice. She looked over to see his eyes glaring at her, and she knew that she had embarrassed him in front of his new friends.

"Well, I'm sorry to have interrupted, but I wanted to meet your friends, Spence. And if it hadn't been for the smoking I would've just come and gone. But you should've brought them into the house and introduced them to everyone—Leah and your grandmother too."

"Sorry. I will." He tapped upon his cymbal impatiently. "Is that all?"

She paused for a moment. "As long as you *all* completely understand about the no smoking policy." She looked directly at Daniel, who was now tuning his guitar.

"We *understand*," said Spencer with impatience. "It won't happen again."

She turned and walked out, leaving the door open behind her. She felt it could use a little fresh air in there. She sighed as she walked toward the house. She was not proud over the way she'd handled the situation, and yet even with hindsight she wasn't sure how she could've reacted differently. Except maybe to have counted to ten before she blew up and embarrassed her son. Still, he knew better. She would discuss this with him later, in private.

Heeding her mother's words of advice, Maggie made a point to communicate openly with Spencer during the next few days, but at the same time she sensed a certain defensive tone when she made any mention of his new friends. She now knew that Ed was Rick Tanner's son, and Rick was a good buddy of Greg Snider's and someone who'd never treated her with an ounce of respect. Yet it seemed unfair to hold the father's behavior against the son. Besides, Ed had displayed some rather good manners, other than the smoking issue, and she wanted to be fair. So she discretely chose not to mention any of this to Spencer. It already felt like walking on a minefield whenever she brought up the subject of his new friends; there seemed no point in carelessly tossing out another bombshell. Still, she felt bewildered at how quickly things could change in the life of a teenager.

One day everything's fine, and the next—well, who knew? Perhaps it was best to be prepared for anything. But after Spencer's amazing turnaround this summer, it seemed senseless that it should all fall apart now. And all she could think was that if it did, it would be due in part to the influence of his two questionable friends.

"What does Sierra think of Ed and Daniel?" she asked after a fairly heated discussion about the increasing popularity of teen smoking.

Spencer shrugged. "I don't know. She has her own set of friends, and even when she tries to get me to hang with them, they act pretty stuck-up to me."

This made her feel sad, as if this whole thing were partly her fault for uprooting him from his home and bringing him here. "Well, maybe you just need to get used to them," she offered hopefully.

He looked her straight in the eye. "Maybe they just need to get used to me."

"But sometimes the newcomer has to take the first step."

"Look, Mom, besides Sierra, Ed was the first person in the whole stupid school to even give me the time of day."

"I know. But you and Sierra are still friends."

"Sierra has her own life," snapped Spencer. "And I have mine."

She blinked in surprise, then sat down on the steps next to him. "Are you saying that you and Sierra aren't very good friends anymore?"

"It's pretty hard to be her friend when Kurt Gilbert is hanging around all the time. He acts like he owns her."

"The guy at the dance?"

"Yeah. I guess he worked at a basketball camp for most of the summer; that's why he wasn't around. But it's pretty clear that he thinks Sierra is his and his alone."

"That seems silly. What does Sierra think?"

"She doesn't seem to mind his attention. He's this preppy kind of sports jock guy. He plays football and basketball and everybody acts like he's real cool."

She nodded knowingly. "And he doesn't like you very much?"

Spencer shook his head. "He treats me like dirt."

"He's probably just jealous."

He looked at her with curiosity. "Oh, yeah, like I'm some real competition. This geeky, freaky, redheaded kid with two left feet."

"You do not have two left feet!"

"Mom, you just don't get it."

She put an arm around his shoulders. "I think Kurt's the one who doesn't get it. And I'm surprised and sorry that Sierra is interested in someone like *that*."

"Well, I probably made him sound worse than he is. Although I'm pretty sure he hates me. I mean, most of the time he just ignores me, or else he says stupid things about me. But the kids think he's cool." Spencer scratched Bart's ear. "And I'm the one who's a geek."

"Well, Sierra doesn't think you're a geek."

"I don't think she does. But she's pretty distracted by Kurt right now. I'm just hoping that when our band plays at the bonfire, she might look at me differently, you know. And maybe a few other people will give us a little respect too."

Suddenly she understood the importance of this whole musical endeavor. As hard as it was for her to accept Ed and Daniel, she'd have to try harder, and for Spence's sake be less judgmental. Besides, she reprimanded herself, God loved both those boys just as much as he loved Spencer. She would just try to reach out to them more.

Nine

By the beginning of October, Maggie still hadn't heard a single word from Gavin, but that didn't stop Clyde from continuing to assume that Leah was his long lost great-niece. Of course, he kept this information between himself and Maggie. But she was aware of how often he found an excuse to frequent the Blue Moose, and had even bought a couple of framed prints from Buckie. Naturally, they were wildlife photos, and he may have purchased them anyway, but Maggie suspected Leah's presence helped to nail the sales. This special bond that Clyde felt towards Leah worried Maggie since it was thus far only theory and unproved. If only she could confirm the link to Gavin! But on the other hand, did a blood connection really mean all that much? Her friend Rebecca had been adopted and firmly believed her adoptive parents were far more important than her biological ones. But Maggie knew how family, or kin as he called it, was vital to Clyde, and the pain he'd suffered from Gavin might lessen some if it turned out that Leah was his kin. Leah had told Maggie how Clyde had promised her a job at the paper if Buckie failed to appreciate her valuable working skills. But it only took a couple of weeks before Buckie began to acknowledge his young employee's progress, bragging (with a wink) that he'd known from the start that this girl had great potential. And when it came time for his Alaska trip in mid-September, he had left without the slightest concern over the welfare of his business, confidently assuming that Audrey and Leah would keep the place "running like clockwork" in his absence. "My only worry," he confessed to Maggie on the eve of his departure, "is that, with these two ladies, I've suddenly become rather dispensable." She laughed and reassured him. "Don't forget, Buckie, you're the guy who takes the photos. Without you, they'd be out of business in no time." In many ways, she'd been relieved to see him go. Sometimes his energy and persistence nearly exhausted her. He was the kind of guy who demanded her attention whether she wanted to give it or not—what she might have once called a "high-maintenance friend." But at the same time, she had to admit Buckie was fun to have around. After only a week, she found herself actually missing his little impromptu visits and lively chats. His absence helped her realize that Buckie, whatever his faults may be, was in fact a very good friend.

Maggie walked by herself to the deli for lunch. Although the sky was cloudless and the sun shone brightly down, the air had a definite crispness to it, as if the mountain atmosphere were too delicate to contain the heat from the sun and the merest breeze could sweep it away. But she liked it and breathed deeply, allowing the clean air to fill her lungs. She was determined to never, never take this beautiful environment for granted. She would never forget decades of breathing yellow-tinted, smog-tainted air. And if, in the dead of winter, she felt the least bit remorseful, she would simply turn up the heat and remind herself of the price she'd once paid to live in a temperate climate.

Already a number of lampposts were in place along the sidewalk on Main Street. Their dark-green enamel paint gleamed in the autumn sun. She noticed the curved hook protruding from just beneath the hurricane-style lantern and imagined how charming the hanging flower baskets would look next spring—a gardening project that Abigail had offered to head up. Pine Mountain was slowly but surely coming around.

"Hello there!" hailed Cindy Jordan, waving from the front steps of the hotel. "Got a minute, Maggie?"

"Sure. What's up?"

"Come on in." Cindy pushed open the large carved door to the hotel. "I'd like your advice on something. I know you've put a lot of work into restoring your house and I'd really appreciate your opinion on this."

"Well actually, Spencer and Jed do the real work..."

"I know, I know. But aren't you the one who makes those never-ending aesthetic decisions like what color, what style, and all that stuff?"

"I guess you're right about that." She followed Cindy past the nearly finished dining room where a wallpaper hanger was applying a strip of attractive tweed wallpaper above the refinished pine wainscoting. "Oh, Cindy," she exclaimed, "this place looks absolutely gorgeous—even better than I remember from childhood!" She glanced at the newly finished wood flooring peeking out from beneath wide protective strips of brown craft paper. "It looks like the floors came out beautifully."

"They did. But I feel like a kid at Christmas; I want to rip off that paper and see what it all looks like together and all done." Cindy beamed as she led Maggie upstairs. "Fortunately the downstairs will be finished by next week. But right now, Brian and I are having a little disagreement over the upstairs bathrooms. And we need to make a decision like yesterday, so I've decided that you're to be the tie breaker."

Maggie groaned, then said sarcastically, "Just great. Nothing I like more than coming between a happily married couple."

Cindy laughed then called down the hallway. "Hey Brian, I found someone to help us with our little problem."

"Are they armed and dangerous?" asked Brian, stepping out into the hallway. "Oh, hi, Maggie. Yes, you might be just the person after all. Now first let me show you why I think we should go with the..."

"Wait a minute," interrupted Cindy. "No lobbying here. We need to present her with the two choices without saying who thinks what about what. Okay?"

"Okay, then let's see if you can present them in a non-partisan way, Ms. Suddenly I'm So Neutral."

"Fine." She turned to Maggie. "It should be a simple decision, really, but I think we've completely exhausted our ability to reason rationally at this point." She led Maggie into one of the high-ceilinged hotel rooms, still in the midst of refurbishing, then pointed to the small bathroom in the corner. "We need to decide on the flooring. We're choosing between the marble or hardwood." In one hand, she held up a sample of white marble tile, and in the other hand a strip of warm, brown oak.

Maggie studied the bathroom. The walls had a beaded-board wainscot painted a clean, milky white, with a pale pat-terned wallpaper above. Very fresh and airy. She then looked at the two flooring choices. "Well, the marble would cer-tainly reflect a lot of light and be easy to keep clean..." She noticed Brian smiling in triumph. "But then again you've already got a lot of white in here." She turned her attention to the mellow oak. "The wood has a charming, natural appeal which seems to complement the rest of the hotel, and I think wood feels a little warmer on bare feet in the middle of the night." She looked at Cindy and smiled. "I'd have to vote for the wood."

Cindy turned to her husband. "There! I knew it!"

"No need to gloat." He looked at Maggie then threw up his hands. "I should've known that the women would stick together."

"Sorry, Brian, but it's my honest opinion."

"It's okay," said Brian good-naturedly. "It's exactly the same rationale I already heard from Cindy. And to be totally honest, I suppose I have to agree. I guess I was just looking for a little controversy to stir things up." He gently poked

Cindy then grinned. "I better go call the decorator and let her know our decision."

Cindy threw an arm around Maggie's shoulders. "And for that, I'd like to take you to lunch—were you on your way to the deli just now?"

"I didn't realize a payment was involved, but it sounds good to me. Any more disputes I can help you sort out?"

"You'll be sorry you asked," called Brian as the two women went back down the stairs.

"Do you want to look around a little before we go?" asked Cindy.

"I'd love to. Last time I was here things were still pretty torn up."

"The kitchen's almost completely done now. And the new tableware will be here any day. But I'll wait for my chef to arrive before I order any more cooking equipment."

"Your *chef*?"

"Yes. His name is Jean-Michel DuPont. He was head chef at Scallions in Seattle, originally from Quebec but trained in one of the best schools in Paris. He's also a good friend of Brian's."

"That's wonderful, but how in the world did you manage to lure him to little old Pine Mountain?"

"Poor Jean-Michel had a bit of a breakdown a few months ago and hasn't been working since. He thinks a small town like this might be just the medicine, at least for awhile. I think he suffered from big city burnout."

"He sounds intriguing. I'd love to do an article on him in the *Pine Cone*, if he's up to it that is. Naturally I wouldn't mention the breakdown. In fact, I'll keep that entirely to myself."

Cindy's hand flew to her mouth. "Oh, I'm sorry. I never should have mentioned his breakdown, even though he's not my patient. I know better! But thank you for your discretion. Goodness, I almost forgot that you're a newspaperwoman. Lucky for me that you have integrity."

"Well, you know how small towns can be. I'm still learning how important it is to keep my mouth closed about certain things. And just for the record, even though I'm a journalist, my own ethics come before getting a story." She ran her hand over the new butcher-block countertops. "Say, did you hear that we're going to get another new restaurant in town?"

Cindy's brow creased. "You're kidding?"

She nodded. "It's true. Scott just told me this morning. Actually, he's a little bummed out about it too. Did you meet Chloe's friend Aaron? He was in town a couple weeks ago."

"Yes. He seemed like a nice young man. Although, I didn't know he was a restaurateur."

"Actually, he's not. But apparently his uncle is, and it seems that Aaron's always wanted to do something like that. He just got his MBA and has been working in his father's business, but after his visit here he decided to go home and see if he could talk 'daddy' into a loan. Scott said that 'daddy' agreed, and Aaron will be back by the end of the month to start looking at properties."

"Hopefully, it'll take him awhile to get set up," said Cindy. "And that will allow us a chance to get reestablished here. At first I thought it was poor planning to open just as tourist season is slowing way down, but Brian thinks that'll give us time to get the kinks out. Then we plan to do some major marketing to draw in some ski traffic once the ski areas open in November. Of course, I *should* be happy to hear of another business coming to town. Growth really is good news for everyone. And we all need to keep working together to get the tourist traffic up so the whole town can benefit."

She continued to show the downstairs including the bathrooms and banquet room, all very impressive with thoughtful renovations. "Well, I guess that's about it."

Suddenly Maggie thought of something. "Hey, can I send Scott over to get some photos while there's still a little work going on here? You know, to show what you guys have been up to."

"What a great idea, not to mention free advertising."

"And I'll write up a piece to go with them about the amazing transformation you guys have managed to accomplish here." Maggie pulled out her little pad and began to jot down some notes and descriptions.

"You might want to mention our new light fixtures. Most of the original lights had been replaced with ugly modern ones back in the fifties, but it was hard to find the old ones in the quantities we needed. So, we went directly to a reproduction artist to have these period lights made." She pointed out the large bronze lights with golden mica shades. "We wanted something that reflected the turn of the century but without the Victorian frills. So we worked together with a designer in the Midwest to create these lights especially for the hotel."

"They look like they work with the Arts and Crafts period," said Maggie, remembering her informative lecture from Jed when she purchased her wardrobe.

"Exactly! And our furnishings are like that too—actually they're a mixture of mission and craftsman, but they really seem to work well with the lodge-style ambiance of this old hotel."

"Have you ever considered having Jed Whitewater make anything for you?"

"Doesn't he just do that rustic log and elk-horn type of furniture?"

Maggie laughed. "Don't let Jed hear you say that. He's also been developing what he calls his Arts and Crafts reproduction style. I just bought a gorgeous fir wardrobe from him. And Buckie has this beautiful table in his shop…"

"Oh, I saw that—did Jed really make *that*?"

Maggie nodded proudly. "He's very talented."

"Maybe I had better talk to him. There are still a few specific pieces I haven't been able to locate. Perhaps I could get Jed to make them for me."

They discussed these possibilities and many other ideas that Cindy wanted input on over lunch at the deli. "This has been such fun, Maggie," she said when it was finally time to part ways. "I don't know how to thank you for your advice and encouragement. We hired a local decorator from Byron, but she's not very imaginative—which is actually a blessing since Brian and I have pretty strong ideas anyway. We mostly have her locating materials and ordering things, and we call the shots. But I have to admit all these decisions are becoming tiresome as we approach the final lap."

"Well, you two have done an amazing job. I can't wait to see it finished."

᎒

After getting his drum set, Spencer's band had practiced nearly every night and most of the weekends for going on three weeks now. Maggie had asked several times how he made time for his homework, but he assured her he was all caught up. Since he'd always been a good student, she decided to trust him on it, and if midterm grades suggested otherwise she would deal with it then. She had made an effort to be more available and to reach out to the other boys, keeping soft drinks on hand and making pizza and foods that could easily be taken out to the barn with them. She found Ed to be fairly friendly and open, but Daniel was another story. The boy seemed to have such a darkness about him that she worried it might be a cloak for even deeper troubles—the kind of troubles she preferred to spare her son from. But what could she do? Audrey continued to tell her not to make too much of it, reminding her that you can't always judge by outward appearances, especially when dealing with a teenager; and not to forget how Leah had appeared to them on that first day they'd met her. Just the same, Maggie tried to keep a careful, if inconspicuous, eye on the boys.

Now with only three days remaining before their big debut at the homecoming bonfire, Maggie knew Spencer's band would be more driven than ever to practice, and she'd picked up some ingredients to make hoagies. Leah offered to help in the kitchen since Audrey had stayed in town to close up the gallery and then go with Elizabeth Rodgers to Byron for dinner. Maggie was glad to see her mother forming friendships with local people. Maybe that would entice her to stay on.

"Their band's really not bad," said Leah as she sliced tomatoes. "I know you're probably not into that kind of music, but I've listened to them a few times and I think they actually have some potential."

"Really?" Maggie layered slices of cheese and meat on a french roll. "It's hard to tell. I mean, I grew up with rock 'n' roll and hard rock, even acid rock, although I usually went in for more mellow sounds. But the stuff these guys play just doesn't sound like real music to me. Sometimes it sounds as if they're all just terribly angry."

Leah laughed. "I suppose it does. But I think it's part of their creative expression. Although I have to admit some of the loud stuff gives me a headache. Back in Phoenix I was in a band for awhile, and sometimes while we were rehearsing I actually wore earplugs. But I always made sure my hair covered them up so the guys didn't know."

Maggie chuckled. "So, did you play an instrument?"

"No, I sang."

"Do you like to sing?"

Leah nodded. "Yeah, it was fun. But I had to quit so I could get a real job. Our band wasn't exactly bringing it in."

Maggie set the last sandwich on the tray. "Want to help me deliver this to the fellas?"

"Sure." Leah picked up a six-pack of sodas and a large bag of chips, and the two of them headed toward the barn. As usual, loud whining sounds were emitting from the old structure. Sometimes Maggie wondered what Clyde would think if he knew what kind of noise came out of the beautiful old barn built by his father so many years ago. Leah slid the door open and the two walked in, Maggie sniffing loudly, as usual, to see if there was any trace of cigarette smoke anywhere.

"Are you guys hungry?" she called over the din of their music. One by one they stopped playing and came over to help themselves to the food.

"Thanks, I'm starved," said Ed, taking a big bite.

Daniel swiped a strand of hair from his eyes and muttered something that sounded like "thanks" then focused his attention fully on the food. That kid could eat more than the other two combined.

"Are you guys about ready for the bonfire?" asked Maggie, trying hard to be congenial.

"Yeah, we've got two songs all ready to go," said Spencer between bites. "But none of us are very good on the vocals."

"Hey," said Maggie suddenly. "I know a singer."

Spencer rolled his eyes. "*Mom*, we aren't one of those seventies bands like The Plumbers or The JeeBees or whatever you call them. We need a singer that understands our kind of sound."

Maggie glanced over at Leah with raised brows and she just shrugged. "Well," began Maggie cautiously. "I just happen to know that Leah used to sing for a band not too different than yours back in Phoenix."

"Really?" said Spencer looking at Leah with fresh interest.

Leah nodded. "They called themselves an alternative-rock band, but they had a different kind of sound. They weren't into electronics at all—everything had to be real."

"Cool," said Ed. "Want to hang around and give us an audition?"

She shrugged again. "I guess I could."

Before long most of the food was gone, and Maggie picked up the remains to take back to the house. Part of her longed to stay and hear how they sounded, especially with

Leah about to sing. But at the same time, she sensed a very definite generation gap drawing itself into a clear line with her on one side and the kids on the other. And even though it made her feel strangely old, she was trying to be sensitive toward Spencer about these things.

"Thanks for the food, Mom," he called as she closed the barn door.

The house was quiet and suddenly seemed overly large and unusually void of voices and people. Maggie puttered around her kitchen, cleaning and straightening what was already clean and straight. She tried to imagine how it would be when her mother finally returned to California after the Harvest Festival. She had, for the most part, melded so easily with their little household. Maggie was sure she'd miss her. And now that Spencer seemed to spend all his spare time practicing music in the barn, it might get a little lonely. But at least, she'd still have Leah—

Just then the phone rang, and she was caught off guard when she heard Gavin's voice speaking earnestly on the other end. "Did you get my letter, Maggie?"

"Yes, I did. I've been waiting for you to call. How are you, Gavin?"

"I'm okay. I really didn't have access to a phone at the rehab center—it was sort of like a minimum security prison. But I'm out now."

"Are you better?"

"Yeah. I've been off the sauce for," he paused, "exactly twenty-seven days."

"Oh, that's so good to hear, Gavin. I'm really proud of you. Clyde will be too."

"How is my uncle?"

"He's doing well." Suddenly she remembered how she was supposed to play detective about Leah. "So, where are you living now, Gavin?"

"I'm staying with some friends in Laguna. Trying to decide what to do next."

"Do you like it down there?"

"Yeah, it's okay if you like living around a whole lot of people. Nothing like good ol' Pine Mountain." He laughed.

"But at least it's a lot warmer down there. It's already starting to freeze at night up here."

"It's going to be quite a switch for you, Maggie. You sure you're up for a Pine Mountain winter?"

"Actually, I'm looking forward to it. Although I don't think my mother can handle it. I've tried to talk her into moving up here permanently. I thought perhaps she could stay here for most of the year, and then go on down to Arizona during the coldest months."

"That's a good idea. Arizona is a nice place to be in the winter."

"Have you been there?"

"Yeah, I lived there once. Didn't care much for the summers though."

So he was there in the summer! "Really? When did you live there?"

"Oh, gosh, it must've been about twenty years ago."

"What were you doing down there?"

"I worked for a developer. We were going to get rich building track houses for old people." He laughed. "Unfortunately for me, it turned out to be the beginning of a recession down there, and I only lasted about a year or so."

"What part of Arizona?"

"Phoenix. I imagine it's changed a lot since then. I heard my old buddy hung in there long enough to finally make himself a boatload of money—guess I should've stuck with it." He paused, and she felt sorry for him. Gavin's life seemed so full of bad timing and disappointments. Of course, she knew he brought a lot of it on himself, but she couldn't help pitying him just the same.

"Anyway, I didn't call to discuss Phoenix. Like I said in my letter, I want to explain to you about what happened with that drug bust."

"*Explain?* But I thought you weren't involved in it?"

"Not directly."

"*Indirectly?*"

"Let me explain, starting from the beginning. You see, back when I first came to work for Uncle Clyde at the *Pine Cone,* I still had some friends. Well, not really friends—acquaintances rather. They heard I was living out there and stopped by to see me one day. They needed a place in Central Oregon to transact some business, and naturally they thought the newspaper office was a handy location."

"I already know all about that, Gavin."

"Yes. But you don't know everything. Well, I didn't think it'd hurt anything, and the money was good and I had some old debts to pay, so I agreed to leave the backdoor to the *Pine Cone* unlocked on certain nights. We often left the doors unlocked anyway—no one ever worried about crime back then. And that's *all* I had to do with that whole thing. But when Uncle Clyde found out what was going on, he threw me out. And that was the end of my involvement with those guys."

"But there's one thing that's always bothered me, Gavin. How did Bart get to Pine Mountain?"

Gavin cleared his throat. "How is good ol' Bart anyway?"

"He's fine. But you didn't answer my question."

"Well, I did come out there for a visit once."

"Whom did you visit?"

"You want the truth?"

"That's usually the best route, in the long run."

"Okay." He sighed loudly. "I was considering letting them use the old homestead as a drop-off place for their...uh...merchandise."

"My house?" she gasped. "You planned to use *my house* for a drug drop!"

"I didn't know anyone lived there then. And in some ways, it still seemed like *my* house. It's where I grew up, Maggie. My dad was even born there."

"I know, I know. But that makes it even worse—that you would consider using your own family's homestead to further the illegal drug trade in this area after they worked so hard to pioneer and your uncle's trying so hard to rebuild this town!"

He didn't answer. And Maggie felt a little guilty about being so confrontational. And yet it angered her. "Why, Gavin?"

"I needed the money. After he threw me out, Uncle Clyde cut me off without a penny. I was flat broke and a little bitter about the whole thing."

"Did you ever consider getting an honest-to-goodness job?"

"I tried. But there was nothing good available."

She sighed in exasperation. "Why are you telling me all this?"

"I want you to tell my uncle that I had nothing to do with that last drug bust."

"*But you did…*"

"Not directly!"

"The fact that they were here, not even a mile from my house, was a direct consequence of your past involvement with them. Can't you see that?"

"I suppose so. But, honestly, Maggie, I *wasn't* involved with them at the time. After I came out I saw someone was living at the homestead, and then Bart ran off into the woods and didn't come back. Well, then and there I just decided to stop being involved with them. Can't you believe that?"

She thought for a moment. "I suppose I can. But I can't see that it changes much as far as your uncle is concerned. After all, he is partly right."

"But not completely. I wanted him to understand that I wasn't *directly* involved. I don't want him thinking I was one of those lowlife guys trafficking and dealing drugs. I know that's what Greg thinks. He wouldn't even listen to me. But really, I'm not. Will you please tell him that?"

"Yeah, I'll try." Maggie considered Leah again, wondering how she could pin him down better. She now knew Leah's mother's maiden name, but wasn't sure if it was wise to mention it just yet. "So, if I do tell Clyde, do you want to know his reaction to all this?"

"Of course."

"Then how will I reach you?"

Once again the line grew quiet. "I'll call you back in a few days."

"Okay."

"Then you'll tell him?"

"Sure. Why not? Clyde deserves to know that his only nephew isn't a completely dirty, rotten scoundrel."

"Thanks a lot," he said with sarcasm.

"Well, you have to admit you have been something of a pain in the old man's life."

"I suppose so. But I'm trying to change, Maggie. Really I am." He sounded sincere, and almost as if he were choking up just a little.

"Good." She softened her tone. "And for your sake, I truly hope so. I know it would make Clyde very happy. Underneath his hard exterior, I believe he still cares deeply about you."

"And I care about him too."

"Hopefully, you'll get a chance to prove it someday."

"Thanks, Maggie. I really do appreciate your friendship."

"I'll be waiting for your next call. Take care, Gavin."

She hung up. She hadn't really learned much in regard to Leah except, and importantly, that Gavin *had* been in Phoenix at the right time. And although it was still circumstantial at best, it gave her hope. She would tell Clyde about it first thing in the morning. Hopefully he'd have some suggestions about what to do next. She couldn't for the life of her imagine how she'd come right out and casually ask Gavin if he'd gotten a high-school girl pregnant during his brief stint in Phoenix. But how else would they ever know for sure?

Ten

*M*aggie knew that Wednesday was Clyde's busy day. He usually arrived around five in the morning to fire up the old press. At first it had seemed unnecessarily early, especially since the paper's circulation was only 500 and it didn't even go out until afternoon, but when she saw how much effort went into keeping the old machinery on task she began to understand. And besides, she knew it was just the way Clyde worked. He thought nothing of rising before dawn to get to the best fishing hole at the lake. Just the same, Maggie was relieved when Scott had recently decided he wanted to learn more about the antiquated press equipment and had begun to assist with the printing process. It took a load off her mind knowing that Clyde wasn't puttering around there by himself in the thin hours of the morning, and of course Scott was always pleased to cut out early on Wednesdays since he got in his full day shortly after lunch. And today Maggie hoped this new arrangement with Scott might allow her to sneak Clyde away for a few minutes.

When she opened the heavy door to the back room, she was met with the loud rhythmic clanking and banging of the press. She stepped inside and smelled the acrid yet clean aroma of fresh ink and paper. She soon spied Clyde over by the large press, then waved and walked over to speak to him. "I hate to disturb you," she said loudly above the din. "But I've had some news," she mouthed the next words, *"from Gavin."*

Clyde nodded, then glanced over to where Scott was maneuvering a large roll of newsprint into place. "I think the boy's got things under control for now," he said loudly. "Let's go to your office so I can hear you."

Behind her closed office door, she started with Gavin's completion of rehab and then went over the details of his "indirect" involvement with the illegal drug operation, emphasizing how he claimed to have quit the drug traffickers long before arrests were ever made.

Finally, Clyde threw up his hands in exasperation. "Is that all you wanted to tell me, Maggie? I didn't come in here to hear about *that* business. I thought you found out something new about our girl."

"Well first, I felt you should hear about Gavin, Clyde. After all, he is your nephew. He deserves to be…"

"He doesn't deserve one single darned thing."

"Look, Clyde," she said in her authoritative voice. "If Gavin *is* Leah's father, don't you think Leah deserves to have his name cleared if it's at all possible?"

Clyde scratched his bristly chin, then leaned forward with renewed interest. "I s'pect you might be onto something there. Okay, go ahead and tell me about Gavin again. I guess I wasn't listening real careful the first go 'round."

She launched into another explanation, making it clear that while Gavin didn't claim complete innocence, neither was he guilty of running a drug operation. "So, even though Gavin's made some regrettable mistakes," she said, wrapping it up, "it's not fair to judge him so harshly. And he's feeling pretty bad that Greg Snider and many others in town—most of all *you*—believe that he was behind the whole drug business from beginning to end."

Clyde nodded wryly. "And that bothers him, does it?"

"Yes, it does. I think now that he's finished his rehab, he'd like to make a fresh start. Have a clean slate, so to speak."

His brow creased. "And you really believe him, Maggie?"

She thought for a moment. "I guess so."

"You don't sound real sure of yourself."

She shrugged. "I suppose I believe that he *wants* to change. Why wouldn't he? His life hasn't been exactly a success so far."

"He's made his bed, I say let him…"

"Clyde!" she snapped, then more gently, "At least consider Leah."

"All right. So, what am I supposed to do about Gavin now?"

"I don't know. Maybe just forgive him."

"Hmph. That's easy for you."

She thought about that. Was it easy for her to forgive? And even if it was, she knew it hadn't always been that way. She studied Clyde for a long moment. She had no doubts about his sincerity in wanting to help Leah, yet dealing with Gavin only seemed to aggravate him beyond words. Finally she said, "There's something I've learned about forgiveness. It's not so much for the one who *gets* forgiven as it is for the one who *does* the forgiving."

Clyde's face grew even more puzzled. "That's quite a mouthful, young lady. You mind explaining exactly what you mean?"

She leaned back in her chair, studying a water stain in the corner of the ceiling as she reflected over a trying time in her past. Finally she spoke. "When I first learned my husband had been shot I didn't really conceive that an actual gunman had been involved, at least not at the beginning. It was hard enough just to process the fact that Phil was dead. I was told that he'd died saving some girl's life and how he was a hero and everything; but not too much of it really sank in, there was just too much to absorb at the time…" She leaned forward, picking up a pencil from her desk and absently rolled it between her hands as she continued. "Then right after the funeral, Phil's friends from the force came up to me and vowed that they'd catch Phil's murderer and make sure he was convicted. They were so angry, almost like vigilantes; they intended to make the creep pay. And for a while I rode on their bandwagon too. After all, they'd been Phil's best buddies. And by the time the kid got caught and the whole thing came to trial, I too was so full of anger and hatred toward this boy that I really wanted to make him pay for what he'd done—and to pay dearly!"

Clyde leaned forward, his faded blue eyes fixed upon her with interest. "And?" he demanded. "What happened?"

She sighed. "The trial had barely begun when I became sick to my stomach. Not surprising since I'd been feeling that way a lot. So I ran into the bathroom and threw up. And then I just kept throwing up again and again—it was so horrible. Finally I stopped, and that's when my friend Rebecca stood me in front of the mirror and said '*look*.' Naturally, I looked awful. She gently told me that I'd been allowing the hate and bitterness to eat away at me, and that it would eventually destroy me completely. 'That kid already stole your husband's life,' she said, 'don't let him steal yours too.' She also told me that even though the kid didn't deserve it, I had to forgive him in order to feel better again. And then she reminded me that that was how God forgave us—we didn't deserve it."

Clyde still looked slightly puzzled. "So, did you?"

She nodded. "At first it didn't seem like much, except my anger began to slowly ebb away, and I stopped having those stomachaches. And then later on, after the kid's conviction and sentence, I sent a note to him in prison saying that I'd forgiven him for killing Phil, and that it was only by God's grace that I could do that."

"Did you ever hear anything back from him?"

"No. But that wasn't the point. Do you see what I'm saying?"

Clyde pressed his lips together then nodded solemnly. "I reckon I do. I guess I could give it some thought in regard to Gavin. I appreciate your story, Maggie, but I can't make you any promises on my end."

She smiled. "That's okay. My biggest concern is that you don't turn yourself into a bitter old man."

"Can't do much about the 'old man' part, but I reckon if I was going to get bitter, I've had me ample opportunity to get bitter during my lifetime. Fact is, I usually get over these things sooner or later." Then his brow grew furrowed and he cocked his head to one side. "'Course I *am* getting up in years. You never know how much time you got left to get over something nowadays. Reckon I better not waste any— eh?" His eyes twinkled youthfully, belying his age.

"Actually, I think that's true with all of us. Who knows what tomorrow will bring? I'm sure my husband didn't have any idea that he was living his last day." She sighed. "But then he was always good at keeping short accounts and a clean slate."

"Sounds like he was a good man, Maggie."

She smiled wistfully at him. "He was. And now do you want to hear about how all this relates to Leah?"

He rubbed his hands together like an eager child. "Now, *that's* what I was mainly hoping for."

She told him about Gavin admitting to having lived in Phoenix at about the right time. "But I didn't know how to pin him down any more—at least, not without coming right out and asking."

"Well, maybe you should ask."

She sighed. "Maybe. But I'm not looking forward to it. I've tried to be his friend, Clyde. I hate to come across like I'm accusing him of something..."

"Being the father of such a fine young lady is hardly a crime!"

"You're right. Leah's a girl I'd be proud to call my own. Why should it bother Gavin at this point in life?"

Clyde chuckled. "Unless he's worried that his daughter might now inherit what he thinks should be coming to him."

A conflict like that hadn't occurred to her. "I suppose that might be a concern."

"It shouldn't be. I've already made it plain as day to Gavin that he's out of my will completely—that is unless he does an about-face, complete turn-around with his sorry excuse of a life."

"I see..." Once again she considered Gavin's potential motives for working so hard to prove himself innocent in his uncle's eyes. Was it possible that he only wanted to trick him into reinserting his name into the family will? And what if he was simply using her as an unwitting conspirator in the whole thing? She despised the idea of being played as a pawn. But then again, what if Gavin was sincere in his desire to turn his life around? It was getting very confusing!

"Next time he calls," said Clyde, shaking his finger at her, "don't you go beating around the bush. You just ask him directly if he knew Leah's mother. Didn't you say you know her name?"

"Yes. You're probably right. And who knows? He may even want to get to know Leah—if she is his daughter."

Clyde frowned. "Poor Leah. She might not want to get to know him."

"You could be surprised. Leah is a very gracious young woman."

He sniffed indignantly. "Don't know how she got that way after all the riffraff she's had to put up with in her life."

"Up until now," she reminded him.

He smiled. "Right. Now she's got family who care about her."

⌒

On Friday morning, Jed called Maggie at work. "I wanted to thank you for dropping my name with the Jordans last week. Cindy and Brian stopped by yesterday and placed a fairly substantial order for some furniture for the hotel."

"That's great," said Maggie. "Cindy didn't realize that you work in a variety of styles."

"Well, I appreciate the advertising. Maybe I should offer you a commission or something." She could hear the smile in his voice.

"That's okay. Although maybe I should be selfishly concerned. You'll probably be busier than ever now, and I still have some projects left to do at my house."

"I can still carve time out for that. And with Spencer getting so skilled at renovating, you might not need me so much anyway."

"I don't know. Spence is pretty caught up with his band right now. He doesn't have much spare time these days."

"Is tomorrow the big night?"

"Yes. How'd you know about that?"

"I was over at the house inspecting his work on your library shelves—by the way, he did an excellent job. Anyway, he told me all about it—even invited me to come." Jed paused. "In fact, I was wondering if you might like to go with me…"

She considered this briefly. Was he asking her out? Or was it just a friendly gesture? And did it even matter? "Sure," she said quickly. "That'd be nice."

"Maybe we could get a bite to eat beforehand," he added casually. "If that works for you, that is."

It was sounding more like a date. "That sounds like fun."

They arranged the time and Maggie hung up, staring at the phone in wonder. For all practical purposes, it seemed that she was actually going out on a date with Jed Whitewater. No, not a date, she reprimanded herself, just friends getting a bite to eat before they went to listen to her son's band. Not a date. Not really.…Still, she wondered what Kate would think about all this.

That evening she casually mentioned this news to her mother as the two of them fixed a late dinner. But her mother's only reaction was to silently stare at her, as if she had not quite understood. So Maggie continued, over-explaining to cover her own discomfort at this reaction. "...and I figured that since you'll have to close up the gallery tomorrow night what with Leah singing and all, I thought I might like to go to see it with another adult..."

"Jed is taking *you* to dinner?" said Audrey as if the words had finally sunk in. "And what exactly does this mean?"

"Oh, nothing really. He just wanted to hear Spence's band and asked if I wanted to go with him. It's really no big deal, Mom."

Audrey's brows arched with suspicion. "Maybe not to you, but I wonder what Kate will think of this new little development."

"It's not a *new little development*..."

"You mean you've gone out with him before?"

"No, not at all. I just mean it's nothing. And Kate has nothing to be concerned about. Besides, don't you remember what Rosa said about Kate and Jed?"

"But that was only Rosa's opinion. And I don't necessarily think Kate shares it."

Maggie studied her mother curiously. "Are you saying you think it's wrong for me to do something like this with him?"

"No, no, of course not. But what about Buckie, dear? Don't you two have something..."

"He's *only* a friend, Mom. And for that matter so is Jed." Maggie shoved the second pizza into the oven with visible irritation. Why did it always seem that her mother wanted to see Kate and Jed paired off permanently? And why did she have to blow this whole thing out of proportion anyway?

"Maggie, I don't mean to interfere, but I do think that Buckie considers you more than just a friend. Why, you two have been dating."

"Dating?" She turned and looked at her mother. "When have we *ever* gone on a real honest-to-goodness date?"

Audrey waved her hand. "Oh, you know. You go to lunch together. You do things with other people. He's over here at the house several times a week."

"But that's only because we're friends. Buckie knows that's all I want right now. I've made that clear. And, yes, it's true I do enjoy his friendship."

"There. You see, a good friendship makes a good foundation for a marriage..."

"*Mom!*" exploded Maggie. "I can't believe you! Don't you realize that I am not even considering marrying Buckie!"

Audrey turned her attention back to the tossed salad. "Sorry, dear. I didn't mean to interfere with your personal life."

Maggie wiped off the countertop in angry swipes. She hated feeling like this toward her mother. But sometimes it seemed as if she were barely fifteen and her mother was still telling her how to live. "I'm sorry too," she said stiffly. "It's been a long week. I think I'm just tired."

"Don't worry about it, honey." Audrey glanced at her watch. "I better go pick up Leah now. We should be back before the pizza is even out of the oven. Then she can practice with the boys. To be honest, I don't much care for their brand of music, but I think I might hop over tomorrow night after I close up the shop and see if I can sneak a peek of their performance, at least from a distance."

"You might want to bring your earplugs with you."

Audrey laughed lightly. "Why, that's exactly what Leah said."

The house grew quiet after her mother left, and Maggie regretted her harsh words about Buckie even more. Her mother's comments may have been irritating, but she knew they were innocent. And even though she doubted if she'd seriously hurt her mother's feelings, she still didn't like losing her temper like that. Perhaps they simply needed to establish some boundaries. Especially if her mother decided to relocate here permanently. Maggie needed her space in certain areas—especially areas of the heart. She didn't want her mother, or anyone for that matter, to dictate whom she should or should not be attracted to. It was tricky enough for her to know her own feelings without someone else sticking their two cents in.

After a casual dinner of pizza and salad, Maggie cleaned the kitchen, then excused herself to her room. Before going to bed, she sent off an overdue email to Rebecca.

RB

For a quiet little town, there always seems to be a lot going on—at least in my life. But today something happened that really took me by surprise. Jed asked me out! Well, sort of. He wants to go with me to hear Spencer's band play tomorrow (we'll have dinner first). But for some reason my mom seems opposed to this. She thinks Buckie and I have something serious going on (although we don't!). And I must admit, if only to you, that I'm a little unsure of this new development. I hope it's not a big mistake. Jed can be a little perplexing sometimes. On the one hand, he seems thoughtful and sensitive, but then sometimes he acts awfully harsh and judgmental. It really throws me off. Sometimes I wonder if it's just because he's trying so hard to be the "good pastor" and maintain a squeaky-clean image, although he's not really an ordained pastor or anything. Actually he's just sort of holding the fort until the church decides on someone more permanent. Just the same, and between you and me, I am very excited about going out with him. There is something about this guy—something mysterious and unexplainable… But it's also kind of scary to feel this way. And I could be all wrong about everything. I also know that feelings can get you into trouble sometimes. I do want to be sensible. Oh my…Well, I'll let you know how it goes.

mc

Eleven

"Buckie gets home tomorrow," announced Leah as she loaded the dishwasher with the breakfast dishes.

"It's a good thing too," said Audrey. "I'm starting to think this retirement business isn't all it's cracked up to be."

Maggie laughed. "I remember not too long ago when you were complaining about retirement being so boring."

"I guess it's just feast or famine with me." Audrey glanced at the kitchen clock. "I'd better go open up the gallery now. I'll see you around eleven, Leah?"

"Is it still okay to catch a ride with you, Maggie?" asked Leah.

"It's fine. I wanted to go in and work out at the fitness center anyway."

"I don't know how you stand it," said Audrey. "Doesn't that Cherise just talk your ears right off?"

"Yes, but I don't really mind. She doesn't have many friends. Besides she's a good source for local news."

"Don't you mean gossip?" said Audrey as she picked up her car keys.

"Whatever." Maggie shook her head and returned her attention back to her *L.A. Times*, not exactly the latest news since it was three days old, but interesting just the same.

"Want the last of the coffee?" offered Leah, holding the pot before her.

"Sure, thanks." Maggie looked up as she refilled her cup. "Are you all ready for the concert tonight?"

Leah shrugged. "I guess so."

"You don't look too excited."

"I think it'll be fun. But I'm not too sure about this weird getup the guys want me to wear…"

"Wear whatever you want to wear, honey. Don't let those silly boys push you around."

"I suppose. But it *is* their band…"

"Yes. But they don't own you. Stand up for yourself. I'm sure Spence doesn't want you to feel like you look weird."

"Oh, it wasn't Spencer's idea." Leah rinsed the coffee decanter in the sink. "It was Ed's."

Maggie considered that. At least it wasn't Daniel's idea—now that kid was definitely pretty weird. Just last week he'd dyed a burgundy stripe into his dark hair. "Well, just the same, Leah, you need to make your own decision about this."

"Yeah, I know."

◦—

Maggie dropped Leah off at the gallery just before eleven; she would work there until five, and then Audrey would close. Those two had been carrying quite a load the past couple of weeks, but fortunately Buckie would be back to help out tomorrow. Maybe that was part of the explanation for her mother's edginess lately. Perhaps the responsibility had been overly stressful for her, and maybe Maggie should have cut her more slack. It was easy to forget that her mother, normally such an energetic person, wasn't as young as she used to be. Maggie would have to remember to encourage her to take it easy the next couple weeks before she returned to San Jose.

The fitness center wasn't very busy for a Saturday, just a couple of young guys working on the weights, and Cherise, as usual, was flitting about in a teal and pink spandex outfit like a big, bright butterfly. "Hey, Maggie," she called.

"Looks kind of slow today," commented Maggie as she stuffed her gym bag into a locker.

"Yeah, but at least that means you don't have to wait." Cherise picked up her ever-present cleaning bottle and cloth and followed Maggie to the treadmill.

Maggie knew her workout routine well enough not to need instruction anymore, but she appreciated the company anyway. And it helped to pass the time, not to mention an occasional scoop like when Cherise knew that a certain NFL player would be in town and arranged for Scott to snatch a photo for the paper. But today as Maggie treaded on the stair-stepper, she noticed that Cherise's normally cheery countenance looked slightly troubled. "Everything okay with you, Cherise?"

Cherise set down her cleaning tools and climbed onto the seat of the nearby rowing machine, glancing over to where the two young men were just finishing up their weight-lifting. "Oh, I don't know…"

Maggie studied her with interest. She'd never seen Cherise quite like this. "You seem really troubled. Are things with you and Greg getting a little stressed again?" Cherise often confided in her, openly sharing the little childish disagreements that seemed to plague their marriage. Yet, she'd never seemed terribly concerned about any of it before.

The two guys went into the shower room and Cherise began to talk quietly. "I'm worried about Greg."

"Is he okay?"

"Oh, sure, he's just fine. But I'm starting to get suspicious."

"Suspicious?" Maggie continued stepping in rhythm.

"Yeah. He's been acting pretty strange lately. He comes and goes all the time without telling me what he's up to—real sneaky-like. I mean, he's always done his own thing, but before I usually knew where he was and who he was hanging with. Now he's gone all secretive on me."

"Oh." The timer went off on the stepper and Maggie climbed down.

Cherise peered into Maggie's face. "Do you think he's having an affair?"

Maggie's brows lifted. "I—uh, I don't really know."

"Well, I did this 'Is Your Mate Cheating?' quiz in *Glamour* magazine and Greg scored real high."

"But that could be a coincidence."

She shook her head. "Something's up, Maggie. I just know it. And I don't think it's good. That thing in *Glamour* said that if your man's ever cheated before—you know, like when he got involved with me on his first wife—well, then it's pretty likely that he'll do it again."

"That doesn't seem very fair. People can change…"

"Yeah, but facts are facts."

"I wonder where *Glamour* gets their facts."

"I don't know, but I happen to believe they're a highly reputable magazine."

Maggie felt sorry for Cherise, but was not really surprised. Their marriage was anything but ideal, and judging by the way Greg had treated his wife, the possibility that he might be involved with another woman seemed rather feasible. But still, Maggie hoped not, if only for Cherise's sake.

"You know what scares me most?" said Cherise as Maggie finished her workout. "That I could end up with *nothing*. I could be a bag lady out on the street."

Maggie laughed. "Now, that's silly. What about your business?"

"It's supposed to be mine, but it's all in Greg's name."

"You're kidding! The fitness center belongs to Greg?"

"Yeah. Lock, stock, and barrel. He handled all the paperwork and he takes care of all the finances and stuff. He's told me more than once, usually when we're in the middle of a big ol' fight, that this whole place legally belongs to him."

Maggie wiped her face with a towel partly in an attempt to conceal her deep concern. "Well, that doesn't seem very fair, especially after all the time and energy that you've invested in this place. Does Greg pay you a salary or anything?"

Cherise laughed, then quickly added, "No, but I *do* get to buy all the sports clothing I want—it's a tax write-off, you know."

"Do you think it's possible to change any of the legal paperwork?"

She shrugged. "I wouldn't even know where to begin."

"I'd start by talking to a good lawyer. But I'd keep it to myself if I were you."

Cherise brightened. "My Uncle Bob is a lawyer over in Byron."

"Then why don't you give him a call and see what he thinks about all this."

"You know, maybe I'll do that."

Maggie reached over and placed a hand on Cherise's arm. "Please, don't get me wrong, Cherise. I'm not recommending that you look into divorce or anything that drastic. Hopefully this whole thing with Greg is nothing. But you guys should come to some fair agreement on your business— at least a fifty-fifty split. You work very hard on it. I think you're entitled to something."

"Yeah, especially when you consider that it was my mom who gave me the money to buy everything in the first place."

Maggie pressed her lips firmly together to avoid saying something she'd regret later. Did Greg Snider think they were living in the nineteenth century? "Well, Cherise," she said, determined to remain calm, "you'd better give old Uncle Bob a little call."

"Thanks for listening. I just don't understand why Greg is so down on you all the time. I always feel better after I talk with you." She smiled brightly, once again the optimist.

"You might not want to mention *that* to Greg." Maggie got her gym bag and left. Poor Cherise. Hopefully her suspicions about Greg were wrong. But if nothing else, this little dilemma might motivate Cherise to get their strange ownership arrangement settled more fairly.

Maggie stopped by the deli for a bowl of soup and was pleased to be joined by Rosa. "I'm so glad you could take a break," she said when Rosa finally sat down. "I've been wanting to catch up with you."

"Oh, it's been so busy—not at all typical for fall." Rosa beamed. "But I'm not complaining! Not a bit."

"Mom says the gallery's turned a pretty fair business in the past two weeks too. Buckie should be pleased."

"When does he get back?"

"Tomorrow." Maggie glanced around the crowded dining area, then lowered her voice. "Which reminds me of something. I wanted to let you know that I'm having dinner with Jed tonight…"

Rosa's eyes lit up. "That's wonderful!"

"Calm down. It's not like a date or anything. He just wanted to go with me to hear Spencer playing at the homecoming bonfire."

"But you said dinner? That sounds a little like a date to me."

"Maybe so…" Maggie sighed. "What do you suppose Kate will think of this?"

Rosa shrugged. "Good question. She ought to know by now that it's hopeless, but affairs of the heart can be a strange business."

Maggie frowned. "I know. I really don't want to see her hurt. I wonder if Jed should talk to her…"

"He has. Many times. She just won't hear what she doesn't want to know."

"It makes me feel bad…"

"Don't let it." Rosa firmly shook her head at her. "It's good that Jed's asked you out. It might even help Kate to see the writing on the wall. Sooner or later she has to face reality."

"I suppose you're right." Maggie took a bite of soup. "This is delicious."

"Thanks. It's a new recipe I found in a magazine. I figure with all the competition coming to town I better make sure the deli can keep up."

Maggie surveyed the crowded room. Most of the faces seemed unfamiliar—tourists passing through town. "It looks like you've got a head start on everyone else. But I know what you mean. Scott told me a little more about the new restaurant that Chloe's friend Aaron plans to start. I think Scott's worried about another sort of competition though."

Rosa rolled her eyes. "That boy! One day he acts like he's going to zip on down to L.A. to work for the *Times*, and the next he's mooning over Chloe. Now explain *that*!"

"Like you said about affairs of the heart..." Maggie glanced up at Sierra taking an order from behind the counter. "Speaking of hearts, my son seems to be spending plenty of time moping around over your daughter these days."

Rosa laughed. "Well, he doesn't need to worry himself. Just last night she was going on and on about what a complete jerk that Kurt Gilbert is and how Spencer is so much nicer."

Maggie smiled. "I'd have to agree with her on that one, but then I might be a little prejudiced."

"It's too bad kids have to go through all this stuff." Rosa poked the fork into her pasta salad. "I've already watched my boys go through it, and there's almost nothing you can do but stand around and wait to pick up the pieces—that is, if they let you. Kids can be so heartless to each other sometimes."

Maggie nodded. "Don't tell Sierra, but that's partly why Spencer has become so involved in this band business. He thinks he has to prove something—I don't know exactly whom to—maybe just himself."

"Well, the good news is that eventually they do grow up."

"And the *bad* news?"

"It's going to take a few years."

‿

Maggie stopped by Chloe's Threads before she went home. Browsing through the racks, she wondered if there was something special she might find to wear tonight. She told herself it was silly and she was making too much of it, but just the same she wanted to look nice, even if she wasn't sure what that meant. She knew that Jed would probably, as usual, be casual. She'd rarely seen him in anything dressier than a denim shirt and jeans, usually sporting his fringed knee-high moccasins.

"Looking for anything in particular?" asked Chloe with a cheerful smile.

"Oh, I don't know. Just kind of browsing, I guess."

"Sure, that's what they all say. You must have something in mind."

Maggie studied Chloe's appearance for a moment. She was dressed in just the simple T-shirt and baggy jeans that most of the kids wore these days, although she'd thrown on what looked like a man's loose vest, which seemed to add an element of style. "I've been a little out of touch with fashion lately," began Maggie apologetically.

"Oh, I don't think so. You always look very classy." Chloe stepped back and checked out Maggie more carefully. "In fact, when I grow up I want to dress just like you."

Maggie grinned. "Thanks, I think. But maybe that's the problem. Maybe I look too grown-up, too stodgy and frumpy. Any suggestions for something that'd be a little more fun? Like, say something for the bonfire concert tonight?"

"Oh, that's right. Spencer's playing. Man, you should've seen what they picked out yesterday for Leah to wear."

"Was it that bad?"

"No, just sort of a wild-and-rock-star kind of cool. Actually, Leah will look really wicked in it."

"Wicked?"

"Oh, you know what I mean, that's just another word for *cool*. Don't worry, she'll look just fine. The truth is, she's so thin she could wear anything and look fantastic. I told her she should come in and do some live modeling in the window for me. But back to you, Maggie. You think you want a younger look?"

"Maybe something a little more with it."

Chloe thought for a moment, then led her to the back of the shop. "I just got these in this week, and I think they're very 'with it.'" She pulled out a smooth black leather jacket.

Maggie grinned. "Now all I need is a motorcycle and some chains."

"No, Maggie, they're not like that at all. Much more Euro-style really. They're popular in France—very chic. Here try one on."

Maggie let her slip the coat on and was surprised at how lightweight and subtle the leather felt. "This is actually kind of nice." She sniffed. "And it smells yummy."

Chloe was pushing her toward a mirror. "Wait until you see how great it looks!"

She stared at the mirror, turning to admire the cut of the coat from all angles. "You know, Chloe, it's really kind of fun..."

"*Fun!*" Chloe threw her long red curls over her shoulder and smiled triumphantly. "Isn't that just what you said you wanted?"

"I suppose so." Maggie giggled. "It's just so unlike anything I've ever had before. I suppose I do tend to dress a little conservatively."

"Then it's perfect!"

"You're a good saleswoman. Okay, I'll take it."

"Great. And I expect to see you wearing it tonight."

"Okay, but what do I wear with it?"

"Anything you want. But it would look very cool with just a white T-shirt and blue-jeans. Maybe with a good sturdy belt. Do you have the right belt?"

Before Maggie left, she'd purchased the coat, a belt, and even a pair of black boots that Chloe had insisted were a must. She loaded the bags into her car feeling very much like a teenager herself. Well, that was okay. After all, she'd spent the bulk of her life being very careful and responsible. It was about time she learned to have a little fun. And besides it wasn't every day that someone like Jed was taking her out.

൦—

After changing her mind several times, Maggie finally decided to wear the outfit that Chloe had helped put together. But as she gave herself one final look in the mirror, she knew it was all wrong. And then the doorbell rang downstairs.

"Want me to get it?" called Leah from down the hall.

"No. I'm all ready to head out anyway..."

"Wow, Maggie," said Leah approvingly.

"What do you think?" asked Maggie.

Leah was standing barefoot at the end of the hall with wet hair dripping down her T-shirt. "You look *very* cool."

"Really? You don't think it's too much for an old woman like me?"

"You're *not* old. And if you think that's too much you haven't seen anything yet!"

Maggie laughed nervously then dashed downstairs to get the door. "Catch you later. Tell Spence I'll see him at the concert."

She opened the door to see Jed dressed in a neat white shirt and pressed khaki pants, far more dressy than his usual jeans and moccasins. In his hands was a small bouquet of daisies. "I picked them at my place on the way out," he said almost apologetically. "They're not much but..."

"I absolutely love them. Do you mind if I run and put them in water right now?"

"Not at all."

She headed for the kitchen, feeling his eyes upon her as she went. Did he think she looked too silly, trying to be too young, too daring? Especially compared to his surprisingly conservative attire tonight. She fumbled in a cupboard for a vase, wondering if she could make some excuse to go upstairs and change. She quickly filled the vase with water, then set it on the table. "There." She turned to face him. "Thanks, we probably won't be seeing too many wild-flowers much longer."

He nodded. "Are you ready?"

She paused, glancing down at her outfit, so unlike her. "I think I look pretty casual. Maybe I should go…"

"You look just fine. And it's perfect for where we're going." He looked at his own clothing then laughed. "I believe I'm the one who overdressed this time."

She still felt unsure as he opened the door of his freshly washed red pick-up for her. Had he dressed like that thinking that she would do likewise? And if he had, it was a good guess, for most of the time she still tended to overdress. She smiled to herself as she climbed into the cab. She suspected he'd cleaned its interior also, for the floor was immaculate and the metal dashboard shined. She slid onto the Navajo-blanket covered seat and waited for him to close the door and climb in the other side, all the while willing herself to calm down, to quit worrying and making such a big deal of this evening.

"I've never mentioned that I really like your truck, Jed. I don't know much about pick-ups, but I'm sure this one must be a classic. What year is it?"

He smiled. "It's a '56. It used to be my dad's. I remember rattling around in it with him when I was a boy. Of course, I've fixed it up some since then. Although he always took excellent care of it."

"Were you and your dad pretty close?"

He thought about that. "I suppose so. But my dad wasn't one to talk much. Even now there's a whole lot I don't know about him, but then I guess that's partly my own fault too."

"I know your mother died when you were pretty young, but do you have any other relatives who can tell you more about your father?"

He shook his head. "Not really. My dad left the reservation under some negative circumstances. I doubt that anyone back there would want to talk about him to me, unless it would be to tear him down."

"So you never went back to the reservation to visit or anything?"

"No. Sometimes my mom wanted to go, but my dad always said we wouldn't be welcome there. You see, after his parents had died and before my dad left, he'd sold off part of the land they'd left him in order to invest in a business. The elders didn't much like that, and everyone gave him a real hard time. So he sold off the rest of the land, collected his share of some federal tribal money, then took his wife and left. He'd had more education than most folks on the reservation, and I don't think he ever fit in with their ways. He was too independent. He wanted to make his own way in the world—and the tribe didn't look too kindly on that. He even changed his name. It was only after he died that I took back our family name. I'm not even sure what my father would think about that now. But at the time it was something I needed to do. I needed to connect to my roots."

"Was your mother from the reservation too?"

Jed nodded. "Yes, and that might've been part of the problem. Her family was more prestigious in the tribe than my father's—at least within the political circles. Her father was on the council. But I think my father's family had been more successful from a financial point of view, which might have been to his ultimate disadvantage."

"Too successful?"

"Maybe. My father's dreams crossed over the reservation boundaries. He wanted to buy a mill and had already begun to log a portion of his land, and some of the elders were opposed. That's when he decided it was time to leave."

Maggie looked ahead to where Jed was driving. This was the same road they used to go to church, but as far as she knew there were no restaurants up this way. "Do you mind if I ask where we're going?"

He grinned. "I was wondering when you would. Actually, I was going to take you to Byron, but I couldn't get a reservation until eight, which would've been pushing it. And then I remembered this special little spot that I thought you might enjoy."

"So you're going to be mysterious."

He nodded and continued to drive down the gravel road. She knew that he lived up here, somewhere near the church. In fact, Rosa had recently told her that the church was originally going to be Jed's own home, but that he'd transformed it when they had decided to make a new church. And there was no denying that it made for a beautiful church, as long as the congregation didn't outgrow it. Finally, they reached the church and he continued to drive, curving around the back on a single-lane road that she'd never noticed before. He continued down the narrow, tree-lined lane until he came upon what looked like a large and well-constructed shop.

"Is that your workshop?"

He parked the truck. "Yes. And I have a little cabin just beyond it."

Suddenly Maggie felt quite honored that he would bring her here. She knew that he was generally a very private person. Maybe this really was a date after all.

He led her around the shop to where a sweet little cabin was situated close to the same ridge that the church sat upon, only this spot was facing west. "It's so beautiful up here, Jed. I remember the first time I saw the church and I thought it was like a little bit of heaven."

He nodded. "That's how I feel. I suppose that's why I wanted to share it. I felt selfish having all this to myself. Do you want a little tour?"

"I'd love it."

First he took her through his shop. Numerous projects were in various stages of progress, and the roomy space was outfitted with what appeared to be state-of-the-art and very large power tools.

"This is impressive, Jed. I didn't realize you had a shop like this. I just assumed you did a lot of your work in the back-room of the furniture store."

He laughed. "Now, that would be a truly amazing feat. I only work on small projects there when I have to mind the shop, but this is where I really work. It's taken a while to accumulate an adequate inventory of tools and supplies, but I'm slowly getting there."

"And have you managed to do all this on what you make at Whitewater Works?"

He shook his head as he closed the door to the shop and led her toward the cabin. "I wish I could say that I did, but the truth is I'm not sure I'll ever see a return on my original investment. But you never know…"

She wanted to ask him how he could afford all this, but at the same time she wanted to respect his privacy. He would tell her if and when he liked.

"This cabin seems older than the church. Did you build it too?"

"I helped a little as a boy. But my dad did most of the work." He patted a hand-hewn log as they stepped onto the small covered porch. "He wasn't a professional, but he taught me a lot about woodworking." Maggie noted a stack of woodworking magazines next to an old wooden rocker. She could imagine Jed spending time out here in the evening. It was a pleasant scene to contemplate.

"I'll show you the inside of the cabin, if you like, but this isn't where we're having dinner." He showed her through the low-ceilinged three-room building. To her surprise, it was tight and cluttered with very little of his own craftsmanship to be seen anywhere. "I've left things pretty much the way it was after my father died. And he hadn't changed it much since my mother died. I guess it's sort of a time capsule for me. I had expected to move on last year after finishing my house, which, as you know, became the church."

"Do you ever plan to use that building as a house?"

"Who knows? Maybe. Right now it seems perfect as a church." He ushered her out of the cramped cabin and down a path until they arrived at a large deck built like the prow of a ship and extending out over the ridge as if suspended in air. Upon this deck were two chairs and a small table, all set for dinner. Nearby were a gas barbecue and an ice chest.

"Wow. This is incredible," said Maggie as she stepped onto the deck and surveyed the mountains to the west.

He pulled out a chair for her. "Well, I have always liked a restaurant with a view."

"And what a view!"

He went to check on the barbecue and she called out, offering to help. "I've got it under control," he assured. "You just relax and enjoy the view. Everything's all ready to go and it'll just be a few minutes." She leaned back in her chair and stared with amazed appreciation at the mountains.

After a few minutes she spoke. "It looks as if the mountains are changing colors even as I look at them."

"It's like that at this time of day. The sun is setting and the light constantly changes." He stepped over and began filling her plate with a thick steak and a skewer full of scrumptious-looking grilled vegetables. Then he leaned over and lit the hurricane lamp.

"This looks fantastic. And it appears you've done this before," she commented as he set a basket of sourdough rolls on the table.

"Not as often as I would like. But I just realized that with winter coming my opportunities for outdoor dining were becoming limited this year." He looked out to where the sun was almost touching the mountains now. "In fact, I was a little worried that the wind might pick up and force us inside."

"It couldn't be a nicer fall day."

They ate congenially. Maggie had never felt more comfortable in his presence. It was as if someone had sprinkled magic happy-dust upon them, or perhaps this was only a dream. Jed openly told her more about his past—about a mother who'd never been able to fit into the small town life of Pine Mountain, but had always loved it up here in "her mountains" as she called them. "Her name was Mary, and after she died, my father always called them Mary's Mountains."

"How sweet."

Then Jed told her about how his father had worked hard logging timber and buying up more land when it was cheap. "I heard that even on the day he died, he still had a chainsaw in his hands. A heart attack. I'd been thinking about coming home about that time, but I waited too long." Jed shook his head and broke open another roll. "So many years lost."

She nodded sadly, then waved her hand toward the land. "But look what your father left you. It must make him so happy that you truly appreciate it."

"I like to think so. And I do remember him saying that he was doing it all for me. But then again I was such a disappointment to him after Viet Nam. Sometimes I just don't know..."

"I think your father would understand."

His face brightened a little. "At least I have this comfort, both of my parents were Christians. I think that's another reason they didn't fit in very well with some members of the tribe at the time. And at least I have the assurance that we'll all be together someday."

"That's worth more than anything."

"I just wish that I could've been a better son while my dad was still here."

"Maybe both your parents are looking down on you now," she suggested as she laid down her fork and knife. "I'm sure they would be very proud."

He pushed his empty plate to the center of the table. "But I've done plenty to shame them too. Come with me and I'll show you something."

He led her down a path into a large area that was fairly wide open, then she realized it looked like a crop of young trees, thousands of them from about two feet to four feet high, growing in neat, even rows.

"Is this a tree farm?"

"Not exactly. It's a reforestation project."

"Was there a fire?"

Jed looked out upon the small trees with sadness. "No. It was a case of greed, pure and simple. After my father died, I came back here. I had all this land, but not a penny of my own to spend. So I went to the bank to see about a loan to start up my woodworking business, and they insisted on using the land as collateral. But I just couldn't agree to that. This land had meant so much to my father, and I didn't want to put it at risk in case my business failed. My father had spent his lifetime logging it, carefully removing one tree at a time without hardly disturbing the land. He was always reading up on forest ecology, even before it was a real issue. Anyway, I thought if my father could sell logs, well then so could I. So I sold the timber in this parcel to a logging company right when lumber was at a premium. The next thing I knew they were in here with huge machines, clear-cutting every single acre. Legally I couldn't stop them. I left town for a while because I couldn't stand to be here. I felt like I'd sold my soul to the devil."

"How awful." She looked over the sea of soft green trees, growing duskier by the moment as the sunlight continued to be swallowed by the mountains.

"When I came back the parcel was completely barren, the soil gouged and torn with ugly, dead stumps all over. It looked like it had been raped and pillaged. It was raining that day, and it felt as if my father's tears were falling on the land." He looked up at the sky, then glanced down at her. "It's getting late."

As they picked up the dishes to take inside, Jed explained to her how he planted the trees as an act of restitution, a peace offering of sorts. And how in turn, the very act of planting the trees eventually brought him to God and to his own personal salvation.

"So, maybe there was a purpose to all of it after all," she said as they set the dishes in the tiny enamel sink inside the cabin.

"Maybe. It's true that God's an expert at bringing goodness out of evil."

She turned and looked at him illuminated from the light of the single bare bulb hanging in the center of the kitchen area. "Thanks for sharing your story with me, Jed. I feel like I know you so much better now."

"I was hoping that would be the case. I know I can come across as unfriendly or overbearing. I suppose it's really just a cover-up."

"A cover-up?"

"Oh, you know the armchair psychologist would say it's probably just a smoke-screen designed to hide my deep insecurities."

"*You* have insecurities?"

He laughed. "See, I do a good job of covering them up." He looked at the clock above the stove. "But if we want to make it to the concert, we had better go. Just leave the dishes here. I'll have the maid take care of them later."

He took her arm as they picked their way down the winding path in the semidarkness. She liked the warmth of his hand under her elbow, strong and confident, directing her safely. Or at least that's how it felt.

Twelve

The bonfire was visible from the edge of the parking lot. Vibrantly dancing orange flames leapt at least twenty feet high into the night sky with a large crowd of high-school kids milling around. Nearby, a makeshift platform was set up where a band was adjusting instruments and the sound system.

"Is that Spencer's group?" asked Jed as they walked toward the crowd.

"No, it doesn't look like them."

"Shall we watch from back here?" he suggested. "Or did you want to mingle with the kids?"

"Back here is fine." Maggie turned up her collar against the cold night air. "I don't want Spence thinking I'm trying to act his age. I remember a mom like that when I was in high school. She'd show up at games and things outfitted like she was still sixteen and acting like she was one of the high-school girls. And her poor daughter was totally mortified. She's probably spent a fortune on therapy just trying to get over it."

Jed smiled down at her. "I don't know. I think you might be able to pass as one of them, Maggie. You don't look much older than eighteen tonight."

She laughed. "Thanks, it must be the dim lighting out here." The band was beginning to play now and the volume was ear-splittingly loud. Maggie actually shielded her ears with her hands and was thankful they weren't any closer. She didn't think the band was very good, but knew she was no judge of this sort of music. However, the kids didn't seem too enthused either. They just continued milling around, hardly paying any attention to the musicians. She was thankful it wasn't Spencer's band, but at the same time grew worried. What if his band received a cool reception like this—or worse—what if they booed them off the stage? Poor Spencer, after only three weeks of working so hard how could he expect that they would be ready for this? She searched the crowd, trying to spot him, but finally gave up in the dim light. At last, the first band finished their final song and began to move away from the stage area. The audience applauded politely but without much enthusiasm. She felt sorry for the musicians; they looked discouraged as they packed up their instruments. Yet at the same time she was relieved that her eardrums would have a rest, if only for a few minutes. And still her concern for Spencer's band was growing. She hated to see him humiliated—especially publicly!

"That was pretty loud," said Jed with a somewhat pained expression.

She nodded. "Leah said we should bring ear plugs. Do you want to move back a ways?"

"You mean to the old fogy section?"

"Call it what you like, I'd like to preserve my hearing for a few more years." They moved back a bit further, but still close enough to see clearly. Soon the second band began to play. Fortunately they kept their volume a little lower, and either Maggie was getting used to this type of music or this group was better than the first. She figured they must be an improvement because now the high-school audience was beginning to respond, gathering closer to the stage and moving a little with the beat. This band seemed more experienced and polished than the previous group, but after their final number the kids applauded with only slightly more energy than the first time.

At last she spotted Spencer moving toward the stage. He'd already told her that the bands had agreed to share the same drum set to avoid taking down and setting up time. She watched as he checked various things on the drums, wondering if he felt as nervous as she did.

"*Good night!*" said Jed suddenly.

Maggie glanced up at him. "What's wrong?"

"What in the world is that girl wearing?"

Maggie looked back to the stage to now see Ed and Daniel setting up. And off to one side was Leah—at least she thought it was Leah. It was hard to tell with all the make-up and strange clothing. Her lips were painted black and her eyes heavily made up with dramatic liner. In contrast her pale skin looked very white. But what was even worse was the short, tight, black plastic mini-skirt and black lace hosiery.

"She looks like a hooker," said Jed in disgust. "Who is she? Certainly not a friend of Spencer's, I hope."

Maggie sucked in her breath. Poor Leah! Why hadn't Maggie asked to see what the boys had picked for her to wear? It was simply awful! Degrading even.

"Hey there," called Chloe as she and Scott joined them.

"Is this where the old folks watch from?" asked Scott as he fiddled with a camera lens. Maggie had asked him to get some photos of the event for next week's paper. Now she wasn't so sure that was a good idea.

She ignored Scott's comment, turning instead to Chloe. "I can't believe you encouraged Leah to wear that outfit."

"I didn't *encourage* her..."

"But I thought you said she looked *good* in it."

"I said she looked like a rock star..."

"Yeah," snapped Maggie, "like Marilyn Manson!"

"Marilyn who?" asked Jed.

"Oh, never mind." Maggie redirected her attention to the stage now. Maybe she was just overreacting. After all, this was a show—they were performing.

"Well, I think she looks disgusting," said Jed. "If I was the principal I'd have her removed from the stage immediately."

This comment made Maggie feel suddenly defensive. "Leah has every right to look however she wants, as long as it's not indecent."

"Who gets to define indecent?" asked Jed.

"I think she looks very cool," said Scott as he snapped a photo. "Give the kid a break."

"Yeah," agreed Chloe. "You two are acting like the fashion police. Lighten up. They're just having a little fun."

Maggie forced a smile to her lips. "You're probably right. It was just a shock at first." Now the band was beginning to play. And it was clear that they had already gotten the crowd's attention, perhaps due to Leah's strange get-up at first, but when they played and Leah began to sing, it became very clear that they were actually quite good. And the audience responded to them very favorably. Kids began clapping and jumping—enthusiasm charged the air like electricity. Spencer's band was a hit! Suddenly, Leah's outfit seemed much less significant, and Maggie focused her attention on the music, even clapping along with the kids to the beat. After three songs, the crowd whistled and cheered for more.

Leah spoke into the microphone. "Thanks, you guys. You've been a great audience. We're a brand new group and we don't have a lot of songs yet. But next time you see us, we will!" The crowd went wild over this, clapping and cheering again. Leah waved to them, and the players began to pack up their things. Kids continued to mill around the band as they moved from the stage. Spencer's face was glowing with pride.

"Wow," said Chloe. "They were *really* good."

"Yeah," agreed Scott as he put his camera away. "And that Leah has a real stage presence."

Jed just shook his head. "If I were you, Maggie, I'd never let her out of the house looking like that again."

"Actually, I was just getting used to it," said Maggie lightly. "And besides, it's not as if I'm her mother. Even if I was, I wouldn't dictate to her how she should dress."

"Hello there," called Rosa as she and Sam approached. "We were in the back having a tailgate party—the noise was a little much for Sam. But Spencer's band sounded really good."

"I think they were the best of the three," said Sam. "In my opinion anyway. 'Course, I'm a bit of an old-timer."

"Well, for once I happen to agree with you, Dad," said Scott.

The small group continued to chat about the music, but Maggie noticed that Jed had become quiet. Perhaps he'd decided it wise to keep his strong opinions to himself. Soon Leah and Spence joined them, still flushed with the excitement of their success.

"You guys were great!" said Maggie. "I hope there aren't any music agents around, they might try and sign you to a label."

"Oh, Mom," said Spencer. But she could tell he was pleased.

"Leah, you have a great voice," said Chloe.

"Thanks. It was fun." Leah had on a coat now to cover up her outfit, but the weird make-up was still a little startling.

Maggie smiled at her and put an arm around her shoulders. "You made quite an impact up there, Leah."

Leah shook her head, then whispered to Maggie. "I think the outfit was a little much, don't you?"

Maggie nodded. "But your talent outshone the outfit."

"Thanks. Did Audrey make it tonight?"

Suddenly Maggie remembered her mother. "I haven't seen her. Maybe she got tired and went home. I think this kind of music might be a little hard on her ears."

"Yeah, I guess…"

"Maggie!" called a man's voice from the parking lot. "Maggie Carpenter? Are you here?"

"Over here," yelled Maggie, waving from the midst of her group of friends.

"That sounds like Buckie," said Leah.

"But he doesn't get home until tomorrow…"

But it was Buckie, and he was jogging over toward them. "Maggie!" he called with urgency. "It's your mom. Something's wrong."

Maggie's heart began to pound in fear. "What is it? Is she okay?"

Buckie was panting. "She says she's okay. But I don't think so. I think she needs to go to the hospital."

"The *hospital*? What's wrong?"

"She's acting strange. She's kind of dizzy, and she says her head hurts. No time to talk right now, come see for yourself."

Maggie turned to Jed. "But I don't have a car, I came with…"

Buckie grabbed her arm. "Then come with me!"

"I'm coming too," announced Spencer.

"Me too," said Leah.

The four of them dashed across the parking lot and piled into Buckie's still running vehicle. "I hated to leave her alone," he said, driving quickly toward his shop, "but she assured me she was just fine."

"Then how are you so certain that something's wrong?"

"Well, I got back early and on my way home saw the lights still on in the shop. I thought it was odd since it was well past closing time. So, I went in and Audrey was still there. I asked her why, but she seemed sort of spaced-out, like she didn't even see me to know me."

"Oh, no!" gasped Maggie. "What could it be?"

"I don't know. Maybe a mild stroke or something. But it alarmed me. I called your house and then Audrey became clear-headed again and remembered you were at the school. She said Spencer's band was playing. I wanted to call an ambulance, but she wouldn't hear of it, so I made her sit down, and then I rushed over to get you."

They pulled up in front of the Blue Moose and Maggie leapt out and ran into the gallery. "*Mom?*" she called. "Are you okay?"

Audrey was still sitting in a chair in the back room. She had a blank expression on her face, then looked up. "Is that you, Maggie?"

Maggie threw her arms around her mother, then gently asked, "How are you feeling, Mom?"

"Oh, I don't know. I'm just a little dizzy, I guess."

"Why did you stay here at the shop?"

"I don't know..." Then her mom's face got a strange blank look. "Maggie," she said in a slightly slurred voice. "I can't see very well..."

Maggie turned to Buckie and whispered, "Call 911. I think she may be having a stroke."

She rode with her mother in the ambulance to the hospital in Byron. Holding her hand, she prayed out loud with the strange, muffled sound of the siren crying in the background. Audrey never fully lost consciousness, but at the same time she never seemed fully conscious either. When they finally arrived after what seemed like hours, Audrey was efficiently wheeled into the emergency room and Maggie was left behind, feeling very much alone and slightly confused. She quickly gave the receptionist all the pertinent information, digging through Audrey's purse to find insurance cards, then she asked if she could join her mother in the ER. The receptionist hesitated, then said she could go in if she stayed out of the way.

Just as she was heading for the ER, Buckie and the kids arrived. Maggie stared in surprise at Leah's strangely made-up face for a moment, then remembered the concert earlier tonight. It seemed like it had been a week ago. "I'm going to join Mom," she explained quickly. "She's in the ER right now."

"Is Grandma...okay?" asked Spencer, tears welling in his eyes.

Maggie gave him a firm hug. "Yes, I think she's okay. Something is definitely wrong, but she is still conscious. They're examining her right now. You guys stay out here and pray for her, and I'll let you know as soon as I know something more." She wrote down a phone number and shoved it into Spencer's hand. "Call Uncle Barry and fill him in on what's going on. He'll want to know."

She went into the ER to find her mother being examined by a physician. Maggie read the nametag pinned to her crisp white jacket: Cynthia Marshall MD. Already an IV was hooked up and a nurse was standing close by with a hypodermic syringe poised as if ready for action. The doctor was carefully checking Audrey's pupils with a penlight, and talking gently to her, asking questions like who was president and what day was it today. Maggie slipped to the other side of the bed and quietly took her mother's hand, waiting and watching as the doctor continued her exam.

"Audrey," the doctor finally spoke, in a clear, well-enunciated voice, glancing over to Maggie as if to get her attention as well. "I think you may have had a mild stroke. But you're lucky your family got you in here so quickly. Right now the nurse is going give you an anticoagulant. And then I will try to schedule an x-ray and a CAT scan for tonight, and hopefully an MRI for tomorrow if we can bump somebody else's appointment. We need to figure out what's causing the blockage of blood flow and see if we can do something to fix it. In the meantime, I'll admit you into ICU for the night."

Audrey mumbled a thank-you to the doctor, then looked over at Maggie with helpless brown eyes. Maggie gently squeezed her mother's hand. "Everything's going to be okay, Mom. I'll stay with you all night, and we'll see what the test results say. Why don't you just try to relax and rest a little right now. You've been awfully busy lately. I guess it's time to slow down."

Audrey blinked her eyes as if to say yes, then closed them. Maggie waited for several minutes until she was certain that Audrey was asleep. Then she slipped back out to the waiting area.

"She's had a mild stroke," she explained to the three worried faces, Leah's was now scrubbed free of all traces of make-up, and it appeared she had been crying.

"That's what I was afraid of," said Buckie sadly. "How serious is it?"

Maggie explained about the testing, then added, "The doctor said it was a good thing we got her here so quickly." She looked at Buckie. "Thank God you came home when you did and that you happened to notice the lights on in the gallery."

He scratched his head. "It's funny. I thought my flight was on Sunday, and that's what I told everyone, but last night when I checked my tickets I was surprised to see it was actually today. I'm glad I didn't miss it."

"Will she be okay?" asked Spencer. "Can I see her?"

"She's resting right now," said Maggie. "And I think she'll be okay. But until we find out the test results we won't know anything for sure."

"She's just got to be okay," said Leah quietly. "She's just got to."

Maggie nodded. "But there's really no reason for all of you to stay here." She turned to Buckie. "Would you mind dropping these guys off at home?"

"No, Mom," argued Spencer. "I want to stay."

"I understand. But I think it would be better if you went home and got some sleep so you can come back fresh in the morning. I'll stay with Grandma all night, but I might need someone to spell me tomorrow. By the way, did you reach Uncle Barry?"

"I left a message on his answering machine and gave him the name and number of the hospital."

"That's good. I'll try calling him later too."

Spencer grew thoughtful. "Okay, Mom, I'll only go home if I can come back first thing in the morning."

"I'll be glad to bring you over before it's time to open the gallery," said Buckie. He glanced at Leah. "I don't suppose you'll want to be working tomorrow."

She shrugged. "I don't know. I really want to be here with Audrey, but I'll understand if you need my help."

Buckie put his arm around Maggie's shoulders. "Don't you worry about us, we'll figure it out. You just make sure you take good care of Audrey. And try to get a little rest yourself—you're looking a little ragged around the edges."

"I can only imagine." She bit her lip, fighting to hold back tears. "Thanks for your help, Buckie." She hugged both kids good-bye and reminded them to pray. "If I hear anything important, I'll call. And maybe you guys could give the Galloways a call and tell them what's up. Rosa has mentioned a prayer chain that the church has all set up for things like this."

"You bet," promised Buckie. "And I'll tell you what, I'll even pray. And you know that's not something I normally do. But I'll do it for Audrey."

Maggie smiled at him. "I'll be sure and tell her that."

Thirteen

y the next morning, Maggie felt like she'd spent the night in the twilight zone. She accompanied her mother as she traveled by gurney and wheelchair all around the hospital for various tests and watched clocks slowly tick under harsh fluorescent lights while she waited and waited, then waited some more. The doctor, satisfied that Audrey's condition was stabilized, had finally settled her into a regular hospital room, where Maggie had eventually fallen asleep in a stiff, vinyl-covered chair.

Her neck had a crick in it that felt like it would take a blacksmith to hammer out. But she forgot all about it when she saw her mother's smiling face. "Morning, dear," said Audrey in a quiet voice. "I must've caused everyone a lot of trouble over nothing."

"Mother," she reprimanded gently, "a stroke is not nothing."

Audrey waved her hand. "But I feel fine now. I think perhaps I was just overly tired yesterday."

"Hello there," called Dr. Marshall as she entered the room. She flipped open the chart and began penciling. "How are you feeling, Audrey?"

"I feel like I should be going home soon."

The doctor nodded. "Well, I don't see why not."

"But what about the stroke?" asked Maggie with concern.

"Actually, I've downgraded your mother's diagnosis from a stroke to a TIA—a transient ischemic attack, which some people call a mini-stroke. It's a temporary deficiency of blood supply to the brain, much like a stroke, only less serious."

"Do you know the cause?" asked Maggie.

"We've ruled out some possibilities, but it could still be a number of things. I'd like to do an MRI this morning. We found an opening at nine. That might tell us something new."

Spencer and Leah came to the hospital shortly before Audrey was to be transported to her MRI. They gave her relieved hugs and wished her luck, then she and Maggie were off to another corner of the hospital. Maggie, though exhausted, wanted to accompany her mother for this last test. She removed all her jewelry, including the belt that she'd bought at Chloe's shop only yesterday, then inserted foam earplugs and went into the small white room containing a large tomb-like machine that resembled an iron lung. There she sat on another stiff, vinyl chair and waited as a series of fairly loud banging and clanging noises occurred. It reminded her of the sound of Clyde's old printing press. Had Buckie called her friends from the paper? Of course, she remembered, Scott would already know and tell the others. After what seemed a very long hour, they were finished. The doctor said that the initial results looked fairly clean, but she couldn't know for sure until a thorough reading was completed and that might take a couple weeks. By now Maggie understood that they wanted to rule out any possibility of a brain tumor or aneurysm.

When she and Audrey arrived back at the room, it was almost eleven and several different flower arrangements had been delivered.

"Oh, my," said Audrey, "did somebody die?"

"Very funny, Grandma," said Spencer. "Oh yeah, Uncle Barry called. He wants you to call him right away. Here's the number at his office."

"How did the MRI go?" asked Leah.

"Fine," said Audrey. "They couldn't find a single thing in there. I always knew my head was empty."

"You *must* be feeling better," said Spencer. "Your old sense of humor is back."

"Do you want me to read the cards that came with your flowers?" asked Leah.

Audrey nodded and leaned back into her bed as Leah revealed one by one who'd sent what. Maggie listened as she waited on hold while Barry's secretary attempted to locate him somewhere in the large design firm's building. It seemed the bouquet of pink roses were from Buckie "the slave-driving boss," the flower basket from the Galloway family, the lovely fall bouquet from the newspaper, and the delicate pot of living orchids was from Jed. "Oh my, how did Jed know that I *love* orchids?" She looked over at Maggie suspiciously. "Did you tell him?"

Still waiting on the phone, Maggie shook her head. "No. I have no idea how he knew. Maybe he's just a good guesser." Just then, she heard her brother's voice. She reassured him that it was going well, gave him the complete medical update, then finally handed the receiver over to her mother. She studied the orchids while her mother reassured Barry that there was no reason to drop everything and come. At last she said goodbye and handed the phone back to Maggie.

Audrey sniffed the fragrant purple orchids in front of her and sighed. Then her brow creased as if she just remembered something. "Didn't you have a date last night with Jed?"

"I suppose you could call it that. We had dinner, and then we went to hear Spencer's band." Maggie didn't want to think about Jed's reaction to the band.

"That's right!" exclaimed Audrey. "The big debut of the band. And I completely missed it. How did it go, Spence?"

He moved a chair right next to her bed. "It was great, Grandma. We did pretty good, and I think the kids actually liked us."

"Liked you?" exclaimed Maggie. "They went *nuts* over your band. You guys were the hit of the night."

"Oh, I wish I could've been there. I don't know what came over me last night. I can't even remember exactly what happened. I just kept getting these headaches, then I'd get all dizzy and forgetful."

"Like Dr. Marshall said, you were having a little blood shortage in the brain."

"Oh, yes, mini-strokes, I think she called them. But enough about me, I want to hear all about your band, Spencer."

"You kids stay here and keep an eye on Grandma," said Maggie winking at her mother. "I don't want to hear about her busting out of here. I'm going to see if I can unearth a decent cup of coffee."

"Why don't you bring me back one too."

Maggie flashed her the thumbs up sign, then turned to Leah. "Do you mind giving Rosa a call and letting her know how Mom's doing? I'm sure she'll be good to get the word out."

With everything feeling somewhat under control, Maggie finally left the room. Now if only she could find a Starbucks somewhere nearby. Just as she rounded the corner to the elevator, she saw Jed walking down the corridor toward her. At first, she smiled to see him striding confidently in his familiar faded blue jeans and fringed moccasins, but then she remembered some of their conversation at the high school and her smile instantly faded.

"How's it going?" he asked kindly. "Is your mother okay?"

"Yes, she's fine. It was only a mini-sort of stroke. I think she'll actually get to go home today."

"Great. But then why did your face look so gloomy just now?"

Maggie bit her lip. "I'm just a little tired…"

"Or perhaps you weren't too happy to see me."

"No, that's not it. Actually, I could use a good cup of coffee."

"There's a kiosk out in the parking lot. Want to give it a try?"

"Sure. I could use some fresh air."

Not having thought to bring her jacket, she shivered in the autumn breeze as they waited for the girl to brew their coffees. The next thing she knew, Jed was slipping his soft woolen coat over her shoulders. "Thanks. I keep forgetting that fall is coming."

They sat outside on a bench and drank their coffee, planning to get another to take back to Audrey when they finished. Maggie squinted up at the blue sky and inhaled deeply. Being inside the stuffy hospital had reminded her of what it was like back in L.A., and it wasn't a pleasant reminder.

"I wanted to apologize," said Jed quietly.

"For what?" She took another sip of her café mocha.

"I acted like a jerk last night."

"Oh, you mean at the bonfire?"

"Yeah. I don't know what came over me. Well, I didn't at the time, but I gave it some thought after I went home, and I think I know."

"What do you mean?"

He sighed deeply. "Well, I think that hearing that loud, rock music sort of snapped something in me. Something from my past. It all seemed remnant of drugs and sin and everything evil."

"Oh."

"It's not that I think Spencer or even Leah is evil. But last night, well, it seemed that way to me. The whole thing just made me really angry."

"Do you think there's something inherently wrong with their music?"

"To be completely honest, I don't know if it's wrong for them. But maybe it's wrong for me. I know that we all have to listen to our own hearts. But I'd hate to see Spencer get involved in something that could be harmful."

"So would I. But he's had such a good time with his music, and you should have seen him telling his grandmother about it just now. His eyes were all lit up."

Jed nodded. "That's good, Maggie. And I admit that I overreacted last night. I'm just glad I didn't say anything to Spencer or Leah."

"It's big of you to admit this to me today." Maggie turned and smiled at him. "Do you want to come say hi to Mom? By the way, she loved your orchids."

He grinned. "She seems like an orchid-sort of lady."

They ordered Audrey a special coffee and walked back toward her room. Maggie wondered how her mother would react to Jed's presence. She knew her mother liked and respected Jed well enough as a person, but for some reason she had an obstacle when it came to Maggie and him together. She had never considered her mother to be bigoted about race, especially coming from an Italian family, but sometimes she wasn't completely sure.

"Brought you some good coffee, Mom," announced Maggie. "And look what I picked up along the way."

"Hello, Audrey," said Jed, as he politely stood by the door.

"Why, Jed Whitewater. What are you doing here?"

He smiled. "I just wanted to make sure you all were doing okay. It got kind of crazy last night, and I, well…"

"Is that pretty Kate with you?" asked Audrey, and Maggie could've sworn she saw a devilish glint in her mother's eye.

Jed shook his head. "No, Kate is minding the shop."

"Speaking of minding the shop," injected Leah, "I told Buckie that if I could find a ride back into town, I'd work the afternoon for him. I know he wants to come see Audrey, plus he's tired from his trip."

Maggie smiled at Leah, thankful she had detoured the conversation and pleased at how thoughtful she was. Maybe that would help improve Leah's image in Jed's eyes.

"I'd be glad to give you a ride." He turned back to Maggie. "Do you know when your mother will be released?"

"The sooner the better," said Audrey. "The doctor said today, but probably not until later this afternoon."

"Well, you just call if you need a ride or anything," offered Jed.

"Thanks. I'll remember that."

They didn't get Audrey back home until nearly six o'clock. And by then Maggie was completely exhausted. Rosa had driven over to Byron to pick them up and helped Maggie get Audrey up the stairs and to bed.

"I think you're next, young lady," said Rosa.

"Oh, I'm okay. Just a little tired."

"To bed," commanded Rosa. "I already have dinner taken care of. And if you're a good girl, I'll bring a tray to your room just like the one Sierra's bringing for Audrey."

"You don't need to do…"

"No arguing or you won't get your tray. And it's enchiladas, but not too spicy."

Maggie smiled. "Off to bed I go. No arguing from me."

"There, that's much better."

⟿

Maggie arranged to work on the paper from home the following week, putting Scott in charge in the meantime. She wanted to keep a wary eye on her mother and make sure she was fully recovered with no more recurrences of stroke. The doctor had pointed out that a TIA could be followed by a real stroke. But each day passed uneventfully, and Audrey was as perky as ever. By Tuesday, Maggie couldn't even keep her out of the kitchen.

"I'll feel better if I'm busy," said Audrey as she wiped off a counter.

"But you're supposed to be recovering quietly," said Maggie. "And I was going to finish cleaning the kitchen as soon as I proofed this article."

"But I like to putter about. I don't like feeling like a helpless invalid."

"Fine," Maggie threw her hands up in the air. "Go ahead, knock yourself out. I don't intend to become your jailer." She went back to the library and continued proofing, trying to push melodramatic images of her mother collapsing on the kitchen floor out of her mind. Her worries helped nothing. She knew she had to let go and trust God. But it just wasn't easy.

The following day, Maggie was finally able to relax. The paper was safely put to bed and being printed. Scott had done a good job keeping things together at the office. Her mother seemed completely recovered with no signs of any recurrences. Spencer was enjoying his new rock-star status at school. It was three o'clock and she was making a pot of Earl Gray tea for them to enjoy before the kids got home. But just as she and Audrey sat down in the parlor, the front door burst open and Leah came in. Her face was streaked with tears, and a copy of what looked like the *Pine Cone* was in her hand.

"Why did you do this, Maggie?" demanded Leah as she held the paper under their noses with a trembling hand.

Maggie blinked. "Do what?" She looked down at the paper, and there on the front page was a good-sized picture of Leah in that horrible outfit from the other night.

"Who is *that*?" asked Audrey, adjusting her glasses to see better.

"What in the world?" exclaimed Maggie. She read the headline out loud, "Bonfire Gets Hot This Year as Leah Hill Cuts Loose."

"Why, that's not you, Leah?" said Audrey, looking up at Leah in amazement.

Leah nodded. "Unfortunately it is. I knew I looked bad, but somehow it looks far worse in a black and white photograph."

Maggie stood up and put an arm around her. "I never saw this before. I've been working at home this week, but mostly just proofing print. I never saw any photos. Scott handled that."

Leah collapsed on the couch. "I'm sure he didn't do it to hurt me. But you should see how people are reacting around town. Buckie is furious. He already got all over my case that night we rode with him to the hospital."

"But why?" asked Audrey. "It doesn't concern him."

"He said since I was his employee, it did. He said I looked like a two-bit hooker."

"That wasn't very nice," said Maggie.

"But he's right. I did." Then Leah leaned her head into her lap and sobbed. "I feel like such a fool."

"Oh, Leah," soothed Audrey. "This will all blow over in…"

"I'm going to get that Scott Galloway on the phone right this minute," declared Maggie hotly. "He had no right to pull something like this." She hit the auto-dial and got Abigail. However, since it was Wednesday and his day to leave early, Scott was nowhere to be found.

"I was a little surprised myself when I saw that photo," said Abigail. "Actually, I was shocked that you'd want to run it, but even more shocked that Leah would dress that way. I thought she was a nice girl. And my goodness, you should have seen Clyde's reaction—you'd have thought the photo was of him in his underwear. Scott had arrived here early and was already printing when Clyde saw what was up. He was absolutely livid. He wouldn't even help Scott with the printing. He just stomped out all furious."

Maggie swallowed. "I'll bet he did. And just for the record, I didn't choose to print it. That was Scott's decision. Thanks, Abigail. I'm sure I'll be hearing from Clyde before long." She hung up and turned to Leah. "I'm so sorry about this."

"Oh, now," said Audrey, "I think you're both making too much of it." She looked at the photo again. "I think it's rather interesting looking. Sort of like a Halloween costume."

Maggie rolled her eyes. "Talk about looking for the bright side."

"Come on, you two. Have a cup of tea. Let's just put this silly old paper aside for right now. It'll all work out."

In silence they drank their tea. A dozen different thoughts shot through Maggie's brain. How could Scott have done this? What would Clyde do? Why was Buckie so upset? When would she hear from Gavin again? Finally, she just had to shake her head to try and dispel all the nagging questions. Then she looked at Leah. "Are you going to be all right?"

Leah looked at her with sad, dark eyes. "I guess I just thought all these people in Pine Mountain were my friends. And now I feel sort of betrayed."

Audrey patted her hand. "It'll all smooth over. You'll see."

"I don't know," said Leah. "Buckie was acting kind of weird about the whole thing. And suddenly I started to wonder what I was doing here in this little town. I walked right out of the gallery. Just like that. I'm sure Buckie thinks I quit. And maybe I did. Then I walked home and as I walked I wondered. What am I doing here? Just hanging on—and to what? And why? Nothing seems to make sense any more." She looked at Maggie with wet eyes. "I think it's time for me to go."

"Oh, Leah," said Maggie. "Surely not because of this?"

Leah shrugged. "Maybe this was just a sign. Maybe I'm trying too hard to fit into someplace where I never belonged."

Now Maggie's eyes were filling with tears. "But we love you, Leah. You're like family to us. I couldn't bear to see you leave. And what about your..." she glanced over to Audrey before she said the word father.

"It's okay, Maggie." Leah looked her right in the eye. "You can go ahead and say it. What about my father? Yes, that's a good question. What about my father? Maybe he doesn't even exist. Or if he does, maybe he's ashamed of me."

"You don't know that."

"I know. But just the same it seems like it's time for me to go."

"Where will you go, Leah?" asked Audrey quietly.

"I don't know. But not back to Arizona."

"How about California?" suggested Audrey hopefully. "How about San Jose?"

Leah's eyes lit up a little. "You mean with you?"

Audrey nodded. "I need to be going home soon. Why don't you come with me?"

"Could I?"

"I wish you would. I could use some help. And you have your driver's license, don't you?"

"Yes. I could drive you all the way home..."

"*Wait!*" cried Maggie, feeling as if her happy little world was quickly spinning completely out of her control. "What are you talking about? You both can't just leave me just like that."

"Why ever not?" asked Audrey.

Maggie stared at the two of them in horror. "Because, because...how will I get along without you?"

Audrey put an arm around Maggie. "Oh, honey, you have Spencer. And your job. And all your friends..."

"*Friends?*" snapped Maggie. "You mean my friends like Buckie and Scott? Look how they've treated Leah. If *those* are my friends I'd hate to have a run-in with my enemies right now."

"Oh, Maggie, you're overreacting. It'll all smooth out."

"Then why don't you stay until it does?" pleaded Maggie.

Audrey shook her head. "Because for the last several days I've been thinking that it's time for me to go home. I've stayed much longer than I originally planned, and there are things I need to take care of at home. And to be honest, I miss my house and my old neighborhood."

"But I thought you liked it here." Maggie peered intently into her mother's eyes, wondering if somehow she had made her feel unwelcome in the past few days. But then they'd always disagreed on some things, why should it be any different now. "We love having you here, Mom. Spencer will be so sad. And what about the Harvest Festival?"

"I know, honey, it'd be fun to be here for that. But there are things I need to take care of. And this little stroke business has left me feeling somewhat unsettled. I'd like to go home and see my own doctor for a complete exam."

Maggie nodded. "Yes, I suppose that makes sense. I guess I'm just being selfish."

Audrey squeezed her hand. "It's okay. I like being wanted."

Maggie bit her lip. She didn't want to see her mother and Leah leave, but she knew it wasn't her decision. She had to let go. And who knew, maybe after a day or two, when this crazy news-photo business blew over and her mother felt back to her old self, perhaps then they would change their minds and forget about this idea of leaving Pine Mountain altogether.

Fourteen

*T*he dinner table that evening was quieter than usual. Leah still seemed to be suffering over the photo in the paper. Maggie had considered calling Scott at home, then decided it could wait until morning, when hopefully she'd be in a more objective frame of mind. The business side of her knew that Scott probably meant no harm, but the other side still simmered over what seemed like a low blow.

"The band is going to practice tonight." Spencer, warned by Maggie about Leah's unfortunate afternoon and the possibility of her leaving, now spoke tentatively. "Do you want to come out and try a new song that Ed is bringing?"

Leah shrugged. "I guess so."

Spencer smiled. "Cool. Ed says that your voice will be perfect for it."

Leah's eyes lit up, ever so slightly. Maggie felt a flicker of encouragement. Perhaps there was hope. Maybe by morning this would all blow over.

Before going to bed, Maggie checked her email to find a note from Rebecca.

MC

How did your date with the mysterious Jed go? I wish I'd gotten your email sooner, I would've called and said, "Go for it, girl. Take some risks. Life is short." And I do think this guy sounds interesting. Okay, maybe a little strange, but interesting. Anyway, it's been so long since you've expressed interest of any kind in a guy, that I figure this one must be special. And if he's not what you thought he was; well, nothing's lost anyway. At least you'll find out. You'll be surprised to hear that I just broke off my relationship with Garrett. I know, I know, I can just hear you saying, "but he was such a nice guy, and you've been going out with him for two years… yada…yada…" But I guess I just realized, or finally admitted, that I wasn't in love with him. It felt unfair to keep him hanging on, pretending we have a future. To be honest, Maggie, it's partly your fault. When I heard your somewhat "veiled enthusiasm" about this Jed character, I realized that I didn't feel anything like that about Garrett—and I never did! So, I'm going to hold out for something else. The funny thing is, once I broke up—I immediately began to miss him desperately. Why is that? All for now, dear.

RB

Maggie smiled as she turned off her computer. She was way too tired to try and tackle *that* one tonight. But Rebecca's comments about Jed were interesting. How had she managed to read so much between the lines of Maggie's email? Or was Maggie that transparent? Perhaps she should be more careful, especially around town. She hadn't heard a word from Jed since his visit to the hospital, and she didn't want to come across as too presumptuous about their relationship. She still wasn't absolutely sure where she stood with him. Rebecca was right. He was sort of mysterious, especially in that regard. But perhaps he was only being cautious. And certainly there was no hurry to rush things along.

After all, it seemed she had plenty of other matters to concern her right now. Unfortunately her thoughts about Jed distracted her from dealing with those other issues.

⟜

The next morning Maggie decided to go to the office. Leah had mentioned how she wouldn't be working for Buckie for the remainder of the week. Whether this was a result of yesterday's walk-out or just due to Buckie being back and the general slowing of tourist traffic, Maggie wasn't sure. But in any case, she knew her mother would be in good hands with Leah around. Only Spencer was in the kitchen when Maggie went down.

"Looks like everyone's sleeping in," she mentioned as she measured coffee.

"Yeah," he muttered between bites of cereal. "Leah probably doesn't want to speak to me this morning."

Maggie turned on the coffee maker, then faced her son. "What do you mean?"

He made a groaning sound. "Well, it wasn't really my fault."

"What are you talking about?"

"Last night," he began, dropping his spoon into the empty bowl with a loud clang. "Ed got real mad at Leah because she didn't want to do this song that he brought over."

"Why didn't she want to do it?"

"She said it was trashy."

"Was it?"

Spencer shrugged. "Well, yeah. I guess it was."

"Did you want to do it?"

He shrugged again. "Not really."

"Then what's the big deal?"

"Well, you know how Ed kind of runs things. Anyway, he got us this gig for a Halloween party, and he wanted us to come up with some new songs. Then he and Leah got into this big ol' fight over the whole thing."

Maggie sank into a chair. "Just what poor Leah needed after her day yesterday."

"I know…" Spencer shook his head. "But I didn't know what to do. Ed's right, we do need some more songs."

"But you don't need to do trashy songs. And you know how Leah is thinking about leaving now anyway…"

"Yeah, and when she told Ed that, he just blew up. Called her names and everything."

Maggie felt her fingernails digging into her palms. "And what did you do, Spence?" she asked with amazing control.

"I was pretty shocked, and I didn't say anything."

"Spencer!"

"Oh, Mom, you'd have to have been there. Ed was just way out of control, and Leah was actually doing a pretty good job of defending herself. Then she got so mad, she just stormed out."

"Good for her."

"And *then* I let Ed have it."

Maggie looked at him. "You did?"

"Yeah, I told him if that's the way he wanted it, he could just leave."

"You did?"

He nodded. "And that's exactly what he did. Just unplugged his bass and stomped out."

"What about Daniel?"

"Well, Daniel's the one with the car. Ed couldn't very well leave without him."

"I see. What was Daniel's part in all this?"

Spencer shrugged. "He didn't say much. Just packed up his stuff and left."

"So what's to become of the band?"

Spencer looked down at his empty bowl. "Guess that's it."

She placed a hand on his shoulder. "I'm sorry, Spence."

He shrugged again. "It's okay, I guess. I mean it was fun and everything. But it's not worth it if everyone's going to fight. And at least Sierra's not hanging out with Kurt anymore."

Maggie tried to hide her smile. "Well, who knows, maybe you'll find some other guys to do a band with."

Spencer picked up his bowl and headed toward the sink. "Maybe."

⌒

Maggie drove slowly to work. For the first time in months, she almost missed the commute in L.A., but only because she wanted time to think. She wanted to figure a way to confront Scott without appearing hostile. But before she knew it, she was parking the car and walking up the front step.

"Hello there, stranger," chirped Abigail. "I didn't expect to see you until next Monday."

"After seeing yesterday's paper, I thought it best to come in." She glanced over to the closed door of Scott's office. "Is Scott in?"

Abigail nodded. "And so is Clyde. He's puttering around the backroom, making lots of huffing and puffing noises. You might want to go diffuse him first."

"You're probably right." She put her briefcase in her office and went to find Clyde. He was pushing a broom back and forth across the floor of the big back-room. "Hello there," she called.

He looked up with a scowl, finished a last sweep, then walked over while brushing his hands on his black work pants. "Abigail told me this morning that you hadn't seen that durned photo until the paper came out. That so?"

She nodded. "It was something of a shock to me too."

He sniffed. "Downright disgusting if you ask me. And I have two questions. First of all, why in the world did you let our girl go traipsing around town in that kind of get-up. And secondly, what did Scott think he was doing, running it in the paper—and on the front page to boot!"

Suddenly she felt the same defenses kicking into gear that she'd felt with Jed at the bonfire. "I don't tell Leah what to wear or what to do, Clyde. She's eighteen years old, and so far has proven herself responsible..."

"What kind of responsible person dresses like that?"

"It was a costume for the band. Perhaps not a very good one, but Ed Tanner picked it out..."

"*Ed Tanner!* Well, that just figures. That family is always stirring one kind of trouble or another."

"That sounds pretty judgmental, Clyde."

"Well, the apple doesn't fall far from the tree."

She sighed. "What good is it to go over all this now?"

"I don't know, Maggie. I just feel so bad about Leah. What went wrong?"

"Nothing really went wrong on Leah's part. And hopefully this whole thing will blow over. But it did hurt her to have the photo in the *Pine Cone*. And I do intend to find out what Scott was thinking. But I seriously doubt that he meant any harm. Knowing Scott, he probably just thought it was a cool shot."

"Hmph. Cool shot, my eye."

"Let it go, Clyde," she advised.

"I suppose you're right." He hooked his thumbs into his red suspenders. "How's your mother doing?"

"Much better. You can hardly slow that woman down."

"Have you heard the results from all the testing yet?"

"Everything but the MRI. That'll take a few weeks. Leah's staying with her today. I thought I'd come in and get some things done, as well as talk to Scott about that photo."

"Better you than me. I'll trust you to take care of it, Maggie."

"Okay, and I'll trust you not to worry about it anymore. It'll all be forgotten in a day or two anyway."

"S'pect you're right."

～

Maggie's conversation with Scott didn't go as well as she'd hoped. He remained stubborn and defensive about the photo, claiming there was nothing wrong with it and that it was an excellent action shot. She told him from now on to run all photos by her before taking them to press. He told her she was being overly controlling, and she reminded him that she was the editor, then walked into her office and loudly closed the door. She didn't like pulling rank like that, but his behavior was unacceptable. Just then the intercom buzzed and Abigail's voice broke in apologetically. "Sorry to bother you, Maggie, but your mother's on the phone."

"That's okay. Put her through." She picked up the phone. "Hi, Mom, everything okay?"

"We're doing just fine, Maggie. Sorry I wasn't up when you left this morning. I didn't realize you were going in."

"No problem. You need your rest. What's up?"

"Well, Leah and I are packing..."

"Packing?"

"Yes, for our trip back home."

"You're packing right now? When are you planning on leaving?"

"Well, we thought we'd go today. We'll take it real easy—drive a few hours, then spend the night wherever seems fitting. Then do the same tomorrow. I figure we'll get home on Saturday. I already made an appointment with my doctor for Monday afternoon."

"Are you sure, Mom? What did your doctor say?"

"Oh, we'll be just fine, Maggie. Leah will do all the driving. And, of course, I have my cell phone just in case. No need to worry."

"It seems so sudden. I mean, when you said you needed to go home I figured you meant in a week or two. And what about Leah's job?"

"She's already called Buckie."

"Oh." Maggie twisted the phone cord in her fingers. "Well, I'll come right home to tell you both goodbye."

"There's no need..."

"Mom!" she interrupted, "I have a need—okay?"

"Sure, honey. That's fine. But we want to be on the road by ten."

ᵒ⸺

It was a teary goodbye. Maggie didn't even know why it was hitting her so hard. It just seemed so wrong. There was her mother's precarious health; and then it seemed like they were admitting failure to allow Leah to leave like this. But once again she reminded herself that this was not her decision to make. She told them she loved them and wanted them to come back—soon. But no promises were made. She watched through tear-wet eyes as her mother's little Honda pulled out of the driveway and disappeared down the road. "Please, watch over them, God," she prayed out loud. Then she wondered how she would explain this hasty departure to Spencer. She felt certain he would feel it as sharply as she. First his band breaks up, then this. She sighed and walked back toward the house. Now it seemed bigger and emptier than ever.

Fifteen

aggie sat down on her front porch steps and continued to cry. She knew it was ridiculous and perhaps only a delayed reaction from a week's worth of accumulated stress, or perhaps it was just part of being a woman. Whatever it was, she couldn't seem to stop the tears. It felt like a big hole had just been cut into her life, and already she missed Leah and her mother terribly. It was as if her happy little home had been divided and plundered. Finally her tears stopped and she wiped her nose. Looking about her, she grew thankful that no one had witnessed her emotional outburst. Not that tears were anything to be ashamed of—she knew crying was a good way to cleanse the soul—but just the same she preferred cleansing her soul in private. Suddenly she noticed the aspens next to her house with the sun spotlighted behind them. Their leaves seemed like a fiery blaze of orange and yellow jewels, topaz and amber, glistening against the blue sky. She watched the trees in fascination as their branches gently trembled in the autumn breeze; and then a few small, jewel-colored leaves fluttered gracefully down to the ground to create a light carpet of orange and yellow. It was just a matter of time before only bare branches would be etched across the winter sky. She studied the richly colored sight for a long moment, trying to imprint its beauty upon her mind, then looked out across the meadow, now flaxen gold from lack of moisture, and saw the mountains in the distance. Although much of their snow was gone, they were still majestic and beautiful. She sighed. Well, if she must be melancholy, at least she had a delightful place to be it in. And this thought almost made her smile, except that it was too soon for that. Instead she stood and stretched and went into her quiet house. She paused in the hallway to phone the *Pine Cone*, informing Abigail that she wouldn't be back in the office until tomorrow, but would instead work at home, taking her calls there.

"Is everything okay, dear?" asked Abigail in a kind and much too sympathetic voice. "Is your mother…"

"She's gone." Maggie felt the tears pressing against her throat, and then her voice cracked ever so slightly. "She and Leah have both gone."

"Oh." She sounded surprised. "My, that seems rather sudden. Was anything wrong?"

"Oh, sort of—but, no, not really. Mom just felt like she needed to get home. She'd made an appointment with her doctor, and Leah is driving her…"

"Well now, that sounds like a nice arrangement. And the girl will be good company for Audrey. How fortunate for you that Leah was free to just pick up and go like that."

"Yes, I suppose you're right. It's just that I'll miss them…"

"Of course you will, dear. But won't they be coming back soon?"

"I don't know for sure." Maggie swallowed hard, determined not to succumb to her earlier despair. "I guess we'll know in time. Thanks for listening, Abigail. I'll see you in the morning."

All afternoon she kept herself busily working and did not allow herself to think about Audrey and Leah. They would be just fine. They would all be fine. Soon she grew so absorbed in an article for next week's paper that she never even noticed the school bus stop along their road and jumped in surprise when she heard the front door bang sharply.

"Mom?" yelled Spencer. "Are you home?"

"In the library."

He burst into the room, dumping his backpack onto the floor with a thud. "Is Leah around?" he asked more quietly, glancing over his shoulder down the hallway.

Maggie closed her laptop. "Actually, she and Grandma have left."

"*Left?*"

For the second time today, she explained the story. This time she gave it a softer, more positive spin, mentioning how good it was that Leah could go along, and how Audrey really needed to see her own physician.

"It's probably a good thing," said Spencer, sinking into the couch and running a hand through his messy hair, which was overdue for a haircut. "Stupid Ed Tanner is going around telling everyone that Leah is a runaway and acting like she was somehow mixed up with those drug guys that got busted here last summer."

Maggie rolled her eyes. "Why in the world is he doing that?"

"'Cause he's an ignorant moron. And because he's really mad at Leah for breaking up the band. It's too bad Leah ever told him about how I found her in the woods. I'm sure she didn't think anything of it at the time, 'cause he was always real nice to her before. In fact, I thought he kind of had a thing for her."

"Maybe he did. Maybe that's why he's so mad now."

"Maybe. Well, at least she's gone for the time being. She won't have to hear all this crud going around about her. When will they be back anyway?"

Maggie forced a weak smile. "I don't really know, Spence. For now, it's back to just you and me again." She sighed then glanced at her watch. "Hey, I'm starving. Do you want to head over to Byron for McDonald's and a movie?"

He grinned. "Sure. There's a new flick I've been wanting to see."

Later that night, Maggie responded to Rebecca's email:

RB

Perhaps it's because we don't know what we have until we lose it (re: your feelings about missing Garrett...). Maybe you were taking him for granted, and after you let him go, you realize what you've lost. Or maybe not. You could just be adjusting to the change. Like when you've had a ho-hum painting on the wall for years, then you take it down and there seems to be this blank space like something's missing. But in time you get used to it, or you replace it with something you really like. Mom and Leah left today. But that was more like taking down a painting that I really loved and enjoyed—and now I really miss it. However, I know it's for the best. Won't go into all the details right now, but Mom was having some health problems and needed to be home. Anyway, I was feeling quite blue today. But I took Spencer out for some pretty bad fast food and a really crummy movie (that he liked!) and strangely enough I feel a little better now. Go figure! I'll fill you in about my date with the mystery man another time. Right now, I'm too drained to even go there. Later.

mc

᎒᎓

The next day, Maggie went to work as usual. She had decided to tell Clyde only that Leah had accompanied her mother on her trip back home, and to leave it open-ended about when the girl might return. The poor guy had been so upset by the photo, it made no sense to trouble him further. Besides, who knew, perhaps Leah would return before long. Scott was holed up in his office with the door closed, and

Maggie figured she'd let it go at that. Perhaps they were at a standoff, or maybe they both just needed some time to cool off. But because of the friction with Scott she found herself wanting to avoid Rosa at lunchtime as well. So instead of going to the deli like she normally would, she popped into Dolly's Diner for a bowl of soup.

As usual, the air in the diner was smoky and grease-tinged. But somehow Maggie didn't care today. She slipped into a corner booth almost unnoticed and quietly observed the chatter of others around her, people she recognized but didn't know well enough to join. She spotted Greg Snider and Rick Tanner in a booth on the other side, deep in conversation with papers spread across the table between them that also included what looked like a map or blueprints of some kind. Rick was furiously jotting down something on a clipboard, while Greg punched numbers into a pocket calculator. Interesting. The reporter in her wondered what the postmaster and farmer could possibly be up to. But perhaps Greg was simply doing some freelance accountant work for Rick's farm.

"Hey there, Maggie," said Dolly with a warm smile. "How are you doing?"

"I'm okay. Do you have some good soup today?"

"You're in luck." She told her the choices, then wrote down Maggie's order. Before she left, she paused as if she just remembered something. "Hey, that was quite a picture of Leah in the paper this week."

Maggie groaned. "Don't remind me."

"No, I'm serious. We loved it. Jinx even cut it out and hung it up on the kitchen bulletin board."

"Really?"

Dolly adjusted her glasses and grinned. "Yeah. He used to belong to this heavy metal band, and he thought it was pretty cool that the *Pine Cone* put it in."

Maggie couldn't help smiling at her. "Well, that's the first positive thing I've heard about it. Thanks."

"No problem. So, how's their little band doing?"

Her smile faded. "Actually, they just broke up."

Dolly shook her head. "Too bad. I heard they were pretty good. But that's not so unusual. Jinx's band would break up about every other week. Then they'd get back together again." She laughed as she walked back to the kitchen.

From the corner of her eye, Maggie saw the door open and to her surprise Buckie walked in. He seemed out of place in his neatly pressed khakis and pale blue polo shirt. And she could tell he wasn't comfortable. She watched with interest as his eyes searched the busy diner until he finally spotted her, then quickly walked over.

"This seat taken?" he asked in what seemed an unnecessarily grumpy voice.

"Hello to you too," she waved her hand toward the seat. "Help yourself."

"Thanks." He sat down and rested his hands on the table, then picked them up again, wiping them as if the table were unclean. "I saw you come in here from across the street, and thought I'd join you, but I had to wait until a customer left before I could close up for the lunch hour."

"I didn't think you liked Dolly's."

"Nor I, you." He frowned without speaking for a long moment. "Is it just my imagination, Maggie, or is your taste degenerating on *all* levels?"

She drew back from the table in surprise. Had she misheard him? "What exactly do you mean, Buckie?"

"You just seem different to me lately. Ever since I got back from Alaska, I mean."

"You know I've had a pretty rotten week, Buckie. Even now I'm feeling a little out of sorts. You might want to rethink the direction of your conversation just a little."

"Okay, okay. I didn't really mean to attack your character..."

"*My character?* What in the world are you talking about?"

"Well, let's see. Where do I begin? First of all, I come home and you and Leah look like something out of a bad seventies movie..."

"I beg your pardon?"

"Oh, you know—Leah in her rock-star outfit and you all dressed up like a teenybopper."

"A teenybopper?" Maggie took a deep breath, then seeing Dolly approaching with her order, she exhaled slowly, mentally counting to ten.

"How about you?" asked Dolly, squinting down at Buckie as if she didn't quite approve of him. Had she been observing their little discourse from the kitchen?

"I'll have what she's having," he answered without even looking up.

After Dolly returned to the kitchen, Maggie turned her attention back to Buckie, determined to disengage herself from reacting emotionally. "You know, Buckie, I think I'll just take your teenybopper comment as a well-disguised compliment. Most women like to be thought of as younger than their age. Now are you finished?"

He slumped down in the booth, then sighed. "I'm sorry, Maggie. That was stupid and totally uncalled for. I guess I'm just upset."

"You mean because Leah left?"

"That's just a small part of it. But, yeah, now that you mention it, it's not easy to come home and find that your only two employees are no more—kaput!"

"And you think that's my fault?"

"Not in regard to Audrey, of course, but if you hadn't let Leah get involved in that questionable rock band..."

"That *questionable* rock band happens to be my son's..."

"Oh, I know, I know. And for the record, I think Spencer would be better off staying away from those guys."

"Not that I need your advice, but just so you won't worry, the band has dissolved."

Buckie ran his hands over his face in frustration. "I'm sorry, Maggie. I know I'm acting like a real jerk. And to be totally honest, I'm just beating around the bush. Do you know what's really getting to me?"

She shook her head. "I have no idea."

"Well, I just found out that the woman I thought I had something going on with has been dating another guy."

"What do you mean?"

"Oh, you know what I mean, Maggie. You've been going out with Jed."

She forced a light laugh. "*Going out* with Jed as in regular dating? Where do you get your information anyway?"

"Kate. And in case you're as oblivious as you appear, she's not too happy with you either."

"Well, I don't know what Kate told you. But if sharing a meal and going to Spencer's concert means we're *going out*, well, then I guess we're guilty as charged. And last night I had dinner and a movie with another guy—is that also called *going out?*"

"Who was that with?" Buckie clearly looked perplexed.

"Spencer." She took a bite of her soup but couldn't even taste it.

"Maggie, I'm trying to be serious. I would like to know what's going on between you and Jed. I want to know where I stand." Just then Dolly plopped down a bowl of soup in front of him, then she winked at Maggie as if to say "hang in there" and left.

"Jed and I are friends," she explained as if speaking to a three-year-old. "Just like you and I are friends. I really don't know anything more than that. If you have a problem with me being friends with Jed, then you'll just have to deal with it."

He looked right into her eyes. "So, are you saying there isn't something between us...something *more* than just friends?"

"Buckie, I like you. I enjoy your company. I even missed you when you were in Alaska. But if you're asking me for something *beyond* that, then…I'm sorry. I've told you all along that friendship is all I have to offer you right now."

"Is that the same thing you'd say to Jed?"

Maggie considered that for a moment.

"You're hesitating."

"I'm thinking. I really want to be honest with you. And in answer to your question: yes, I would have to tell Jed that before anything else I want to be friends. After that, we'd have to see what develops. But if I can't first establish a good friendship with a man, then I'm not interested in anything else later on down the line."

"Don't we have a good friendship, Maggie?"

"I thought so. But you've given me reason to question that today, Buckie."

"I said I was sorry. I meant it."

"Okay, forgiven." She tried another bite of soup, but found it hard to swallow.

"You said you'd be honest with me, Maggie. I want to ask you a question, and I want an honest answer." He paused as if to carefully arrange his words in a neat little package. "Do you think there's any chance that we will ever evolve into something *more* than friends?"

She looked him square in the eyes. "I don't know for sure. But if you forced me to answer that question today, I might have to say…I don't think so."

He looked down at his untouched soup. "That's what I was afraid of."

"I'm sorry, Buckie. I'm just trying to be honest. And I could be all wrong. I know my mother would definitely think so."

He smiled stiffly as he stood. "Yes, your mother has her own opinion about us. Give Audrey my regards." Then he paid his bill at the cash register and left. Suddenly Maggie understood exactly how Rebecca must have felt when she broke up with Garrett. It *was* like losing something. It was, in fact, the loss of a friend. But the worrisome part was the wondering if whether the relationship should have been, or might have become, something more. Now she would probably never know. Maggie looked down at her luke-warm soup. Well, this certainly seemed to be her week for losing people. She thought of the aspens next to her house, their leaves steadily swirling into the wind and falling to the ground. At this rate she feared her own branches might be stripped clean before long.

Maggie couldn't eat her soup. She tried to munch on a cracker, but even that tasted like cardboard. She glanced across the room to see both Greg and Rick staring at her as if they had witnessed the whole thing with Buckie. In fact it appeared that several sets of eyes were turned this way. *How embarrassing*! What could Buckie have possibly been thinking to have initiated an intimate conversation like that in Dolly's Diner of all places. They might as well have run the story on the front page of the *Pine Cone*!

"Anything wrong with the soup?" asked Dolly with con-cern. "Or was it just the company?"

"The soup was fine, Dolly. I guess I just lost my appetite."

Dolly shook her head, then whispered, "Plum crazy to try and sort these things out in public like that. He may be some hotshot, slick, big-city photographer, but he still has a lot to learn about women!"

Maggie sighed deeply. "You're right about that."

Dolly tore up her tab. "This one's on me."

"Dolly, you don't have to..."

"I know. But I get to. And next time you come in here, you had better eat your soup, girl. You might give me a bad reputation."

Maggie smiled. "Thanks." When Dolly turned away, she laid a nice tip on the table and then left without looking at any of her spectators.

So it was official, she thought as she walked back to the office. The word was out. Kate knew that she and Jed had gone on a date. Well, what of it? Like Rosa had said, Kate should've known by now that it was useless. But just the same, Maggie felt bad for her. And she felt equally bad for Buckie. It had hurt her to see the pain in his eyes. Why did it have to turn out this way? Why couldn't people simply be friends? Why did the mere suggestion of romance have to fall like a wedge, splitting and permanently parting relationships between men and women? And what if this were merely a sneak preview of what could and perhaps *would* happen between her and Jed?

She shuddered at the thought of it, pulling her woolen sweater more snugly around her. Glancing up at the sky, she was surprised to see it had turned the color of lead. Heavy, dull lead. When had those storm clouds rolled in? And yet, it seemed fitting with her mood and circumstances. She quickly turned the corner next to the Pine Mountain Hotel, consciously diverting her eyes away from Whitewater Works where she had just spotted Kate Murray outside sweeping the sidewalk around the planters. It might have been her imagination, but she was certain she felt Kate watching her as she walked, felt Kate's pretty blue eyes like focused laser beams slicing right through her. Maggie had never meant to hurt Kate. She truly liked the woman. But what could possibly be done to change anything now? Furthermore, what could she do to prevent feeling, herself, the very same hurt that Kate was probably experiencing at this very moment? She knew there were no guarantees for anyone.

Sixteen

everal weeks earlier, Maggie had mentioned to
Jed her need for a desk for her library. She'd told
him that she hoped to find an old, flat-topped
desk, perhaps in mahogany to go with the bookshelves. But
so far her search had been fruitless. When she got home from
work on Friday, she found a message on her answering
machine from Jed, asking her to stop by his shop and see a
desk that he thought might work for her. She glanced at her
watch. It was after five, and although she knew the shop
stayed open until seven on Fridays, she had no desire to drive
back into town and risk coming face to face with Kate.
Besides she was tired. She went into the kitchen and noticed
a note from Spencer on the table. He was with Daniel. They
were going to the football game and he would be home later.
Maggie stared at the note. The thought of Spencer spending
the evening with Daniel brought her no comfort. She remembered, for no specific reason, how Spencer's hair had been
getting long and shaggy lately, and how he'd resisted her suggestion of a haircut. Now suddenly she envisioned him
coming home looking just like Daniel, with facial piercings
and tattoos of who knew what. Oh, if only she could talk to
her mother right now! And why hadn't they called just to
assure her that all was well and the trip was going fine? Of

course, she knew that no news is good news, but it would be nice to hear their voices. As it was, she felt like she'd been cut off from them cold turkey!

She jerked open the refrigerator and stood looking blankly inside its interior in much the same way Spencer would do when he was hungry and too tired to fix something. After her non-lunch at the diner today, she was ravenous. And yet she had no desire to cook anything. Plus she needed to go to the grocery store.

"*I need my mommy!*" she said out loud.

Just then the phone rang. It was Jed. "Did you get my message?"

Maggie closed the refrigerator and sat down on a kitchen stool. "Yes. I just got home and heard it."

"Are you going to come in?"

"Right now?"

"Sure, unless you're right in the middle of something." He paused as if checking something. "I suppose it is the dinner hour. I often forget about such conventions, one of the curses of bachelorhood."

She laughed. "I think I know exactly how you feel. With Mom and Leah gone..."

"They're gone?"

"Oh, I guess I haven't seen you. Yes, they left just yesterday—although it seems like days ago. Leah is driving Mom back to San Jose."

"Is Leah a good driver?"

Maggie's stomach rumbled as she considered this potentially disturbing question. "I guess I don't really know. I certainly hope so."

"Sorry, I didn't mean to worry you."

She sighed. "Right now, I seem plagued with all kinds of worries. What's one more to add to the pile?"

"I didn't mean to bother you, Maggie. I just thought you might want to see this desk."

"Sorry. I didn't mean to sound so glum. But it's been a long week, and I'm not in the best frame of mind. Anyway,

I suppose I could come on over to the shop and see the desk. Spencer's gone for the evening and I don't have anything going on here." She paused. "But there is something that's bothering me, Jed."

"What's that?"

"Well, it probably sounds silly, but is Kate working there tonight?"

"Actually, I just sent her home—and not in a very cheerful mood, I'm afraid. Why don't you come on over and we can look at this desk and talk. Then maybe we could go to Byron and get a bite to eat."

"You just said the magic words. I'm starved."

"Well, come on over. You can see the desk, then I'll close the shop early."

"I'm halfway out the door."

As Maggie drove toward town, she felt slightly encouraged. The prospect of spending an evening with Jed seemed both comforting and exhilarating. A strange combination perhaps, but it appealed to her. She parked in front of Jed's shop and climbed out of her car. But just as she was closing the door, she noticed Buckie locking up the Blue Moose on the opposite side of the street. Unsure of whether he had spotted her or not, she turned her head away and quickly ducked into Whitewater Works, feeling somewhat like a criminal on the lam.

"Everything okay?" asked Jed as she hurried into his shop. Seeing him standing there, so tall and strong and his dark eyes full of concern, made her want to throw herself into his arms. But of course, she checked herself. *That* would be ridiculous. But just the same his mere presence made her feel safe. "Is something wrong?"

She frowned, then looked over her shoulder. "I'm just feeling guilty about…someone."

He glanced toward the rapidly darkening street outside. "Buckie?"

She nodded. "It's been a really lousy day, Jed."

"I know what you mean. I may be placing an ad in your paper for a new employee next week."

"I'm sorry. Is it what I think?"

He pressed his lips together. "Let's not talk about this just yet. Why don't you come see this desk, then we'll get out of here. You may not even like it, but a tourist stopped in today and wanted to buy it. I'd already told Kate that it wasn't for sale until you saw it, and I think she was trying to sell it just to spite me."

Maggie couldn't help but laugh over this. "You're kidding."

He shook his head. "No, and I didn't think it was very funny."

Despite his seriousness, she began to laugh harder. "I'm sorry, Jed. But it just strikes me as so funny, Kate in here trying to sell a desk that she thinks I might want..." She burst into fresh laughter, and to her relief he also began to chuckle too.

"I suppose it is slightly humorous. Usually when your employees want to get even with you, they try *not* to sell things. But here Kate is trying to unload your desk—well, not actually *your* desk, unless you want it, that is." He stopped in front of a large, flat, dark-stained desk, exactly the color of mahogany. Like the wardrobe that he'd made for her bedroom, this too was created in a craftsman style—smooth even lines, and very classic.

"I love it." She smoothed her hand over the top, then tested the drawers, which not surprisingly, slid perfectly. "Cedar," she said as she breathed in the aromatic wood.

He laughed. "I remember the first day I met you, Maggie."

She stood and looked at him. "You do?"

"Yeah. This city lady comes in here and asks me why I waste cedar to line desk drawers. Do you remember?"

She felt her cheeks grow warm as she nodded. She remembered it as if it were yesterday. "Well, if it makes you feel better, I no longer consider it a waste."

He grinned. "Good. You're coming around then."

"I want this desk, Jed. I guess I should've asked the price before I said that. I've never been very good at bartering."

"Let's not talk about money on empty stomachs. I just wanted to make sure you really wanted it before that guy came back." Jed securely tied a large "sold" sign on the knob of the top drawer. Then he turned off most of the lights and locked the front door. "My truck's in back."

"It seems darker than usual for this time of night," said Maggie as they drove down the highway toward Byron.

"It's always like that this time of year," said Jed. "Plus those clouds are pretty thick and heavy. They're about to dump some snow in the mountains."

"Really? How exciting!"

He chuckled slightly. "I keep forgetting that all this is still new to you. But the truth is, even though I've lived here all my life, I still enjoy watching the seasons come and go. Some more than others."

"I hope I *never* take it for granted."

"It'll be interesting to see what you think after you've survived your first Pine Mountain winter."

"I'm looking forward to it."

They drove along in comfortable silence for awhile, then Jed spoke. "About Kate..." he began, then cleared his throat. Suddenly Maggie felt herself holding her breath. She exhaled quietly and waited for him to continue.

"I feel really bad about Kate," he said sadly. "She's a nice girl. I hate to see her being hurt. In fact, if I saw somebody else hurting her, I'd take him to task. But it seems like I'm the one who's doing the hurting. And I don't like it."

Maggie glanced over at him, then away. "I think I know how you feel."

"It's not that I haven't seen this coming, at least lately anyway. For a long time, I though Kate and I were just good friends and that she was a good employee. And I must admit, I enjoy her company. But in the past few months, she's said and done some things that send a different message—a message I didn't want to hear. So I tried to give her hints.

Sometimes I've even been fairly blunt. But, man, that woman is determined!"

Maggie laughed. She wanted to say something like, "well, consider the prize," but fortunately thought better of it. Even now she wasn't completely secure about where she stood with Jed. Although she was feeling more and more hopeful all the time. "So, what are you going to do?"

"That's just it. I don't know for sure. I'd really hate to lose her at the shop. She's been very valuable to me. But if she's only stayed because she thinks..." He paused.

"Because she thinks there's a future with you," she finished for him.

"Yes. Now I can see that's probably what's kept her here all along. Although, I've asked her many times why she stays. She's smart, she could easily find other, better jobs. But she has always said she liked the town, liked being able to hike and ski and fish in her own backyard. And I know that's true. But I feel guilty just the same. If I'd set her straight, right at the start, maybe she would be living somewhere else right now, and probably be a whole lot happier."

"But, Jed, she's a grown woman. She makes her own choices. You didn't entice her to stay on. She's not dumb. She had to know she was taking a chance."

"I suppose you're right. But it just feels lousy to hurt someone like that. Especially when they've been a good friend to you. I mean, she's really loyal, Maggie. She's stood by me through some really tough times."

Maggie swallowed hard. Maybe Jed wasn't absolutely sure about Kate even now. Maybe he did have feelings for her, but was only just figuring it out now. She remembered how she'd felt when Buckie had walked out of the diner—as if she were losing something that she might actually need. "It's confusing," she said simply.

"What's confusing?"

"Oh, I was just thinking how difficult relationships can be." Maggie paused to consider what she was about to say. In some ways it felt like she could be sealing her fate with

Jed, but in other ways it seemed it needed to be said. "Take you and Kate, for instance. Almost everyone in town, including my own mother, perceives you two as a happy couple. You seem like good friends, you work well together, you even have similar interests. A match made in heaven."

Jed groaned.

"Bear with me for a minute. Anyway, there are folks in town who would say *you are one lucky guy, Jed Whitewater.* I mean, think about it, a beautiful woman like Kate at your side, she believes in you, works hard for you—what more could you want?"

He thought for a moment. "I suppose it would seem that way. But just the same, something is missing. And believe me, there have been plenty of times when I've tried to convince myself otherwise. I'm not blind, Maggie. And I'm sure not dead."

"Well, how do you feel about Kate now, Jed? Now that you could be losing her altogether? Does that change anything for you? Do you wonder if you might be letting go of something that was really right all along, but you just took for granted?"

"That's an interesting premise. It sounds as if you've given this some thought."

"Actually, I recently received an email from a friend in L.A. She's just broken up with a guy she'd been seeing for a couple of years, and suddenly she's feeling a gaping hole in her life."

"Uh-huh. I can understand that."

"So can I." Maggie knew that it was her turn to become more transparent. But it wasn't easy laying her heart on the line. And she didn't want Jed to feel any pressure from her. Especially in light of all the pressure he already felt from Kate. Just the same, she needed to be honest. "Actually," she began hesitantly, "I had something like that occur today with Buckie."

"What happened?"

"He'd learned from Kate that you and I had been 'going out.' Anyway, that's how he put it. He made it sound like we'd been together the whole time he'd been gone. He confronted me about our relationship—his and mine, I mean. And finally he asked me if there was any future there."

"And what did you say?"

"I explained that I thought any serious relationship between a man and woman had to begin with a good, solid friendship, and that I really did value his friendship. But if I had to answer him today, then I'd have to say no, I don't think there's a future in it."

"And what did he say?"

"I could see he was hurt, and I felt really bad. He didn't say much, just walked away. But when he did, it felt like I'd just lost a very good friend. It made me sad."

"*Exactly!*"

"Why does it have to be like that, Jed?"

"I don't know. But there seems to be no getting around it." He was pulling into the parking lot of a restaurant now. "Do you like Italian?"

"Love it. I've seen this from the highway, but I've never been here."

He turned off the engine, then faced her. "Let's make a deal. No more talk of Buckie and Kate for now. Let's just enjoy a good meal together. Deal?"

She smiled. "Deal."

The lobby of the restaurant was already crowded, but the dark-haired hostess smiled and greeted Jed by name as if they were old friends. It appeared that he had called ahead and secured them a reservation, so they were ushered to a quiet corner and seated at a table covered in a red-checked cloth with a wax-covered wine bottle for a candle holder.

"What a sweet place," commented Maggie as she scanned the menu.

"The family who owns it came from Tuscany," said Jed. "I've know one of the sons for years." He glanced around the room. "But I don't see him tonight."

The meal was fantastic, and the conversation flowed smoothly with no further mention of either Buckie or Kate.

"So when will your mother and Leah make it home to San Jose?" asked Jed as the waiter poured coffee to go with their desert.

"Tomorrow. Mom wanted to take it easy, which was smart. But I wish I'd made her promise to call. And then when you said that about Leah's driving…"

"Sorry about that. I'm sure they're fine. Speaking of Leah, what's the story on that awful picture you ran in the *Pine Cone* this week?"

"I didn't run it. Scott is responsible for that little number. And we're still not speaking."

He laughed. "Poor Scott. Not very discerning on his part. But you can't blame him completely."

"Why not?"

"Well, Leah's the one who went public in that little getup."

Maggie rolled her eyes. "Haven't we already been over this, Jed?"

He nodded, then sipped his coffee. "Yes. But after I saw that photo, it made me think that I might not have been completely wrong in some of my observations about the girl."

She sat down her cup with a loud clink. "Jed, Leah is very dear to me. I know you seem to think she's twisted or evil or…"

"I never said that."

"Not in so many words. But you need to understand that I care about her. I miss her very much, and I really hope that she comes back. She is welcome in my home anytime, and I've even considered adopting her."

Jed's brows lifted. "Well, you sure know how to put a guy in his place."

She smiled. "Sorry. But I've gotten used to being on the defensive when it comes to Leah."

He leaned forward. "The only reason I come down hard on her is because I care about Spencer, Maggie. I hate to see him exposed to bad influences."

"I appreciate that. But I don't believe Leah is a bad influence. Now, if you knew who he was with tonight, you might have cause to worry."

"And who would that be?"

"Oh, just that weird Daniel from the band. I mean, he may be okay. But his appearance sort of bothers me..."

"Ah-hah!" said Jed in triumph. "Those things *do* make a difference to you."

She shrugged ruefully. "I suppose so. Sometimes anyway."

He grew thoughtful. "It's hard to know though. I am the first to admit that I can be overly judgmental sometimes. I think it's usually a backlash from my days of being so messed up. You know, like the pendulum swinging from one extreme to the other. I try to ask myself how Jesus would look at people, and that usually helps. But a lot of the time I forget to ask."

"I know what you mean."

"Like this Daniel, for instance. What do you really know about him?"

"Probably about as much as you know about Leah."

"Maybe that's our problem." Jed set down his cup as if he'd just made a discovery. "Maybe our judgmental attitudes are just a result of being uninformed. We see the surface and assume we know what lies beneath. In some cases we're right. In others, we couldn't be more wrong. Like that first day I saw you." He laughed. "I thought you were a snooty Californian who wouldn't last a week in Pine Mountain."

"Gee, thanks."

"But then I got to know you."

"And now what do you think?" She leaned forward with interest.

"I think I'm still trying to figure you out."

Seventeen

When Maggie got home, she saw Daniel's orange VW parked in the driveway and the house all lit up. She opened the front door to hear music blaring from upstairs, probably from Spencer's CD player cranked to full volume.

"Oh, hi, Mom!" yelled Spencer from over the balcony. "I'll turn it down now."

She nodded at him and mouthed, "Thank you."

He disappeared for a moment then came back. "It was getting too cold at the football game so we came home to listen to this new CD. Is it okay if Daniel spends the night here?"

"Sure," she answered, although she felt somewhat unsure. "Did you guys get something to eat already?"

"Not really. Got any suggestions?"

"I think I saw a pizza in the freezer. Want me to pop it in the oven for you?"

His eyes lit up. "Sure. Thanks, Mom."

She puttered around the kitchen while the pizza baked, making carrot sticks and a small bowl of ranch dip. She was uncertain as to how she should react to this continuing friendship with Daniel, especially after she'd been so secretly relieved to hear of the band breaking up. Now it looked like she wasn't getting off the hook so easily. She reminded herself of her words regarding Jed's harsh judgments toward Leah. Why should things be any different in regard to Daniel? Then she remembered what Jed said about ignorance making him become more judgmental. Perhaps she should try harder to get to know this weird kid.

"Pizza's ready," she yelled up the stairs. She considered leaving the boys to themselves to devour their pepperoni pizza in private, but then thought perhaps she should make an attempt to be sociable. Besides the refrigerator needed to be cleaned out. So as the boys came into the kitchen, she ducked down to check outdated containers of leftovers and wipe down the shelves.

"Man, I wish the band hadn't split up," said Spencer with his mouth full. "I bet we could've done a good job on that last song."

"Yeah, but we would've needed Leah to sing lead."

"Well, she's gonna come back. If Ed hadn't gone all ballistic on us, I think it could've all worked out."

Maggie dumped the contents of an overdue cottage cheese carton down the disposal, then glanced over to the table.

"Thanks for the pizza, Mom," said Spencer.

"Yeah, thanks, Maggie." Daniel actually spoke to her. And when he did, she noticed something missing.

She stepped closer to the table and studied his face. "Something about you looks different, Daniel."

He grinned. "It's the lip. I took out the studs."

She blinked in surprise. "Why?"

"I didn't really want them anymore."

"It was all Ed's idea," explained Spencer. "He talked Daniel into them when the band first started getting together. Ed had this idea of what we all should look like."

"Yeah. Pretty stupid," said Daniel.

"And the tattoo?" asked Maggie, almost afraid to know the answer.

"It wasn't real," said Daniel. "But I might still get one—someday. But if I do, it'll be because I want to, not 'cause someone else tells me to."

"Yeah, that's one thing I don't miss about the band," said Spencer. "Ed was always running everything. And, man, could he be bossy."

"He wasn't always like that," said Daniel. "I think he's just getting a big head 'cause he thinks they're going to be so rich."

"Rich?" asked Maggie as she dunked a carrot in the dip.

"Yeah. His dad is into this big land development deal. And Ed says they're going to become millionaires." He laughed. "I'll believe it when I see it."

"Yeah," said Spencer. "Ed kept bragging that his dad was going to buy him a Corvette when this deal closed."

Suddenly Maggie remembered Greg and Rick deep in discussion at Dolly's Diner. "Is Greg Snider involved in this deal?" she asked hesitantly.

"I dunno," said Daniel reaching for another slice of pizza. "Ed said the whole thing is supposed to be real hush-hush."

"Well, that sure didn't keep him from talking about it," said Spencer.

"Interesting."

"Why's that, Mom?"

"Oh, I saw Rick and Greg all involved in something and I'll bet this is what it is. But the whole thing seems pretty weird since they both act so opposed to any kind of development."

"Maybe they're just hypocrites," said Daniel in a matter-of-fact tone.

"Why don't you do an investigative report on it for the newspaper," suggested Spencer with enthusiasm. "An exposé."

She grinned. "I might just do that. But right now, all I want to investigate is my bed. You guys keep it down, okay?"

"Sure. Good night, Mom."

✑

The next morning Maggie looked out the front window to see a fresh, clean coating of white on the mountains. Jed had been right about the snow. She smiled as she sipped her coffee and recalled their pleasant evening. Just what she'd needed, and yet so unexpected. Then suddenly, she remembered her desk. She went into the library and imagined the piece centered against the back wall facing the fireplace. It would be perfect in there, and she felt certain Jed had designed it especially for this room. She didn't care if it cost a fortune. It was worth it, and besides it was a tax-deductible business expense. She would do her writing while sitting at it—perhaps finish that novel, or maybe just some magazine articles. Whatever she did, it was sure to be inspired when created from a desk like that. Jed had promised to deliver it to her today, but they hadn't decided on a time. Nor had they discussed the price. She wanted to leave a check with Spencer in case he came while she was working out in town. She considered calling the store but didn't wish to get Kate on the phone. Finally she decided to simply drive by on her way to the fitness center and see if she could spot his truck.

Sure enough, it was there. She hoped that meant Kate was not. She glanced at her watch. Nearly eleven. Perhaps Kate was working the afternoon since it was Saturday and a late closing night. Maggie hurried in with her checkbook in hand, ready to just turn around and run, if need be. She spied Jed behind the counter writing something down.

"Hey there," she called from the front of the store. "I was hoping you'd be here. We forgot to decide what time you're bringing my desk by…"

"There's a little problem," he said.

Maggie stood at the counter and spread open her checkbook. "Oh, that's okay. You don't have to deliver it today. But why don't I go ahead and pay for it…"

"The desk's been sold."

She leaned her head to one side. "What?"

"That's right!" snapped Kate, coming from the back of the store. "The desk's been sold. And it's all my fault. And now Jed is mad at me. And you might as well get mad too. Then we can all just get mad together!"

Maggie didn't know what to say. She looked at Jed, but his face seemed blank, or perhaps it was just a mask hiding some deeper feelings. "Oh," she finally said weakly. "My desk is sold?"

"Normally the furniture in here doesn't belong specifically to anyone—until they've purchased it, that is!" Kate looked Maggie directly in the eye, almost in defiance.

"But Jed put a sold tag..."

"The tag was gone," said Kate, turning to Jed. "Just like I told him. Only he didn't believe me. And now I suppose you won't either." She threw her hands up in the air. "I don't even know why I care." Then she collapsed into a rocking chair and burst into sobs.

Now Maggie really didn't know what to say or do. She looked over at Jed, and he looked even more perplexed than she felt. She turned back to Kate and spoke quickly. "Look, Kate, it's okay. No big deal. I mean it was a really great desk and everything, but I'm sure you made an honest mistake. And it's only a piece of furniture, right?" She turned back to Jed, held up her hands helplessly, then just shook her head. "I'd better go now."

She drove to the fitness center with shaking hands. This was craziness. She was getting all upset about a silly piece of furniture. But in the same moment, she knew it wasn't about furniture. She knew that whole nerve-wracking episode in Jed's store had precious little to do with the missing desk. It was about dashed hopes and broken hearts. And perhaps it was all her fault.

"Hey you," called Cherise cheerfully as Maggie walked in. Then she came closer. "Say, what's wrong. You look like you just saw a ghost or something."

Maggie forced a smile, then actually told an outright lie. "I almost ran over a cat and it shook me up a little."

Cherise patted her shoulder. "Oh, I hate it when that happens. But at least you didn't actually hit it. Come on. Let's get you started."

Towards the end of her workout, Maggie began to feel calmer about the desk dilemma. It was probably a blessing in disguise. Maybe the whole thing just needed to happen— a way to bring things to the surface so they could all deal with them. Poor Jed. She couldn't quite get the troubled expression on his face out of her head. The sooner they all got past this the better.

"Hey there," said Cherise as if trying to awaken Maggie from a deep dream.

"Oh, sorry, I guess I was just zoning out."

"That's okay. But you've been on that thing for about ten minutes. Ready to move on?" She waited nearby while Maggie started on the next machine. "I wanted to let you know that I talked to my uncle," said Cherise in a quiet voice.

"Your uncle?"

"Remember, the lawyer," whispered Cherise. "Anyway, he was pretty concerned too. He's going to try to straighten it all out with Greg."

"Are things any better with you and Greg?"

Cherise shrugged. "I don't know. But I finally came out and accused him of having an affair and he just laughed. Then he said he had more important things to think about."

Maggie wondered how to ask this next question, and finally decided to take it head on. "Is Greg involved in some sort of land development deal?"

"Huh?" Cherise looked clueless. "What do you mean?"

"Oh, I just heard that Rick Tanner is involved in some land development, get-rich-quick scheme, and I thought that maybe…"

Cherise considered that. "Well, Greg hangs with Rick all the time now. But he never told me anything about Rick coming into any money. Are you sure about this, Maggie?"

"Nope. It's second- or third-hand information. But I'd like to find out from the original sources if it's true. I'd really like to do an article for the paper on it if I can get any facts. I think the citizens of Pine Mountain would be interested."

"Okay, now play this by me again, Maggie. Did you say there's a land development deal involved?"

Maggie nodded and climbed down from the machine. "That's what I heard."

Cherise folded her arms across her chest and slowly shook her head. "I seriously doubt that it's true. You know how opposed both those guys are to any kind of development. No, you must've got your information wrong, Maggie. But I'm glad you came to me with it so I could straighten you out."

Maggie shrugged. "Well, I'm sure whatever it is, you'll get to the bottom of it. And by the way, I really am happy that you don't think Greg is having an affair anymore."

"Yeah, that was a big relief. But I'm glad I called Uncle Bob just the same."

"Yes, you're smart to take care of those things before they become real problems." Maggie wiped her forehead on her towel. "Well, I think that should do it for me."

"But you didn't do the stepper yet..."

"I know. But maybe I'll take a walk today instead."

◌

Daniel and Spencer were practicing music in the barn. Maggie wondered how they could accomplish much with only guitar and drums, but they managed to produce plenty of noise. When she opened the front door, the phone was ringing and she dashed to answer it. She heard her mother's voice on the other end.

"Mom," she cried with relief. "I'm so glad to hear from you. Are you okay?"

"I'm fine, dear. Just a little tired is all and very glad to be home. Little Leah is a good driver. She got us safely here without a hitch."

"You do sound tired, Mom. I hope you'll take it easy."

"Don't you worry, honey. I'm just road weary. I'll be back to my old self in a day or two. What's new with you?"

Maggie thought for a moment. She had no desire to tell her mother about the unhappy episode with Jed and Kate this morning. "Well, I just got home from working out. And you'll never believe what I heard yesterday..." She told Audrey about what Daniel had said about Greg and Rick.

Audrey chuckled. "Well, wouldn't that be something. So you say Daniel spent the night?"

Then Maggie explained how she felt about Daniel, now that she knew him a little better. "It's funny, Mom. I used to think that Ed was the better of the two boys just because he seemed to have such good manners. But I can see now that I had them both all wrong."

"You just never know." Audrey paused for a moment. "Leah says to tell you and Spencer hi. I think she misses you already. I know I do. And now I think I'll go lie down for a bit."

"That sounds wise. Let me know how the doctor appointment goes on Monday."

Maggie hung up and sighed. She wished they were still here. But at least they had made it safely home. She absently flipped through the little calendar next to the phone, then noticed with surprise that the Harvest Festival planning meeting was scheduled for that evening at seven. And she had promised to take her mother's place on the committee. Brian and Cindy Jordan were hosting the get-together at their hotel. Cindy had told her last week how everything in the downstairs was finally done, and she planned to make this meeting very special as an impromptu celebration for their major accomplishment. Maggie knew it would be well worth going to.

She fixed some lunch for the boys, then took Bart for a long walk in the woods. The air was cold, crisp, and invigorating.

As she walked she allowed herself to finally consider the situation with Jed and Kate. This morning had been shocking and offensive to her. She hated feeling like she was the cause of all this. And although part of her knew that it wasn't really her fault, another part took the blame. Poor Jed. He'd seemed so frustrated. She could tell this whole thing was as distasteful to him as it was to her. But what could be done? Perhaps her only option was to wait it out and let the pieces fall where they may. She considered calling Rosa for advice, but suspected she would be working at the deli. And besides, she hadn't spoken to her since the fallout with Scott. Perhaps Rosa would be at the meeting tonight. But then, Maggie remembered, so would Scott. She'd asked him several weeks ago to cover the Harvest Festival developments before she knew she'd be on the committee. How had life become so complicated? Or was this merely the price one paid for living in a small town? It seemed that everyone's life entwined around another's—and another and another. And right now too many lives seemed at odds with her own. She watched Bart running through the pine trees, leaping on small bushes of sagebrush with carefree abandon. Lucky dog! His life was so simple. Finally it seemed the only thing to do (and why hadn't she considered this sooner?) was to hand all these troublesome relationships over to God. He could sort them out. And so she did.

As she turned back towards home, a sense of restful peace washed over her. She breathed in the pine-scented air, and enjoyed the play of sun and shadow in the tall pine trees as she walked along the dusty path. She threw sticks for Bart. She even paused long enough to notice a couple of does less than thirty feet away. All these things she had failed to see during the first half of her walk, and only because she'd been so absorbed in her own problems. She reminded herself of her commitment to never take the beauty of her environment for granted. This was God's country and if she allowed it, she could find healing here. On the other hand, if she only focused on her problems and troubles (problems and troubles that would always come and go), she might as well be living in downtown L.A. She was here in Pine Mountain for a purpose. She might as well enjoy all the benefits!

Eighteen

aggie took her time in getting ready for the meeting. She suspected it would be a festive occasion and decided to use the opportunity to dress up a little, at least something more than her usual jeans or khakis. She finally decided on a pair of sage-green pleated trousers and a matching silk blouse. She hadn't worn the slacks for a year and was surprised to find them loose around the waist. She smiled to herself as she tightened her belt—Cherise's abdominal plan must be working. She tied her hair back with a fall-colored paisley scarf and stepped back to view her image. Very uptown—at least for this town. But it was fun for a change.

Several cars were parked near the hotel, and white twinkling lights adorned the nearby trees and entrance. Very inviting. Maggie walked inside the foyer to see several softly glowing candles and a pretty fall arrangement of flowers and gourds on an entry table that now held the guest book. She heard soft classical music playing in the background as she signed her name and noticed by the signatures just above hers that Sam and Rosa had come in before her.

"Hello there, Maggie," called Cindy as she placed a wooden tray of cheese and crackers on a large table in the dining area. "Everyone else is checking out the kitchen right now."

"Oh, Cindy, it looks absolutely beautiful in here." Maggie skimmed the lovely room with her eyes, taking in the polished wood floor as it reflected the light of a small, crackling fire in the huge rock fireplace. Overhead, the reproduction light fixtures cast a soft, golden glow over the rich hues of carefully placed paintings and carpets. "You've done a fantastic job!"

"Why, thank you." Cindy beamed. "I'm rather pleased with the effect myself."

"You should be. It all came together so perfectly—better than I even imagined."

"How's your mother?" asked Cindy. "Did she make it home okay? I can't believe she decided to take off like that. Such a long drive after her stroke!"

"I know. I didn't want her to go, but she was determined. And you know how she is. But luckily Leah was able to drive her..."

"You let Leah drive her?"

Maggie blinked. "Well, it wasn't really my decision. But Mom wanted her and Leah was willing."

Cindy frowned with concern, then lowered her voice since more people were now coming in the front door. "But I thought that Leah was in some kind of trouble. Brian told me he heard she was involved with drugs and had been selling them to high-school kids. When I heard she was gone, I was relieved for your sake. But I had no idea she went home with Audrey."

Maggie felt as if someone had just punched her. "Well, I don't know who's feeding these rumors, but they're not true..."

"Hello," called Clara and she and Lou came into the hotel. "My but this is lovely, Cindy. What a wonderful decorator you are! Ah-hah, I see the china bowl that you bought from my shop last week. It looks so nice on that buffet hutch."

Maggie greeted the Hendersons with Cindy, but her words sounded false and tinny to her own ears. She couldn't stop thinking about what Cindy had just repeated about Leah. She wondered how many others had heard these horrible rumors. And how could she begin to squelch them? Poor Leah. Thank goodness she wasn't around to hear.

Soon the others flowed out the swinging kitchen doors, and Maggie saw Buckie among them. Just great. She hadn't realized he was on this committee. This evening was not looking very promising. Then with relief, she spotted Rosa and Sam, and was just about to go say hello when she noticed Scott and Chloe also emerging from the kitchen. They joined his parents. She told herself it was silly, she should just go on over and pretend that nothing whatsoever was wrong between her and Scott. But after hearing Cindy's derogatory comments about Leah, the whole photo issue seemed just as fresh as before. Perhaps she would speak to Rosa alone later. Elizabeth Rodgers now had Buckie by her side and the two were amiably chatting with the Hendersons. Maggie went to see if Cindy needed any help in the kitchen. It turned out she had hired a high-school girl to give her a hand for the evening.

"No, we're just fine in here, Maggie. You go out and socialize. Have some fun before the meeting starts."

So Maggie went back out into the dining room and tried to appear as if she were occupied with studying the art upon the walls as she casually sipped a glass of punch. The sooner this meeting started, the happier she would be.

"It's Jed and Kate," announced Elizabeth in an enthusiastic voice. "Well, you both finally made it to a meeting at the same time! And here I'd decided that if you two didn't show up tonight, I'd put you both on the clean-up committee." This brought peals of laughter from everyone, and Maggie stiffly turned to see Jed and Kate in the foyer. Jed was reaching to help Kate remove her long cream-colored coat. Then Kate walked in, smiling brightly, and looking every bit like royalty in her sleek and well-designed navy dress. Freshwater pearls provided a perfect touch of elegance—very classy combined with her pale blond hair. Maggie felt as if one of Cindy's expensive Persian carpets had just been jerked out from beneath her as she was assaulted by a startling jolt of jealousy unlike anything she'd ever felt before. But she focused every ounce of her willpower on maintaining an expression that she hoped was completely void of emotion as she turned back to view the pastoral painting of a farm girl bringing home the cows. Fortunately everyone else was making much over the couple, which allowed Maggie to slip away, she hoped unnoticed, toward the back. But just as she reached the hallway that led to the bathrooms, she saw Buckie's eyes fastened on her. And she wasn't sure whether it was pity or triumph she saw registered there. But either way she had no desire to find out. The hallway to the bathrooms also looped around to the stairway, and Maggie decided that perhaps a tour of the second floor would be in order. After all, she had helped pick out the flooring up there. Perhaps she should see how it looked. The second floor was still under renovation, but probably much improved since she'd last been up. A dim hallway light lit her way as she tiptoed up the stairs feeling very much like a trespasser. Upon reaching the top landing, she realized she had no actual desire to inspect the bathroom floors and instead she paused at the top of the semi-dark balcony and listened for the sounds below. At first she heard little more than her heart pounding in her ears. But then taking a long, deep breath, exhaling slowly, she willed herself to regain a sense of composure. In her hand was the half-filled glass of punch, which she drank slowly, allowing the sweet, cool sips to trickle down until the glass was empty. Then she sat down upon the top step and sighed. Lilting voices sprinkled with laughter filtered up the stairwell, perfectly wrapped in the festive notes of Mozart. It was the sound of a delightful party in full swing with everyone having a good time. Another wave of envy washed over her, this one not rooted so much in the gorgeous Kate, but more a result of missing out on something she'd looked forward to enjoying. She shook her head as if to dislodge these negative feelings. She knew it was childish to feel this way. But right now, knowing and feeling were two very different and unrelated things. She considered simply slipping out the backdoor. Certainly no one would miss her—not much anyway. Or perhaps she could create a believable excuse to exit, something that wouldn't draw undue attention—maybe something do to with Spencer. Or perhaps she should behave like a mature adult and just go downstairs and face the music. How bad could it be?

As she tiptoed back down the stairs she heard the distinct ringing of a utensil against a crystal glass and the crowd quieted. "It's time for everyone to begin finding seats," came Elizabeth's authoritative voice. "As much fun as all this is, we do have business to attend to. And if we're lucky, we can wrap up early and enjoy some more socializing later on."

Maggie hurried into the dining room, hoping that her absence had gone unobserved. She found a chair toward the back of the room and quietly sat down, then opened her purse to find her little notebook. As Elizabeth spoke she pretended to be focused on her notes, scribbling unreadable words as if she were gathering vital information for an important newspaper article. It was a painfully long hour, and even though Maggie obediently raised her hand to volunteer for a committee, she couldn't recall which one it had been, and it certainly wasn't in her notes. She would ask Elizabeth later. Finally the ordeal was over, and Maggie snapped her notebook closed, then quickly rose from her chair and made her way to the foyer without even glancing back. Not that she was worried about being noticed since everyone else seemed to be migrating toward the refreshment table anyway. Only moments ago, Cindy had just placed on it a scrumptious-looking array of desserts. But Maggie had no appetite. And it wasn't until she was safely in her car and driving home that she felt she could even breathe again.

At home, she emailed Rebecca.

RB

Oh dear, I think I am becoming completely neurotic. I went to what should have been a lovely gathering tonight (actually a planning meeting) in the beautifully refurbished hotel with wonderful refreshments, etc. And just because Jed walked in with the gorgeous Kate on his arm, I went all to pieces. Well, not so as anyone would notice—at least I hope not! But inside, I completely fell apart. I was so jealous, I felt like I was back in junior high school again. And hence, I have decided I want nothing to do with such feelings. I want no involvement with men (at least not in a romantic way). I shall live the life of a celibate writer, quietly content to surround myself with the local scenic beauty, some good books, my son, of course, and a few good friends. Although, that may be a problem too. For it seems my list of friends is shrinking each day. In no time, I shall most certainly be left with none. Well perhaps Dolly (from the diner) might stick around—actually she does seem like a loyal and understanding person. But that will probably be it. Just Dolly and me hanging out together in Pine Mountain. Oh my....

mc

∽

If she'd had it her way, they wouldn't be going to church today. But Spencer was already up and ready to go. How could she say "no, I don't really want to go today" and live with herself tomorrow? So they went, but Maggie carefully timed it so as not to arrive too early or too late. They sat near the back, for the church was surprisingly full—it seemed to grow each week. She wondered what Jed would do if the church continued like this. To add on and destroy the perfect dimensions of this building seemed a shame, but already it was getting crowded. She barely heard the musicians play, and the announcements drifted right over her. She tried not to notice (but how could she not?) the blond head sitting in her usual spot in front, chin tilted attentively just so. Maggie checked her watch again, willing the minute hand to move faster. Finally, Jed approached the pulpit. As usual he was clearing his throat as he set his Bible on the hand-carved stand. She fixed her eyes on the view of the mountains behind him, thankful for their distracting beauty, for she was unwilling to chance a direct look at him. If their eyes were to meet, she felt certain hers would fill with tears. And she tried not to listen to his voice or hear the meaning of his words. But it was useless. Especially considering the unusual tone of his voice. He sounded very serious and somewhat unhappy.

"I'm coming before you this morning with a heavy heart," he said, and the quiet room became even more hushed, as if everyone were leaning forward and cupping their ears to hear better. "I have difficult news to share. But I know, after much soul searching, that it's right. Unfortunately, right isn't always easy." He paused and looked over the congregation, his eyes sweeping over the rows and looking at the people, one by one. She averted her eyes when he came to their row. And then he continued to speak.

"I have decided to step down from my position of leadership in this church." Heads turned slightly from side to side, as if people were trying to determine if they had heard right, then soft murmurs could be heard. Even Maggie sat up straighter, her head cocked slightly. What was this all about?

"I know it may come as a shock—to everyone, including me. But I honestly believe it's God's leading for my life. I know the first question everyone will want to ask is: *why?* And I want to try to answer it for you today. As you know, I offered this building when our church was in need, and somehow along with that I began to share from the pulpit upon occasion. Before long the elders decided that I should take over this position indefinitely, or at least until a real pastor happened along. And I've enjoyed sharing on Sundays.

It always challenges me to come up with something new, and I believe the experience has helped me to grow in the Lord— immensely. But lately I've felt checked in my spirit. I've felt undeserving of this position. As you know, I am relatively young in the faith compared to many of you. And as a result, I've been seeing more and more how inadequate I am to lead you. I find that I am often judgmental, critical, and some- times downright ungracious—in other words, not very Christlike. And after much soul searching and Bible reading, I believe this behavior is simply a result of my own spiritual immaturity. So for the health of this church, and for my own spiritual health, I have decided to step down. I feel I have a lot of growing and learning to do, and being in a leadership position can be deceptive—it can make me feel as if I should have already arrived. I know we never really arrive, but in order to lead I feel I need to have a little more spiritual mileage under my belt."

He paused, as if giving them a moment to digest this news, then continued in a more positive tone of voice. "In the meantime, I will stay very involved in the church. This building is still dedicated to our services. But I'd like to rec- ommend that we return to the sharing of the pulpit like we did after losing Pastor Jack. And for next Sunday, if the elders agree, I'd like to recommend that Sam Galloway preach." Jed smiled down at Sam. "I know this might come as a shock to some of you—and maybe a relief to a few others." He laughed. "But I know it's the right thing to do." Then he opened his Bible. "Now, and because I don't want you to feel like you got cheated out of a sermon, I do have a little something for you." He then read the portion of Scrip- ture where Jesus warned about judging others, then launched into what Maggie later felt was his best sermon ever—about the perils of judgment and how it was better to try to see things through the nonjudgmental eyes of Jesus.

After he finished the congregation crowded around the pulpit, some expressing gratitude for his service, and some encouraging him to rethink his decision about stepping down.

Without standing, Maggie watched for a moment, then turned to Spencer. "Are you ready to go?"

"Don't you want to go say something to Jed?"

She shook her head. "You go on up, if you like. I can talk to him another time."

He shrugged. "I guess I can too. He looks pretty busy at the moment. We might as well go."

They drove home quietly. Maggie had mixed feelings about Jed's decision. On the one hand it seemed, especially today, that he was doing a good job of leading; the church seemed to be steadily growing and she'd heard no complaints. But on the other hand, she felt relieved for his sake. She had often worried that he took his position too seriously, often acting as if he carried the entire world, or at least Pine Mountain, on his shoulders. Perhaps he did need to grow more spiritually before assuming such a responsibility. Anyway, she figured he must've done what he believed was right. How could anyone argue with that?

"Do you think Jed's sermon was about Leah?" asked Spencer.

"What do you mean?" Maggie glanced over at her son curiously.

"I mean the part about judging. Ever since that stupid news photo, it seems like people have been judging her all wrong. And there's all those rumors and everything."

"I don't know. I suppose that could be part of it. I think it also might just be the nature of small towns to be pretty judgmental."

"Why's that?

"I suppose it's because everyone knows everyone else's business. Or at least they think they do. And rumors get going. And then people often make judgments based on inadequate information. And to be honest, Spence, it's not just people from small towns. I have to confess that I had judged Daniel all wrong. But now that I know him better, I really like him."

Spencer laughed. "Yeah, I remember once when you were acting like Ed was more together than Daniel, and I thought: Man, she doesn't have a clue!"

Maggie laughed. "I guess we can all fall victim to being judgmental occasionally."

"Yeah, I suppose I'm like that about stupid, old Kurt Gilbert. I mean, he's probably not so bad, and Sierra says he's a good snowboarder."

"Maybe you'll get to know him better and even become friends."

"Let's not push things, Mom."

⌒

That afternoon, Maggie found an email response from Rebecca:

MC

Bet you're surprised I'm getting back to you so quickly. But you sounded rather desperate. Neurotic? I don't think so. In love? Maybe. Infatuated? Probably. Now, before you shut down your computer and permanently strip me from your address book altogether, let me inject right here that I could be all wrong. But I do think you're acting strangely. For you anyway. And that makes me think you must have some pretty strong feelings for this guy. The questions are: Are they real? Is he worth it? Is the potential for a relationship worth it? Do you recall the time I had it real bad for that attorney down in San Diego? We were working on that pharmaceutical case together...Anyway, it turned out to be a big, fat mistake, remember? I wish I had thought it all through better from the start (because in hindsight I can see there were plenty of clues and red flags). I could have avoided some serious heartache. Now, I don't know this Jed from Adam, but it sounds to me like he may be a little too handsome for his own good. And to show up with a beautiful blond on his arm is a BIG concern. Maybe you just need to step back and try to get some objectivity here. I wish that Audrey were still there. She has such a level head. But anyway, Maggie, give yourself some space. Do a little soul searching. And what about Buckie? I was really starting to like him from your little email comments—and it seemed you had so much in common—you know, writers and photographers…. Perhaps you shouldn't have given up on him so soon. But as always, I warn you to take my advice with a grain of salt. I am just an outsider looking in. Listen to your heart, dear one. And, by all means, don't forget to pray!

RB

Nineteen

For the next couple of days, Maggie tried to "give herself some space" as Rebecca had suggested. She went to work. She came home. She spent time with Spencer and then worked on her novel until her eyes refused to focus and all she could do was to fall into bed and hopefully sleep. By the end of the week it had all slipped into a somewhat comfortable, if not slightly sparse, routine. She had hoped to hear from Jed in the next few days but had not. Not even a message on her machine. And since she was still trying to give herself "space" she didn't watch for him or his classic red truck on her way to and from work, nor did she allow herself to think of him. Besides it was easier that way. But she also avoided Rosa, knowing how she'd be tempted to discuss her confusing relationship with Jed with her understanding friend. Rosa had left a sweet, concerned message on her answering machine, explaining how she'd been so busy with the deli and how she'd missed seeing Maggie, and so on. But Maggie still hadn't returned her call. Despite feeling rather guilty about avoiding her, she knew it'd be tough to chit-chat with her good friend while her little stand-off with Rosa's son remained somewhat unresolved. Although some headway had been made just this morning when she and Scott had actually exchanged some polite, albeit chilly, greetings. And she might've actually dropped into the deli at lunchtime except that she had no desire to bump into Buckie in town. As a result she continued to avoid Main Street altogether. Instead she carried her lunch from home in a brown paper bag, and as a consequence she worked like a slave all through the noon hour.

"You seem to be turning into something of a hermit," commented Abigail dryly as they finished a Harvest Festival planning meeting in Maggie's office. Maggie had finally discovered which committee she'd actually volunteered for last week at the hotel, and it turned out to be the decorating committee chaired by Clara Henderson. The two of them had convinced Abigail to join forces and today they'd met for lunch in Maggie's office and made surprisingly good progress. They had decided to keep the decorations fairly simple, relying on harvest items such as corn stalks, hay bales, and pumpkins; all to be provided by a farmer friend of Abigail's and then arranged next to the new lampposts now gracing Main Street. As a final thought, Maggie had suggested they also host a scarecrow building contest for the local kids to participate in. They would place the finished scarecrows around town for people to vote upon, and the winners would receive prizes which Abigail would persuasively solicit (with promises of free ad space) from several local businesses. Maggie would prepare the announcement for next week's newspaper, and Clara would report their progress to Elizabeth. Hopefully it would all work out as planned.

"I'm not a hermit," argued Maggie as she tossed her yogurt carton in the garbage and dusted crumbs from her desk. "Look, I just sat here and spent nearly two hours gabbing with you and Clara."

"Spending time planning decorations with a couple of old crones is hardly a social occasion, Maggie. No, I've been watching you and you've definitely been acting like a hermit lately."

Maggie rolled her eyes. "Well, maybe I just need some quiet time to think about a few things."

Abigail grew concerned. "Is everything okay? Is your mother doing all right?"

"Yes, Mom says everything's fine."

"How about you then?" She peered into Maggie's eyes as if looking for symptoms of some strange ailment. "Is your health okay? You have been looking a little pale lately."

Maggie sighed. "I'm fine. Really. Probably just staying up too late working on my novel."

Abigail just shook her head. "There's plenty of time to write books when you're my age, Maggie Carpenter. Right now, you should be out having a good time while you're still young enough to enjoy it!"

This made Maggie laugh. "I don't see what age has to do with it. Just the same, I hope I have as much spunk as you when I'm your age, Abigail. You're truly an inspiration."

Abigail stood a little taller, straightened her bright periwinkle jacket, and smiled. "Why, thank you."

ᔍ

When Maggie got home, the phone was ringing. She grabbed it up to hear Leah on the other end. "Hi, Maggie. I hope I'm not bothering you."

"Not at all. How's everything going?"

"Actually, I'm a little concerned about Audrey..."

"What's wrong?" asked Maggie anxiously. "Mom told me she was just fine on Tuesday. What's going on?"

"Well, she may be fine. But I think she's acting kind of strange. Almost as if she's getting her affairs in order, if you know what I mean."

"You mean, like she thinks she's going to die?"

"Oh, I don't know. Maybe...She just keeps going around her house and putting things into neat little piles and attaching all these post-it notes—like 'this is for Barry' and 'send these to cousin Judy' and 'save this for Maggie.' Stuff like that, you know."

"Maybe she's just trying to get organized."

"Maybe..."

"But you don't think so?"

"I don't know. I guess I'm just worried. I love your mother so much, Maggie. I don't want anything to happen to her."

"How does her health seem? Have you noticed any changes?"

"Not really. Except that she still tires easily and some-times she gets these headaches and has to lie down."

"That doesn't sound good—especially the headaches. Did you go in with her to her doctor's appointment on Monday?"

"I stayed in the waiting room."

"Did she say anything to you afterwards? I mean other than she was just fine."

"Well, she was pretty quiet on the way home. But I just thought she was still tired from the trip."

Maggie considered this. "I don't know what to say, Leah. I guess you should try to keep an eye on her—and not to worry so much—but if you see anything unusual, don't be afraid to call me or her doctor. What's she doing right now?"

"She's asleep. That's why I can talk like this."

"Well, I'm glad you called. I want you to keep me informed about everything. And besides, it's nice to talk with you."

"Thanks. It's good to talk to you too. I really miss you guys." Her voice cracked slightly, and suddenly Maggie wished she could hug the girl.

"Oh, honey, we really miss you too. I hope you'll come back to Pine Mountain eventually—when you can. Although I must admit it's a great comfort having you there with Mom. Thanks for doing that."

"I'm glad I can be here. I just don't want anything bad to happen to her."

"Neither do I. Be sure and let me know if *anything* changes. And you take care."

Maggie hung up and leaned her head against the wall in the hallway. Suddenly her mother seemed so far away and removed from her life. What if something did go wrong? How difficult would it be to get there in a reasonable amount of time? Pine Mountain was so isolated. She wondered if she should call back and talk to her mom and really question her about her health. But then she remembered she was sleeping. There seemed no point in waking her now. And it wouldn't be wise to alarm her with their concerns, it might only increase her stress and she probably didn't need that. She'd just have to call first thing in the morning, and under the pretense of sharing the latest local news, she'd also try to detect exactly how her mother was doing.

The phone rang again and Maggie picked it up. This time it was Spencer. After a brief greeting he asked if he could spend the night at Daniel's house. Maggie paused uneasily. She hated to sound negative about Daniel, especially after their recent progress, but she still felt she didn't know him that well.

"Where does Daniel live?" she asked, stalling for time.

"He lives on this really cool ranch just south of town—he lives here with his grandparents, Tom and Linda. And they have horses, Mom! They're—what did you say they were called, Daniel? Oh, yeah, quarter horses. The kind they use in rodeos. And Daniel is a really good rider, and he's teaching me how to ride too. It's really cool, Mom."

She smiled. It all sounded pretty harmless and actually quite fun. "Okay. Just let me write down the address and phone number and stuff. Then I'll pick you up in the morning after I work out at the fitness center and meet his grandparents." They worked out the details and she hung up. So, Daniel was a cowboy—who ever would've guessed!

Once again, her house seemed overly large and almost unbearably empty. Her footsteps sounded hollow and lonely as she walked down the hardwood floor of the hallway.

What could she have been thinking when she'd purchased this drafty old place? It badly needed people and voices, laughter and music. Right now it felt cold and dead. She went into her library, still minus one desk, and sighed. This room had the potential to be a somewhat cozy retreat with its rapidly-filling bookshelves, colorful area rug, and the soft leather sofa. But right now it was only partially furnished and missing any special decorative touches to add personality. Perhaps this was a project she could focus her energy upon during the weekend, something to distract her from the other discouraging areas of her life. But for the time being, she suspected a fire in the fireplace would cheer up the room considerably. After arranging paper and kindling, she soon got a small fire crackling, then went to the kitchen to fix herself some dinner. She hated cooking for one. It seemed such a waste of time. She wondered how her mother had managed for all these years—and actually seemed to enjoy it! She opened a can of vegetable soup to heat in the microwave, then sliced up some swiss cheese and an apple. Arranging these items on a tray with some crackers, she then proceeded back to the library and sat down on a footstool to eat in front of the fire.

"Is this to be my life?" she asked herself out loud. "Sitting all alone, huddled by the fireplace, in my big, old, empty house? Is this what my life has finally come down to?" Suddenly, she imagined herself on a cold winter's night—perhaps even snowed in. Stuck out here all by herself, isolated, lonely, cold...She shuddered and moved her stool closer to the fire. She knew she was allowing her imagination to get carried away, over-dramatizing her situation. But at the same time, she knew there was some truth to it. And if something was actually wrong, she'd much rather look it straight in the face right now, and be honest with herself, than to have it creep up on her later—perhaps when it truly was the middle of winter! She remembered Abigail's comment today. Was she becoming a hermit? And if she were, was it merely the result of some recent unhappy circumstances, or was it perhaps an unconscious choice on her part? She looked at the flickering flames and sipped her soup. Many writers did have the tendency to hole up and keep to themselves.... She knew of some sad stories. But at least she had the newspaper to keep her going. Her job forced her to get up and go to work everyday. But then what? Spencer grew more independent each day. And, of course, that was part of growing up—she wanted that for him. Her mother and Leah showed no signs of coming back anytime soon. And her few, recent friendships suddenly seemed delicate and unsteady, not to mention dwindling fast. She thought specifically of Buckie. He might have been a pain on occasion, but he was fun to have around. She sighed. Yes, she definitely seemed to be on a downward spiral in the area of friendships lately.

Finally, she allowed herself to consider her relationship with Jed. Naturally, he'd been popping in and out of her thoughts all along, but she had managed to keep him suppressed, like someone bound and gagged and thrown down into the cellar, and yet he persistently knocked upon the walls in hopes of attaining her attention. Her self-control had been amazing as day after day she refused to acknowledge his presence in her mind. Perhaps she'd hoped that time and space would eventually and miraculously make everything plain and clear. And yet everything was just as murky, if not murkier, than it had been a few weeks ago, the night they'd first gone out. She considered all that had happened in the past couple of weeks. The unforgettable dinner on his property on the mountain. Their misunderstanding over Leah. His apology. Another nice dinner. The desk. She paused and looked at the wall where the desk would've gone. He had made that desk just for her—she knew it. But why would he go to such trouble? Certainly not just to make a sale? Yet when Kate had sold it, he'd said very little. And then he had escorted Kate to the hotel that night, with Kate looking a little like the cat who'd just swallowed the canary. Well, it just made absolutely no sense. No wonder she had avoided thinking about it altogether. But still she couldn't help wonder…what exactly was going on inside that man's head? Did he even know? Was he as confused as she? She thought about his decision to step down from the pulpit. That had been a shock to everyone. Perhaps he, like she, was going through a difficult season of his life, a time of pruning. And, of course, he had to deal with the situation with Kate— that couldn't be easy. But then again, *what was* the situation with Kate? Employee, friend, potential soul mate? Maggie shook her head. Too many unanswered questions! Maybe she'd been wise not to consider these things during this past week. It only seemed to frustrate and confuse her now. If only she knew what he was thinking. Perhaps if she'd been raised differently, she'd simply pick up the phone right now and call him. But an old-fashioned part of her resisted this urge. If he wanted to talk, he could call her. In the meantime, she would continue to wait, trying not to think about it too much. And, of course, she would continue to pray about the whole thing. All week long she had prayed specifically for the strength to accept the possibility that Jed might not be right for her. And with each passing day, it seemed more and more likely that perhaps he wasn't.

She threw another log on the fire, then wrapped up in a soft afghan that her mother had knitted several years ago. She curled up on the couch, pulling a thick, hardback novel onto her lap. A book Elizabeth had convinced her to buy last summer, but she'd postponed beginning until she had time enough to really immerse herself in it. She had the time now. *There's nothing wrong with being alone*, she mentally reassured herself. She'd never been afraid of solitude in the past; in fact, there'd been times when she'd longed for it. And, of course, she knew that God was *always* with her—that was comforting in itself. Perhaps all this worry about hermitting and isolation was pure nonsense. Sure, she probably needed to reach out to others a little more as well as to continue maintenance on what few relationships she still had. But just the same, there was nothing wrong with being alone. She opened the book and inhaled the fresh, pulpy smell of new paper. She ran her hand over the smooth white page and smiled. Yes, being alone definitely had its benefits. And then she began to read.

⌐

The next morning she called her mother. "How's it going, Mom?" she asked brightly, careful to not convey any unnecessary concern.

"Just fine, dear. It's a beautiful day here. Sunny and warm. How's it where you are?"

"It's sunny here too—lots of blue sky. But the wind's blowing a little and it's pretty brisk outside. The mountains look gorgeous with their clean white jackets on."

"Oh, I'd love to see that!"

"So, what've you been up to?" asked Maggie.

"This and that. Mostly just puttering around. Taking care of things that were neglected while I was gone. Molly, next-door, watered my plants but they looked a little sad. I think they need some fertilizer. Leah's a great help. But I keep telling her she should find herself a job or maybe look into going to college next term. I want to pay her tuition at the local junior college, if she's willing to attend."

"That's nice. She's lucky to have you, Mom."

"I think *I'm* the lucky one. Leah's a true God-send."

"I know. So…are you really feeling okay, Mom? I mean health-wise."

"Just a little tired is all. I guess I'm just getting old."

"And everything with the doctor was okay?"

"Well, he still has to read some tests from the hospital. They hadn't come yet. But he didn't seem too concerned."

"How about you, Mom? Are you concerned? Please, be honest."

There was a long pause. "Well, Maggie, you know I'm not getting any younger. I suppose this little stroke episode has reminded me that I won't live forever…"

"But you're only 64, Mom. That's not old by today's standards. Why just look at Abigail and Clara, not to mention old Clyde Barnes!"

Audrey laughed. "Yes. They do give one hope. I didn't mean to go all maudlin on you, honey, but you did ask. And I guess I've been feeling rather old and feeble lately. It's not a very pleasant feeling."

"I appreciate your honesty, Mom. And I do want to know what's up. If it's any comfort to you, I've been feeling old lately too. Maybe it's just that time of year. Say, have you heard from Barry? I thought he might be flying down to visit by now."

"He called again and offered to come, but I told him not to bother. He's so busy with his job right now. I don't want him going to a lot of trouble for nothing."

"Mom, you aren't nothing. We love you."

"I know, honey. But I'm going to be just fine. I just need to slow down is all."

"Okay. Then just do it. Take it easy. Let Leah wait on you."

Audrey laughed. "Poor Leah. I must feel like a ball and chain around that little girl's neck."

"I happen to know for a fact that you aren't. She loves you, Mom."

"Well, it's mutual."

"Call me as soon as you hear from the doctor about the tests, okay?"

"I will. Now, don't forget to give Spencer a big hug for me."

Maggie hung up and glanced at her watch. She had promised to pick up Spencer after her work-out. But at the moment, the idea of working out had absolutely no appeal. Still, she realized, that's usually when she needed it the most—both physically and mentally. She pulled on her gym clothes and headed off to the fitness center. At least Cherise would be a happy face. And as strange as others thought it seemed, Maggie actually appreciated Cherise's sunny disposition.

It wasn't until midway through her workout that Cherise was able to extract herself from the telephone and come over to say hello. "I think I just sold another membership," she said brightly. "And the lady said she saw my ad in the *Pine Cone*."

"Chalk one up for the *Pine Cone*," huffed Maggie as she finished another set of reps.

"Hey, I wanted to tell you something, Maggie." Cherise bent over and lowered her voice. "You might be right about Greg and Rick doing a little land development deal."

Maggie suddenly sat up. "Really? Did you actually ask him about it?"

Cherise nodded. "Yep. And at first, he got all grumpy and acted like I didn't know what I was talking about. But then I told him how you wanted to do an article..."

"You told him *that?*"

"Yeah, I figured it might be good advertising for him and whatever it is they're up to. Well, it turns out that they're trying to develop Rick's farm property along with the sixty acres that belongs to Greg's family into some sort of time-share condo outfit."

"You're kidding? That doesn't sound like Greg."

Cherise's eyes grew wide as she nodded emphatically. "I know. That's exactly what I thought too. But it turns out they've been working on this deal for a couple years now. The problem is that the land between their two farms belongs to Arnold Westerly and he's not interested in selling, at least not for what they're trying to pay. And I guess his property is the best piece, because of a natural spring, plus it's the biggest—almost two hundred acres. Anyway, I asked Greg how come they were doing this when all along everyone thought they were so opposed to development. And you know what he said?"

Maggie leaned forward. "I have no idea."

"He said they were just trying to keep everything hush-hush to keep other investors away and to prevent Arnold from jacking up his price."

Maggie shook her head in disbelief. "Now I think I've heard everything."

"But the problem is, now Greg's all worked up about you putting something in the *Pine Cone*. He says it'll just drive Arnold's price up even higher and probably blow the whole deal to boot. And he says they were just about to get him to sign papers."

"I see. But you must realize this is really big news, Cherise. Front page stuff." Maggie was ready to dash out right then and there and start writing her story.

"I know," Cherise's brows lifted in a pleading appeal, "but I told Greg you were my friend, Maggie, and that even if I told you everything, you wouldn't print a single word that would hurt me or him."

"You told him that?"

"Yeah, and then he laughed right in my face. He told me I was stupid to trust you. And for sure you'd try to ruin us with this."

Maggie felt sick. "Well, I *am* a journalist, Cherise. My job is to report the news."

"I know. But I told Greg you were better than that. I told him that you valued people more than that paper."

"That's true," she said meekly.

"But Greg said I didn't know anything about anything. He said that if you'd run that photo of Leah, then you'd run anything."

"*I* didn't run that photo of Leah."

"Oh. Well, see, that proves my point then." Cherise tilted her head to one side curiously. "Say, is it really true what they're saying about Leah?"

"What do you mean?"

"You know, that she was involved with those drug people who got busted last summer—is that really true?"

Maggie scowled. "No. Not a word of it. In fact, I think we can credit Rick Tanner's son with that nasty little rumor. He got ticked at Leah just because she didn't want to sing, and I think this is how he's getting even."

Cherise's eyes narrowed. "That little sneak. He always acts real smooth on the outside, but ever since I caught him peeping in the lady's dressing room here, I've never trusted that kid. Man, I feel sorry for Leah. How's she taking it?"

"Fortunately she doesn't know."

"So, Maggie, was I wrong? Are you going to print that stuff about Rick and Greg's plans?"

"The newspaperwoman in me says that I should." Maggie blotted the towel on her forehead and sighed.

"But what about the *real* Maggie?"

Maggie slid the towel from her face and looked at her, so naïve and trusting. "Well, how about this, Cherise. How about if I sit on the story until the boys get things squared away with Arnold. But the minute the deal's finalized I want to run the story. This town deserves to know."

"That seems very fair. Do you mind if I tell Greg?"

"No. But you should know that if someone else, besides you, had been my source on this story, then I wouldn't have hesitated to print it. But since you're the one who told me, and it is in essence your story too, then I'll respect our friendship and keep quiet, but just for a while."

Cherise's face was beaming now. "You think of me as a friend, Maggie?"

Maggie smiled. "Yeah. And, believe me, friends can be a pretty precious commodity nowadays."

Cherise reached over and hugged her. "Thanks. That means a lot to me."

Twenty

Maggie and Spencer went to church on Sunday. Sam Galloway led the service, and Jed was nowhere to be seen. Maggie felt concerned by his absence and looked around the congregation for someone she could make an unobtrusive inquiry to. And at the end of the service was when she noticed that Kate was also missing. A coincidence perhaps, or was something going on? She tried to curb her imagination from speculations as she quickly made her way to the door. What business was it of hers? She and Jed were little more than good friends anyway. She waved goodbye to Spencer, who was now talking with Sierra near the front of the building. He'd been invited to join her and Scott and Chloe as they attended a jazz concert in Byron. Then Maggie quietly slipped out and headed to her car. She chastised herself for not being more outgoing and friendly and for not staying to visit after the service. But suddenly she had felt like an outsider, an alien; even more so than when she'd first moved to Pine Mountain. Not only that, but she was upset by the absence of Jed and Kate. But as she drove toward home she tried, once again, to push thoughts of Jed to the recesses of her mind. Whatever would be would be.

She spent an hour outside under the clear blue sky, raking aspen leaves into neat, golden piles. The air was brisk and cold, but the exercise was invigorating and a good distraction from uncomfortable thoughts. Finally, she stopped to take a break and went in to fix herself a late lunch. Just as she was washing her hands in the deep kitchen sink, the phone rang. It was Gavin Barnes.

"Gavin," she exclaimed as she grabbed for a towel. "I'm so glad you called."

"Really? You're *glad?*"

"Yes. I've been wanting to ask you about something. But you go first. Tell me why you've called."

"I just wanted to find out if you've talked to my uncle yet. I was thinking about coming up there to see him, but I thought I better find out if he's still planning to string me up first."

She laughed lightly. "I don't think he wants to string you up. But he might still be a bit irked. He has a hard time believing that you're completely innocent…"

"I never claimed to be *completely* innocent."

"I know. But I guess he still thinks you were fairly responsible for the whole thing. It's all been very hard on him. I'm not sure what you can do to change his mind. Although I did mention to him that it would help to simply forgive you and move on, and I think he's considering it."

"Thanks, Maggie. I appreciate it. I was thinking about writing him a letter of apology. That was something they recommended in rehab."

"That sounds like a great idea." She thought for a moment. "You might even want to consider putting together an open letter of apology to the entire town. I could run it in the paper for you."

He didn't speak for a moment. "I suppose I could do that," he said slowly. "Although it might be a little embarrassing."

"Any worse than it's been already?"

"I guess not. Tell you what, I'll think about it and then let you know. Okay, now what did you want to ask me?"

Maggie tried to arrange her words carefully in her mind. This wasn't going to be easy. "Well, do you remember when I asked you about living in Arizona?"

"Yeah. Is your mom still planning to go down there for the winter?"

"No, that's not what this is about. I just wanted to ask you about any relationships you might have had down there..."

"Gee, Maggie, that was a long time ago. And I didn't really know that many people when I was..."

"Actually, I'm thinking specifically of only one person, Gavin. Someone by the name of Claudia Hill. Do you remember her?"

After a long pause, he answered. "Yeah, I think I remember a girl named Claudia. A pretty little blond girl. But I didn't know her all that well. Why?"

Maggie tried to think of a way to put it delicately, then remembered Clyde's advice that she get straight to the point. "Well, she became pregnant around the same time that you were there..."

"Now hold on a minute—back up the truck. If you're saying what I think..."

"Just let me finish. Apparently she was involved with a guy from Pine Mountain, and she..."

"I might have messed around some. But I didn't get anyone pregnant."

"Gavin, will you let me talk? Anyway, the child is all grown up now, and she was having some hard times and came to Pine Mountain to find her father..."

"Well, she's barking up the wrong family tree!"

"She happens to know that her father is from Pine Mountain and that he came from money..."

"Oh, so that's it. Some kid just waltzed in with this cock-and-bull story and thinks she can move in on my inheritance!

Well, I'm giving you my word, Maggie, I didn't get this Claudia gal pregnant..."

"But Gavin, all the pieces fit."

"I don't give a hill of beans about the pieces. That kid's not mine! And she sure as heck had better not be out there buttering up old Uncle Clyde—"

"*Gavin!* She doesn't even know that you exist...not yet."

"What d'ya mean, *not yet?*"

"Well, Clyde is aware that this girl might possibly be your daughter, and his great-niece, and he's actually quite fond of her and would like to help—"

"She's *not* my daughter!" He was yelling now. "Can't you hear me?"

"I can hear you. Please calm down and listen. It's not like we're accusing you of something horrible. She's really a wonderful girl and you'd be proud—"

"I don't care if she's Mother Teresa reincarnate. *She's not my daughter!*"

Maggie's fist tightened around the phone cord as she tried to keep her voice even. "Would you be willing to take a blood test?"

Another long silence. "There's absolutely no point in a blood test. I know she's not mine. And if she's smart, that little gold-digger will get herself out of town just as quickly as she showed up."

Maggie had lost all patience now and was sorely close to losing her temper as well. "She's *not* a little gold digger, Gavin! And for your information, she's already left town."

"Well, good riddance!"

She almost hung up, then decided to try a more effective route. She forced herself to speak in a quiet, yet almost threatening tone. "You know, Gavin, blood test or no blood test, we're 99 percent sure that she's your child, and this denial act of yours doesn't convince me of anything except your stupidity. Furthermore, Clyde has already accepted her as if she were his own flesh and blood. And if you were smart, you'd be a whole lot more helpful about the whole thing, because at this rate, she has a much better chance of inheriting the Barnes estate than you ever will." *Then* she hung up. But she was still fuming and her hands were shaking.

Without even fixing lunch, she went back outside and attacked her raking project with a vengeance. Whipping the rake around like a weapon, she swept up golden clouds of aspen leaves and began heaping them all into one large burn pile. Finally, she stopped long enough to hear someone calling her name. She turned to see Jed walking directly towards her.

"You look like a yellow tornado," he said with a little half smile as he approached her. "Did the leaves do something to offend you, or is this just your normal raking pace?"

She dropped her rake across the pile, then pushed a stray strand of hair from her face. "No. I guess I'm just taking out my anger on them."

He frowned, then glanced down at his moccasined feet. "Any special reason you're feeling angry?"

She could tell by his demeanor that he suspected it might be due to him, and for some reason that thought was reassuring. Perhaps he did care. Just the same she was relieved to be able to answer otherwise. "Oh, I just had a distasteful phone conversation with good old Gavin Barnes."

Jed looked up with curious interest. "And why, may I ask, are you having phone conversations with Gavin Barnes?"

"He called to find out something about Clyde, and then I tried to extract some sensitive information from him— and...it just sort of blew up in my face."

"I see."

She looked into his dark eyes and saw compassion there. Perhaps it wouldn't hurt to tell him what was going on, especially now that Leah was gone, and what with Gavin being such a jerk about the whole thing. Maybe he would have some helpful suggestions, especially since he could see it from a guy's perspective. "Do you want to hear the whole story?" she asked tentatively. Deep down inside she wondered if she were perhaps simply swapping this dilemma for the one she really wanted to solve with him. But then again, any opportunity to talk to Jed right now seemed worth a shot. And perhaps this conversation would pave the road to another.

"Sure, but you look like you could use a break. Maybe you should sit down."

"Good idea. Let's go sit on the porch and I'll tell you all about it."

After getting sodas, they sat down in the rockers and she slowly began to unravel her story. Starting from the beginning, she gradually worked her way up to today's explosive confrontation with Gavin. The whole while Jed listened in what appeared an intent and very focused silence. It comforted her to see how much he seemed to care.

"And it's not so much that I think that Gavin should get to know Leah, although perhaps in time...I mean, he's not a completely bad person, and he has quit drinking and all. But I do think the relationship with Clyde is worth preserving for Leah. And it would be so helpful for her to know some of her roots, especially when everything is such a mess on her mother's side. And to be perfectly honest, I really miss her, almost as if she were my own, and I would love to have an excuse, any excuse, to bring her back here." Maggie sighed, then looked out toward the mountains. "Although I must admit I'm thankful she's with my mom right now." She turned and glanced at Jed, still sitting in silence. It surprised her to see such a look of consternation upon his face, as if he felt this whole thing just as keenly as she. She smiled at him reassuringly. "It's not like I expect you to come up with any answers, Jed. But I really do appreciate you listening..."

Then he turned and looked straight into her eyes. "I've got to go, Maggie. I'm really sorry. But I'll talk to you later." And he abruptly stood and walked over to his pick-up; then climbed in and drove off in a cloud of brown dust. She just sat there stunned for several minutes, staring at her deserted driveway in shock. What in the world had come over him like that? Had she only imagined that he'd been listening, or that he had even really cared for that matter? Was she completely dense? Was she simply losing it altogether?

She went inside the house and numbly fixed herself some lunch. Perhaps it was only hunger that was making her feel as if she'd just visited the Twilight Zone. But even after consuming a thick roast beef sandwich she still felt confused. In a desperate effort to make sense of the last hour, she emailed Rebecca.

RB

You might have been right on the money in regards to "my mystery man" Jed. I think I may need to cut my losses and move on as far as he is concerned. And yet, it makes me very sad. This has been a most frustrating day. All alone, and then a phone call from the man I suspect to be Leah's father. Naturally, he denies everything. And now he's afraid Leah is moving in on his inheritance—as if he'll get any! I may need some legal advice about this. Can we force him to do a DNA test to prove paternity? Does that take a court order? Oh my. What I wouldn't give to be able to zap myself down to L.A. and meet you at Henri's for an espresso and a nice, long chat. Right now it seems that nothing is going my way. I'm even having doubts about why I came to Pine Mountain in the first place. Certainly it wasn't to feel this lousy and lonely. Yes, now I remember, it was partially for Spencer. And I should be glad because it seems things have turned around for him a little. But personally, I could take or leave this place at the moment. Of course, I will change my song when I go outside and see several does standing out by the pines with the mountains in the background. At least, I think I will. Right now I don't know anything for absolutely sure. I think I'll take a nap. Don't take anything I've said just now too seriously. I'm sure it'll all look better when I wake up.

mc

Twenty-One

The shrill ringing of the phone startled Maggie awake. She glanced at the clock by her bed as she reached for the phone. Only two o'clock. She'd barely lain down for a nap, and yet she'd fallen soundly asleep.

"Hello?" she answered groggily, resenting the caller's interruption of her restful escape. They had better not be selling vinyl siding or carpet cleaning.

"Maggie!" It sounded like Leah, but her voice was shrill and urgent. "Thank goodness you're home. I'm at the hospital with Audrey."

"What's wrong?" Maggie sat up straight, her fingers wrapping tightly around the receiver. "Is it Mom? Is she okay?"

"I don't know. She was having one of those headaches today and it just kept getting worse. And at lunch time her vision became blurry and then she became confused—kind of like when Buckie found her at the Blue Moose. Anyway, I didn't know what else to do, so I called 911. We're at the hospital now. She's being examined, and they're trying to reach her doctor."

"Is she conscious?" asked Maggie, a weak feeling churning within.

"She was sort of in and out. Because I'm not family they won't let me go into the ER to see her."

"It's okay, honey. I'll come right away."

"Oh, could you, Maggie?" Leah's voice choked in a sob.

"Of course. I'll see what it takes to get a flight out of Byron. Or maybe I can drive to Portland and fly out from there. I'll hitchhike if I have to. Whatever it takes I'll be there. Hopefully by tonight." Maggie hung up and prayed as she impatiently searched the phone book for the airlines that flew out of Byron. She knew flights from their slightly isolated locale were limited at best; and then to connect with another flight out of Portland going directly to San Jose could be tricky. Fortunately she got what sounded like a knowledgeable woman on the other end, and when Maggie quickly explained her dire situation the woman was both sympathetic and helpful. Maggie listened to the steady clicking of the keyboard keys as the woman searched her computer for flight connections from Byron to San Jose.

"You're in luck," said the woman finally. "The connection in Portland will be tight, but if all goes well we can get you into San Jose by seven o'clock tonight. That is if you can get to Byron by three-fifteen."

Maggie glanced at her watch as she headed for her closet. "I'm in Pine Mountain right now, but I think I can make it. I'll leave immediately. Thanks for your help."

"Don't thank me. I think you must've had a guardian angel or something. It's very unusual to get connections as good as this at such late notice."

Maggie was already stuffing clothing into her carry-on bag. "Yes, I was actually praying even as I dialed the airport. I think God was listening."

"I guess so!"

Maggie called Rosa on her cell phone as she drove to Byron. No one was home, so she left a message telling her what was up and asking Rosa to explain everything to Spencer. Maggie hated leaving him behind like this, but she didn't know what else to do. Besides, he was almost fifteen.

It wasn't as if he couldn't be home alone for a day or even two. Perhaps she could arrange to fly him to San Jose on Monday or Tuesday. She arrived at the airport just in time to check in, and was soon loaded onto the plane and flying over the Cascade Mountains to Portland. She looked out her window at the craggy surfaces below, already coated with snow. It looked cold and fierce down there, and suddenly she felt very vulnerable in the small twin-engine commuter plane as it bumped and bobbed like a child's kite in the turbulent mountain air currents. I'm in God's hands, she told herself as she leaned back into her seat, attempting to relax during the short flight. Then she prayed that her mother would also be in God's hands right now, and that the medical staff would diagnose and treat whatever was causing these problems. After about twenty minutes she saw the outskirts of Portland sprawling below. The turbulence had delayed their flight some and now it seemed they were being forced to circle the airport, losing even more precious minutes. She knew this would push her tight connection even tighter, but she simply closed her eyes and fervently prayed to make her next flight. She grabbed her bag as the small plane taxied, moving slower than a slug, down the runway. And at last the passengers were unloaded and she began to jog past the rest across the tarmac and into the terminal. She'd only packed her carry-on in order to speed things up when she finally landed in San Jose, but now as she slung the unusually heavy bag over her shoulder she wished she'd traveled even lighter. And now there was no choice but to dash the length of twenty-some gates, running almost full speed, to make her next connection. And she knew she was late. Arriving out of breath, she found a deserted gate and the counter attendant now closing the door that led out to the plane.

She waved her ticket in the air as she cried frantically, "*Wait!* Has the San Jose flight left yet? *This is an emergency!*"

The man stopped and stared at her, then quickly spoke into his walkie-talkie as he reopened the door and disappeared down the walkway toward the plane. She followed him in time to see the heavy door on the plane opening up, and then he grinned as he took her ticket and returned to her a boarding pass. "Lucky for you this flight was running a few minutes late."

"Thanks. I'll never complain about a late take-off again." She entered the plane with more thanks and apologies and quickly made her way to her row, breathing a prayer of sincere thanksgiving as she finally collapsed into her aisle seat.

"That was cutting it pretty close," commented the young woman next to her with impatience. "At this rate, we probably won't land in San Jose until nine."

Maggie thought about snipping back at this insolent, selfish woman, but managed to control her tongue as she answered pleasantly, "I don't think you need to worry. I overheard the steward assuring first class that the pilot will make up for the delay in the air. They still plan to make San Jose by seven."

"Well, that's a relief. My fiancé is meeting me and we're supposed to have a late dinner with his family. It's the first time I've met them and I didn't want to make everyone wait."

Maggie chatted with the woman as they flew, eventually explaining how this trip was something of an emergency. And to her surprise the woman suddenly became very understanding. "I'm glad you made your flight then. Where did you fly in from?"

"Byron. Although, I live in Pine Mountain."

"Pine Mountain!" exclaimed the woman. "Why, I just love that little town. I saw a news blurb on TV about it last summer and ever since I've been wanting to get over there to do a story."

"*A story?* Are you a journalist?"

"Yes. I'm the arts and leisure editor for the *Oregonian*."

Maggie grinned. "Boy, did I sit next to the right person." She formally introduced herself and learned that the woman's name was Jessie Edwards. By the end of the flight, they had exchanged their business cards and personal history, along with a rather pleasant conversation.

"Will you be at the Harvest Festival?" asked Jessie as they made their way slowly down the crowded aisle.

"I'm not sure what's going on with my mother yet. My commitment will be to stay with her as long as she needs me."

Jessie nodded. "I understand. I'll be sure and send you a copy of the feature I do on Pine Mountain. But I sure hope to see you at the festival."

As the steward had promised, they had landed in San Jose right on schedule. From there Maggie was able to skip baggage claim and quickly hail a taxi to take her directly to the hospital. It had been nearly four hours since she'd talked to Leah. She wondered what had happened with her mother during that time. What would her condition be? Would she even be conscious? Making her way to the front desk at the hospital, she shot up another prayer, then paused to ask for information and directions.

After a seemingly endless search on the computer, the volunteer finally said, "It appears that Audrey Martin is scheduled for surgery right now."

"*Surgery?*"

The woman nodded. "That's all I can tell you, dear. Surgery is in the west wing of the third floor and there's a nice waiting room nearby with coffee and tea."

"Thanks." Maggie took off toward the elevator, then up to the third floor. She quickly spotted Leah in the waiting area, looking very much like a small child as she sat upon a peachy floral couch with her knees pulled up to her chest and her head bent down, almost in a fetal position. Maggie's heart went out to her. "Leah?" she spoke gently as she placed a hand on the girl's hunched shoulder. "What's going on?"

Leah stood up and threw her arms around Maggie. "I don't know for sure. The doctor came and he had all her MRIs and things. He thinks there's a tumor that might be blocking an artery. He said the best thing was to go inside and look."

Maggie tightly held the trembling girl. "A tumor?"

Leah's voice was muffled against her shoulder. "I don't understand why the doctors in Byron didn't spot it."

"I don't know either. Was Mom conscious before she went into surgery?"

"I never even got to see her." Tears were streaming down her pale cheeks now. "I've been so worried. I didn't know what to do—besides to pray, that is."

"I think that's about all we can do right now." Together they sank down on to the couch and Maggie put her arm around Leah's shoulders. They both bowed their heads and prayed quietly for several minutes.

"I'm so glad you came," said Leah after they both said amen.

"Believe me, it was no small miracle to make it here this quickly." She looked up at the clock on the wall. "I'll try to reach Spencer now. I had to leave without even talking to him." She dialed her home number and was relieved to hear Spencer answer. After explaining everything she knew to him, she finally apologized for having to leave so abruptly without taking him along. "I just didn't know what else to do. I wish I could've brought you. And I'll arrange for you to fly..."

"It's okay, Mom. I'm just glad you're there with Grandma right now. If you want me to come, I will. Just let me know what you want me to do. We're having midterms at school this week, but I don't care if I miss them."

Maggie smiled at her son's honesty. "Well, let's not decide anything right now. If you don't hear from me tonight, it means everything's going okay. I'll call and let you know what's up in the morning. Then we'll determine whether you need to miss any midterms or not. For the time being, let's just think positively. And I know that you'll be praying for her."

"You can count on that. And don't worry about anything, Mom. Bart and I are just fine. Tell Grandma I love her."

She felt her eyes fill with tears. "I will, Spence. That means a lot to her. I love you, honey."

"Love you too, Mom."

She hung up, then returned to the couch to continue her waiting vigil with Leah. She attempted to read a home and garden magazine, but her mind refused to stay focused even on the glossy photos. Finally she just leaned back and closed her eyes—more praying and waiting. There seemed little else to do.

It was nearly nine when someone in surgical scrubs finally approached them. He was an older man, small and slightly bald, with the tidy look of a surgeon. "Hello, are you here for Audrey Martin?"

Maggie stood and introduced herself, eagerly shaking his hand and introducing Leah as well. She spoke quickly, as if to fill in all the spaces, as if she were almost afraid to hear what he might have to say.

"We've had a successful operation. The tumor was not very big and actually fairly neat as tumors go. We've sent it out for a biopsy. It was blocking an artery in her neck, and the loss of blood flow was what brought on the symptoms of stroke. The location of the tumor at the base of her neck was quite likely the reason it was overlooked, at least initially. I suspect the doctors were looking for something higher up."

"How is she?"

"Like I said, everything went as well as possible. The blockage on the artery was about fifty percent, not excessive but enough that she may have incurred some minor brain damage. Although I'm sure her physician can make a better assessment tomorrow. Hopefully if she has suffered any damage it is only minor and perhaps will diminish with therapy. Of course, we won't know any of this for sure until she recovers from the procedure."

Maggie nodded. "So, generally, you're saying that it sounds like she'll recover?"

"I can't give any guarantees on recovery. But like I said, the operation was successful. It's fortunate she got in here as quickly as she did, and that we were all on hand. Plus her doctor brought in the scans to read from her previous tests. She was very lucky. This whole thing could've gone very differently."

"Thank you," said Maggie weakly, still unsure whether she should be relieved or not. "When can we see her?"

"She'll be under observation in the recovery room for about an hour or so. Then we'll move her to ICU."

"ICU?"

"We need to keep her under close observation to assure that no hemorrhaging occurs." He took off his glasses and peered at her as if to question whether she'd been really listening to him. "It was a very serious procedure."

Maggie nodded. "I understand. Thank you."

Seemingly satisfied, he turned from her and went over to the nurses station and began to make a phone call. Maggie felt certain there must be more questions to ask him, but she couldn't think of any. She turned to Leah and forced a tepid smile to her lips. "It sounds like everything went as well as it could. I guess we'll just have to keep waiting. Have you had anything to eat since you got here this afternoon?"

Leah shook her head. "I'm not hungry."

"I know, but I think we need to eat something. I saw a Chinese restaurant across the street from the hospital parking lot. Why don't we walk over there? It sounds like Mom will be sleeping for a while yet anyway."

Leah looked unsure. "I just hate to leave her, Maggie."

"I know. But sitting here with an empty stomach won't help her a bit, honey."

"You're probably right." Leah agreed. "In fact, Audrey's always the one telling me that life will look better on a full stomach."

Maggie chuckled. "Blame it on those Italian roots.

Twenty-Two

Somehow Maggie managed to convince Leah to go home and get some rest. Once again Maggie began what promised to be another long night in the hospital as she waited for her mother to wake up. As exhausted as she was, she could not find sleep. Instead she alternated between prayers for her mother and trying to figure out what had gone wrong with her life so recently. She felt completely uprooted, like a rowboat that had been cut loose upon the sea, and there seemed to be no place that really felt like home to her anymore. Not back in L.A. where she'd sold her house in the suburbs last spring. Not here in the San Jose area where she'd grown up. And now even Pine Mountain no longer felt like home. What was going on with her? She sternly reminded herself that ultimately heaven would be her home. But just the same she longed for a place that felt like home here on earth. But what made a place home? She knew she'd felt at home in Pine Mountain before, but something had changed. And now the small, quaint town seemed far removed, not only geographically, but also in an alienated and almost hostile sort of way. Maybe it was ridiculous, but she suddenly felt as if she were no longer welcome there. What did she really have back there anyway?

(Besides Spencer, of course, although he'd never wanted to move in the first place.) There was an old, drafty farmhouse, still in need of a number of repairs and renovations. A tiny hole-in-the-wall newspaper to run. But what else? The mountains? Surely even their beauty wouldn't be enough to sustain her. How could she have made such a mess of things? Hadn't God led her there to start with, or had she simply deceived herself in order to have her own way? Round and round her thoughts went, one tumbling over the next until she wasn't even sure what she really thought anymore. And probably it would be better *not* to think at all.

Finally she was distracted by a sense of movement nearby and she turned to see the hospital bed and was reminded once again of where she was and why. She saw her mother's pale face twitch and her eyelids seemed to flutter slightly. And then her eyes opened, and she looked at Maggie with what seemed an almost amused expression.

Maggie stood up and moved closer to the bed, taking her mother's hand in her own. "Mom?" she whispered. "How are you doing?"

A slight smile played across her mother's pale lips as she whispered, "I've been better."

Maggie squeezed her hand gently and smiled in return. "But I think you're on the mend. They got the tumor out."

"Tumor?" Audrey's eyes flickered with curious concern.

"Yes. I suppose you weren't aware. They discovered a small tumor at the base of your neck that was slowing the blood flow of a main artery. That's why you kept getting those headaches and that light-headed feeling."

"Did they get all of it?"

"Yes. And the doctor said it looked pretty clean, but of course they're sending it in for a biopsy."

Audrey closed her eyes and sighed. "I had a feeling…"

Maggie nodded. "You knew something was wrong, didn't you, Mom?"

"Yes."

"Well, at least you're sounding like your old self now. The doctor was concerned you might be left with some stroke-related effects, but you seem very clear to me."

"You look awful," said Audrey.

Maggie made a face. "Thanks, Mom. I needed that."

Audrey smiled slightly. "Go home, honey, get some rest. I'll be just fine."

"I don't want to leave you."

"Go, Maggie. I'll rest better if you do."

She finally agreed. "Okay, if you promise to rest, I'll go." She bent over and kissed her mother's smooth cheek. "I'm so glad you're okay, Mom. I was feeling very lost just now. I think I still need my mommy."

"I'm glad you do." Audrey smiled and closed her eyes.

Instead of going to her mother's house, Maggie went back into the deserted waiting room and curled up in a corner of the peachy floral couch. It was only a few hours until morning anyway, and with the fresh assurance that her mother was okay, perhaps she'd finally be able to rest. If she could only block out all her troubling thoughts and allow sleep to drift over her. She tried to envision herself curled up and protected in the hand of God, and finally she managed to relax. Right there under the harsh fluorescent light and the constant humming of foreign hospital noises, she fell soundly and completely asleep.

When she awoke she felt surprisingly refreshed and peaceful. She stretched her arms and looked about her at the strange hospital surroundings, taking a moment to remember how she'd come to be here and why. And there, in a sea-foam green easy chair directly across from her, sat Jed Whitewater! At first he smiled sheepishly, then walked over and sat next to her on the sofa.

"Hi there," he said quietly.

"What are *you* doing here?" she asked in surprise, blinking her eyes as if to test if this were only a dream.

"I drove down."

"You *drove*?"

"Yes, last night."

"But why? What are you doing…"

"I called at your house last night to talk to you, and Spencer told me the news about Audrey." He nodded down the hallway to ICU. "He's in there with her right now. She's doing much better, by the way."

Maggie shook her head incredulously. "Spencer is *here*? I still don't get it. It must have taken all night to get here. All that trouble just to bring Spence? I could've had him flown…"

"It wasn't just to bring Spencer. Although that was part of it."

"But why then?"

He sighed deeply. "It's a long, long story, Maggie. Do you want me to start into it right now? Or would you rather go check on your mother first? They're about to move her out of ICU to a private room."

"Of course I want to see Mom. But I also want you to explain everything to me later."

Spencer and her mother were chatting amiably. Audrey's color had fully returned, and she looked far better now than when she'd left Pine Mountain over a week ago. She glanced up at Maggie and smiled. "What a pleasant surprise to wake up and see my grandson this morning."

"I'm pretty surprised too." Maggie put a possessive arm around her son's shoulders. "But I'm also very glad to see him." She turned back to her mother. "You're sure looking perky this morning."

"Other than a sore neck, I feel completely well. I don't know how long they think they can keep me in this bed, but I'm ready to get up and get going right now."

"Take it easy, Grandma," warned Spencer. "We'll bust you out of this joint just as soon as we think it's safe."

"Yes, be patient, Mom. You've just been through major surgery. I'm sure they'll want to keep you a day or two."

Audrey groaned. "Goodness, I hope not. I have so much to do."

"Now, what can you possibly have to do that can't wait a day or two?"

"Well, first off, I need to call a realtor…"

"What do you mean?" With horror, Maggie suddenly imagined her mother vegetating in a long, stucco retirement home with old folks shuffling around in their bathrobes.

"Well," began Audrey, "do you still have that sweet little carriage house for rent or perhaps lease?"

Spencer grinned. "You bet we do, Grandma!"

"Are you serious, Mom?"

"If your offer is still good. I certainly wouldn't want to impose…"

"It's no imposition! You know good and well that we'd love to have you with us. But what about all that snow and ice that'll be coming this winter?"

"Well, I just happen to have a good friend in Tucson who might let me visit her if things gets a little too chilly up there in the northlands." Audrey smiled. "But you never know. I might be more adaptable than you think."

∘⌒

They caught Leah in the lobby as they were waiting for Audrey to be transferred into her new room. Surprised to see Spencer and Jed, Leah listened with wide eyes as Maggie told her the good news about Audrey's amazing recovery.

"Wow," she said. "That's so great. Can I go see her?"

"I suppose she might be settled in by now." Maggie glanced at Spencer. "Do you want to show Leah where Grandma's new room is while Jed and I go down to the cafeteria for a cup of coffee?"

The two pairs headed in different directions. And before long Maggie and Jed located the hospital's cafeteria. Then, finding an empty table in a quiet corner, they sat down across from each other with their coffee between them. Maggie lifted her cup, taking a slow sip as she studied Jed with perplexed curiosity. Finally she leaned forward, deciding to cut straight to the chase. "Okay, I give. Why in the world did you spend a whole night just to drive down here?"

"Like I said, it's a long story. And I've been trying to think of where I should begin. Maybe I should try to tell you the condensed version—at least for now." He set down his cup and looked into her eyes. "You see, yesterday…was it only yesterday when I stopped by your house? Anyway, yesterday when you told me about your phone call from Gavin—and about how he'd been living in Phoenix twenty years ago—and how you were certain he was Leah's father, well, it just totally shocked me. You may have noticed that I was speechless. What you said completely threw me for a loop."

"I'm not following you. You're shocked just because I think that Gavin is Leah's father?"

He waved his hand. "No, I mean the *whole* story was shocking. What you said about Leah coming from Arizona to find her father, who was from Pine Mountain and all that…" He looked down at his coffee as he meticulously rotated the cup in perfect stationary circles, turning it round and round on the orange plastic-laminate table. Finally he looked up and continued to speak. "You see, Maggie, I spent some time down in Phoenix while Gavin was there…"

"That's good. Maybe you could be a witness that Gavin might possibly be Leah's father."

"Maggie," he said in a pleading voice. "*I* am Leah's father."

Her cup met the table with a dull thud. She shook her head as if to clear her ears. Perhaps she had heard him wrong. "*What?*"

"I was never really sure before, and over the years I had nearly convinced myself that it had all been an expensive and cruel hoax. Even back then, when Claudia told me she was certain that I was the father, I had my doubts. It seemed so unlikely, and I'd heard that she'd been involved with lots of guys. But just the same, I knew I couldn't deny the possibility. And I felt responsible to help out…"

"*You're* the one who gave Claudia the money?" She still couldn't believe it. "You're really Leah's father?"

He nodded somberly. "Like I said, I wasn't absolutely certain at the time. But I feel certain now. Something about Leah has always seemed oddly familiar to me. And yesterday, after leaving your house, I went home and dug out an old photo of my mother when she was young. Leah really resembles her, especially through the eyes."

Maggie shook her head again. "This is all so strange, Jed. I can hardly process it. And after a somewhat sleepless night I'm still pretty tired. You're not playing a trick on me, are you?"

"It's no trick. The whole crazy thing happened a long time ago. I was a totally different person then. Remember what I told you about my post-Viet Nam years—back when I was into all kinds of crummy stuff—anything to help me escape the memories.... Well, I'd gone to Phoenix to stay with an old army buddy and had just gotten work on a construction crew with him when I ran into Gavin Barnes at a wild party. And since we were both obviously using pretty heavily back then, we finally seemed to have something in common." He shook his head, as if in disgust, then continued. "Gavin invited me to another party with some of his friends. Claudia was there that night, and we were all pretty high. I didn't realize she was only eighteen, and anyway I wasn't much older. It was just a very regrettable one-night stand that I had nearly forgotten by the next week."

"But...how did she know you were really the father? How did she find you?"

"She'd given me her phone number, and in return I'd given her the number of the guy I was living with. I never called her. But about a month or so later, she called me. She told me that she was certain she was pregnant. And she said I was the only one who could possibly be the father."

"And then you paid her off?" Maggie's eyes narrowed accusingly.

"It wasn't a payoff. I just felt responsible. She was young and frightened and I wanted to help her. I was flat broke at the time. It was one of the hardest things I ever did, calling up my dad and asking to borrow that kind of money." Jed's head hung sadly. "And he never even asked me why."

"But you told her not to contact you after you gave her the money."

"I just didn't want her to bother my dad. She seemed to think that since I'd given her so much cash that we must've been loaded." He sighed deeply. "I know it emptied his savings to loan me that money. But it wasn't just the financial part. I didn't want him to know what I'd done. I was so ashamed, and I knew the whole thing would really upset him—he was pretty old-fashioned. Claudia was still living with her mom, and I figured what I gave her should've taken care of her for some time. And I sure wasn't in any position to take on a family—I could barely take care of myself back then. I would've made a lousy father, not to mention that I didn't love her."

"So *this* is why you drove all the way here last night." Maggie felt her cheeks grow warm as she recalled her initial thrill when she'd first seen him this morning. She'd actually hoped that he'd come for her sake. How foolish could she have been!

Jed laid his hands on the table. "I think Leah deserves to know the truth. I won't blame her if she wants nothing to do with me. But I want to tell her face to face. And I want to apologize for abandoning her."

"Does Spencer know about any of this?"

"No. I thought I should tell Leah first."

She nodded. "That seems right." She glanced up at the cafeteria entrance to see Spencer and Leah now walking directly toward them. "Well, it looks like you could be getting your chance very soon. Perhaps it would be best if Spencer and I got out of the way."

Jed looked understandably nervous. "I guess now is as good a time as any."

"They're giving Grandma a bath," explained Spencer as he approached the table. "And I'm getting hungry."

Maggie stood up. "I know. How about if I take you over to Grandma's and maybe we can find something decent to eat there, better than this old hospital food. Plus we can both take showers and rest a little."

"Sounds good to me."

As Maggie got the keys to her mother's car from Leah, she smiled and gave her a warm hug. "I sure love you, Leah," she whispered. Then she glanced over her shoulder to Jed with a *you're on your own* expression, then she and Spencer left.

She still felt numb as she slowly maneuvered her way through traffic towards her mother's house. It almost seemed as if she were trying to escape the hold of some strange dream.

"You okay, Mom?" asked Spencer.

She looked at him, almost surprised to see him sitting beside her. "Yes. I guess I'm just in a daze or something."

"Yeah, me too. Driving all night makes me feel like I have jet lag."

She nodded. "Do you know why Jed wanted to come down here?"

"I guess just to see Grandma and give me a ride. It was sure nice of him."

"There's a little more to it than that." She cleared her throat, trying to think where to begin. It seemed only fair to tell Spencer. It would also spare Jed and Leah from having to explain—they would have enough emotional issues to work through. "Remember when Leah first showed up at Pine Mountain? Well, it wasn't a coincidence that she came there. She had specifically come to try to locate her father…"

"Her father lives in Pine Mountain?"

"Yes. That's what she thought. But after her search, she'd had no success. And that's when you found her. She was pretty discouraged."

"Yeah, I remember. At one point, I was actually worried that she was going to do herself in."

"Thank goodness she didn't. Anyway, we have just discovered that Jed is actually her father…"

"You're kidding! Jed's her father? Man, how lucky could she get?"

Maggie blinked. "Well, her life hasn't exactly been lucky. She's had it pretty hard."

"Oh, I know. But at least she has Jed now. I'm sure he'll be a great dad to her. She must be really happy. Does she know yet?"

Maggie explained that Jed was talking to her right now, and then she continued to field and answer the rest of Spencer's many questions until they finally pulled up into her mother's driveway.

"This is so cool," said Spencer as he climbed from the car. "Grandma's moving back to Pine Mountain. Leah is Jed's daughter. Man, this is so cool!"

"I suppose…" Maggie unlocked the door to her mother's house. "But right now I'm just too tired to try to figure it all out."

Twenty-Three

After breakfast, a shower, and a short nap, Maggie called Clyde and told him of her mother's progress. Then she carefully began an explanation of how she'd just learned that it was Jed, not Gavin, who was actually Leah's father. After a long silence, Clyde finally expressed his pleasure for Leah's sake, but Maggie couldn't miss the sting of disappointment in his voice. And suddenly she realized how very much she'd wanted for Clyde to be related to Leah. It had seemed so perfect.

"If it makes you feel any better, Clyde, I happen to know that Leah would love to adopt you as an honorary grandparent. She told me so several weeks back."

"She did? Well, that was sure sweet of her. I suppose that blood relation isn't everything it's cracked up to be."

"Speaking of blood relation, I now owe your nephew a great, big, fat apology." She told Clyde about the unpleasant conversation she'd had with Gavin after he'd, quite honestly it now seemed, denied her harsh accusation. "I feel so bad, Clyde. I really got on his case. Poor Gavin, as if he doesn't have enough troubles already."

"Probably serves the varmint right." Clyde chuckled. "And that part about losing his inheritance to young Leah

252 •— Melody Carlson

will surely rattle his cage some. But don't you worry, he'll get over it. He always does."

She then told Clyde of her plan to stay with her mother for awhile, at least until she came home from the hospital. But she promised to continue working on the paper off-site by sending files back and forth online. She then asked him to transfer her to Scott.

"Hi, Maggie, how's your mom doing?" asked Scott in a surprisingly cheerful tone.

Once again she recapped the story of the successful surgery; then, clearing her throat, she began a sincere apology over their recent misunderstanding over the photo of Leah, but before she could even finish her sentence Scott cut her off.

"Maggie, it was all my fault. And I'm really, really sorry. I acted childish and stupid, and hopefully I won't ever do something like *that* again. I'm surprised you didn't just hand me a pink slip and send me packing with no hopes of ever getting a recommendation to the *Times*. My only excuse is that I was having a crummy week with this Chloe and Aaron Jackson thing."

"How's that going?"

"Better, I guess. But then I don't really know for sure. Chloe tells me she's not the least bit interested in him. But then sometimes she acts as though she enjoys his attention. I think she just likes to see me get jealous."

Maggie laughed. "Well, maybe you just need to reassure her of your true feelings for her; that way she won't need to resort to game-playing."

"Hmm. You ever consider doing a romantic advice column for the paper? *Dear Maggie: Hints for the Love-lorn.*"

"What a joke! Come to think of it, disregard what I just said. I've got no business handing you advice in that area."

How nice it was to be on friendly terms again with Scott! Together they smoothed out some details regarding the paper and coverage of the upcoming Harvest Festival activities.

She then told him about the Portland reporter she'd met on her flight who would be in contact with the *Pine Cone*. Then she searched her mind for any other possible news leads or interesting tidbits that she'd meant to look into. She longed to ask him if he'd heard anything about the land development deal being cooked up by Greg Snider but, remembering her promise to Cherise, kept this little morsel to herself. There would be time to deal with that later. And then as she was wrapping it up, Scott promised not to run any more questionable photos without her approval first.

❧

Maggie hated to disturb Spencer's sleep, but she was eager to get back to the hospital. Just as she was about to leave him a note and go, he came thumping down the stairs. As she drove through town, she wondered whom she most wanted to see right now: her mother, Leah, or Jed? How would Leah have taken the news? How was Jed dealing with suddenly being cast in the role of father? Would her mother still be improving so wonderfully?

"Have you recovered from your 'jet lag' yet?" she asked her son as they walked through the large sliding glass door into the hospital.

"I guess so." He glanced at his watch then grinned slyly. "And right now I happen to be missing my last class of the day...*and* my geometry test!"

"Oh dear, will you be able to make that up?"

He rolled his eyes. "Probably."

They found Audrey alone in her room, propped up against pillows as she read a paperback that Leah had brought her from home. Other than a stiff neck, she still seemed to look and feel quite well. They visited with her for a while, then Spencer went off in search of a pop machine.

"Jed and Leah were here earlier." Audrey allowed the words to trail at the end, as if to invite further conversation.

"So did they tell you?"

She nodded. "Unbelievable! I'm still taking it all in myself. Poor Leah seemed rather stunned by the whole thing. Of course, I can't really blame her."

"I hope she's okay with everything. I'm sure it must be hard—for them both." Maggie helped her mother adjust the pillows behind her then sat back down.

"I think Leah's very fortunate; Jed's a *good* man."

"Really? I never got the impression that you cared for him that much."

"Oh, I don't know whatever gave you *that* idea. I've always liked Jed a lot. He and I have shared some wonderful conversations while he's been out working on your house. I just never felt certain that he was exactly right for you, and being the protective mother that I am, I didn't want to see you get hurt. Because, as you know, there was always the Kate factor."

"Yes, the Kate factor." Maggie sighed. "Well, I don't think Kate has anything to worry about concerning Jed and me anymore."

"Was she worried?"

"Let's just say…I don't think she was too happy with me. And I would've listed her with the people in town who were thoroughly disgusted with me."

"You actually have a list?" Audrey's brow raised with interest. "Just how many are on it?"

"Fortunately, I have decreased the list by one. Scott and I are back on track again."

"That's good. But who are all the others?"

"Well, besides Kate, there's Buckie." Maggie grew thoughtful for a moment when no other names occurred to her. "Hmm, maybe it's not as bad as I'd imagined. But honestly, Mom, just a few days ago it felt as if I had no one."

Audrey laughed. "No one?"

She nodded. "I'm serious. You and Leah were gone, and Buckie was mad at me. Jed was pretty much ignoring me. And Kate, well, if looks could kill…. Plus there was the thing with Scott, which sort of alienated me from the whole

Galloway family. It really did feel like I had no one. Even last night I didn't think I ever wanted to go back to Pine Mountain again."

"Really? Why not?"

"It just didn't seem like home to me anymore. It seemed like there was nothing there for me. No friends. Nothing."

"And now?"

Maggie smiled faintly. "It's looking a teeny bit better. But this whole thing's been a little unnerving. I kept imagining myself living all alone in my big, old house. It wasn't a very pretty picture."

"No, that doesn't sound like fun." Audrey peered into Maggie's eyes. "So, be honest, Maggie, do you really feel like Pine Mountain *is* your home?"

She shrugged. "It seems I don't know anything for sure anymore. But I hope it is."

Audrey grew thoughtful. "Something occurred to me this morning as I was lying here, stuck in this silly bed."

"What's that, Mom?"

"Well, I was thinking about how as a young woman I always cared a great deal about what *other* people thought..."

Maggie nodded. "Yes, I suppose I can relate to that."

"Then I hit my middle-aged years, and I cared more about what *I* thought..."

Maggie considered this. "I guess that's a sign of maturity."

"And now that I'm entering my latter years," Audrey grinned, "I don't care what *anyone* thinks."

Maggie laughed. "Sounds good to me."

Twenty-Four

aggie stayed with her mother for two weeks to
help out and to ensure she made a complete
recovery. During that time, besides working
off-site on the newspaper, she managed to sort, sell, ship, and
even give away a lifetime's worth of her family's accumula-
tions. Until finally only the "keepers" remained—the pieces
Audrey used daily or else held significant keepsake or family
heirloom value. Jed and Spencer had stayed on a couple
more days, leaving on Wednesday in order to get Spencer
back to school before he'd missed the entire week. Jed had
generously agreed to keep Spencer and Bart out at his place,
although Spence had assured her that they would be fine on
their own. Just the same, she felt relieved not to have to
worry about him. And perhaps it would be good for Jed to
get some parenting practice, Maggie wondered how he'd
handle his new role of dad with Leah. Hopefully he wouldn't
try to be too fatherly too soon.

During those two days, the majority of Jed's time had
been spent with Leah—hours spent talking and getting to
know each other better. Naturally this was understandable,
but as a consequence Maggie had barely spoken to him since
that first morning in the hospital cafeteria. But, she convinced herself, it was all for the best. Confused by what was,

or what wasn't, between them, it seemed much easier to just let their tenuous relationship quietly slip away—like the faded, withering October rose petals that steadily fell from her mother's prized bush by the front walk. And it seemed more than ever that her mother had been correct all along with her subtle warnings that they might not be right for each other.

After recovering from the initial shock of Jed's incredible revelation, Leah had adjusted rather quickly, becoming quite comfortable with the news that he was truly her birth-father. She told Maggie that she'd always admired him; and now that he was gone, she spoke of him constantly, elated that she had finally made a genetic connection that seemed to fit and make sense. She looked forward to returning to Pine Mountain, where she said she would finally feel like a real member of the community. "I have roots!" she had exclaimed out of the blue one morning as she and Maggie were rummaging through the attic—the last bastion of Audrey's stashed and nearly forgotten family mementos and heirlooms.

Maggie had picked a cobweb from Leah's hair and smiled. "Yes, you certainly do! And what fun you'll have getting to know more about your father and your grandparents. They seem like interesting people. And wait until you see his place, and all the trees—it's really quite beautiful!"

"You've already seen it?" A hint of shadow crossed over Leah's face, as if she already felt slightly possessive over Jed and the peripheral areas of his life.

"Yes, but only briefly." Maggie's tone grew apologetic, with no intention of spoiling even a fragment of Leah's happy anticipation. "It's just past the church, you know, up there on the ridge."

"It's funny. I've always loved it up there. I mean, from the very first time I saw it, I thought it was so special. And every time we went to church, I always felt amazingly at home. Do you suppose it's possible that I knew, somewhere inside of me, that I was actually a part of all that?"

Maggie pressed her lips together thoughtfully. Again not wanting to diminish Leah's joy, she dared not admit how she had also felt just like that. She finally said, "I think it's possible that you felt something kindred up there—that perhaps something in your spirit knew."

Leah had smiled beautifully. "I think so too."

⌒

Maggie stood and studied her mother's house in the early morning light. The home of her childhood looked somewhat forlorn as it sat like a large abandoned child on Meadowlark Street. It's faded blue siding needed a fresh coat of paint and a for-sale sign leaned slightly to one side in the center of the small front yard. The house's interior was stark and barren now, stripped of all furniture, goods, and boxes. The moving van had come and gone yesterday, and would probably begin unloading Audrey's things in the carriage house by noon today. Last night Maggie had walked through each of the empty rooms for a final inspection to ensure that nothing was left behind. As her heels echoed over the hardwood floors she couldn't stop the flood of memories—both good *and* bad. A trace of sadness washed over her as reality hit— was it Thomas Wolfe who'd so aptly put it? *You can never go home again.* Yet at the same time, she wondered what was home anyway—four walls and a roof? Certainly there was more to it than just the structure that protected one from the elements. And how could she grieve over the loss of this house when it was simply the necessary sacrifice that allowed her mother to relocate in Pine Mountain? She straightened the blue and white for-sale sign and removed an old soft drink cup that had been tossed into the boxwood hedge.

After she'd returned from taking Leah and Audrey to the airport yesterday, the realtor had called saying that an offer on the house was forthcoming, and she'd told him what time the two should arrive in Pine Mountain and to call Audrey then. Maggie had remained behind to finish cleaning the house and then drive her mother's car to Pine Mountain. Audrey had tried to talk her out of it, but Maggie had insisted the peace and quiet of a long drive would be good medicine, allowing her time to gather her thoughts. She had known her mother would be in good hands with Leah. And just as she had suspected, the two arrived safe and sound, and Jed was there to greet them at the airport. Audrey had called her when she got home and cheerfully reported that they'd even found the kitchen freshly stocked with groceries, all compliments of Rosa!

And the drive, though long, was soothing. She used the cruise control and alternately enjoyed both the silence and some classical tapes her mother kept in her car. The hours passed quickly. And just as Maggie started getting a little stiff and road-weary, she began her ascent up the mountain pass. The sun dropped low in the sky, but enough light remained to backlight the startling white snowcapped peaks. Framed by dark, green pines, this familiar yet ever-changing sight breathed new life and fresh energy into her. And, yes, it felt as if she were coming home!

The newly surfaced road leading to Pine Mountain gleamed dark in the dusky light, and the lack of potholes cut the commute by half. As she approached the edge of town, she observed clean streets, softly glowing street lamps, and an overall aura of serenity and contentment. And as she paused at the stop sign, she knew with almost certainty that she had truly come home. This was right where she belonged. Okay, so everything wasn't perfect, but then neither was she. And she could admit she had some work to do, especially in the area of relationships. But she could do that. She *would* do that!

For fun she didn't turn down the road that led to her house, but continued going straight into town, driving down Main Street and soaking in every detail. To her dismay, things seemed rather quiet. No shops were open. Even the hotel looked closed. But then she remembered how the shops had planned to resume winter hours following the Harvest Festival. She'd completely missed that celebration last week, and now searched the quiet streets for some sign of leftover decorations. Abigail had described everything very colorfully over the phone, saying how it all had turned out so well; even the scarecrow contest had been a big hit with Jennie and Jason Hollingsworth winning first prize with their grandma scarecrow design. But unfortunately, other than a few stray pieces of straw still blowing across the sidewalk, the decorations were all gone now. Oh well, surely Scott must've gotten some good photo coverage. And there would always be next year.

She turned around and headed for home, suddenly excited by the prospect of being in her own house again. Yes, it was *home*—her home! Why had she ever concerned herself with such silly worries? Why, everyone always said that *home is where the heart is*, and with great relief she realized that her heart was here—had been all along.

As she pulled into her driveway, she noticed several cars parked about. Alarmed, she wondered if something was wrong. Had her mother experienced another health problem? She haphazardly parked the car, leaped out, and began to run towards the house. *What was going on?*

"Hey!" called a man's voice. "You're going the wrong way." She turned to see Jed waving at her from near the barn. "The party's over here."

"Party?" she asked weakly as she slowly walked toward him.

He grinned. "That's right. Since you couldn't come to the Harvest Festival, some of your friends thought you might like it if we brought the Harvest Festival to you. Actually, it's more of a Harvest Party."

She stared at him in dumb surprise. "A Harvest Party?" But the part that really stuck in her mind was when he'd said "your friends." *Her friends* had planned this. That meant she did have friends!

He pointed to some pumpkins, cornstalks, and even a scarecrow leaning casually next to the closed barn door. "See, Abigail even thought to have the decorations saved and brought over here."

"How thoughtful." She studied him more carefully now. Dressed in a handsome sage-green shirt and dark trousers, he looked unusually festive. She looked down at her own attire—a dark coffee stain, attained somewhere on her journey, streaked down the front of her pale denim shirt. "Do you think anyone will mind if I go into the house to freshen up a little?"

"Actually, we weren't expecting you quite yet—you must've made pretty good time. Audrey said you weren't supposed to arrive until around seven."

"So *that's* why she was so interested in what time I was going to leave this morning."

He nodded. "Do you mind if I walk back to the house with you?"

"Sure, that's fine." She walked back slowly, taking time to inhale deeply of the fresh mountain air. "Ah, I almost forgot how incredible the air up here smells. It's good to be home."

"I'm sorry we didn't get to talk much in San Jose," he began as they walked in the front door together. "I had some things I wanted to tell you, but the timing seemed all wrong. And there was Leah, and she had so many questions..."

"You certainly can't blame her for that." Maggie waited for him to close the door, then turned to face him as she suddenly recalled her somewhat hostile reaction when he'd told her about being Leah's father. "Actually, Jed, I've been wanting to tell you that I'm sorry for the—"

"*You're* sorry?" He laughed, then shook his head. "Good night, Maggie, what can you possibly have to be sorry about? I'm the one who's behaved like a lunatic. I should be doing the apologizing. And I am truly sorry. To tell you the truth, since my dad's death, this has been one of the most difficult months of my life."

She blinked. "Really?"

He nodded. "You have no idea. At first, I thought it was just because I needed to step down from my position as pastor, and although it was right, it sure wasn't easy. I might also add that decision had something to do with you..."

"With me? But why? I never..."

"It's a long story, and I'll tell you all about it some other time. But on top of that, there was my relationship with you to consider, plus that business with Kate, and then to top it off, finding out about Leah..." He stopped himself. "Now, don't get me wrong. I couldn't be any happier than to find out she's my daughter—it's like an amazing miracle. But it's just been so much to deal with..."

"I know. And I may understand all this better than you think. I've had a pretty hard month myself—one I hope never to repeat. There was one point when I was almost ready to give up on Pine Mountain altogether—just move away and start a whole new life."

Jed looked astonished. "Would you really do that?"

She shook her head. "No, of course not. But at the time I felt so alone and confused, I just wasn't thinking clearly."

He placed a hand on her shoulder. "And I'm sure that was partly my fault. I'm really sorry. I hope you'll forgive me."

She smiled up at him. "Forgiven."

"And do you suppose you can give me another chance?"

"Another chance?"

"You know, a chance for me to prove that I'm worthy of your friendship...and whatever else may come."

She felt the slight frown creasing her forehead. "But what about Kate?"

Jed threw back his head and laughed. "Kate? I'll have you know that Kate Murray is doing just fine, thank you very much. And I can most happily report that she no longer works for me, but has recently moved across the street to take a position at the Blue Moose Gallery."

"Kate works for *Buckie?*"

"Or he works for her. It depends on which way you look at it. She already has him considering a line of decor accessories that she feels would fit in with his gallery—and who knows what else. That woman definitely has plans."

Maggie laughed. "But what about you—your shop?"

He smiled confidently. "*I* have Leah. She's agreed to begin working for me starting next week."

She felt her eyes misting with pure happiness. "Oh, I'm so glad for her—and for you, Jed. You have absolutely no idea…"

"I think I do. In fact, I still remember you cutting me down to size in Leah's defense that night at the bonfire. And then afterwards you said how you'd be proud to have Leah as your own daughter." He shook his head sadly. "What a complete fool I was. Again, I'm truly sorry."

"Please don't apologize anymore. All that matters is that you've figured it out. You know that Leah's a rare jewel."

"I know." He brightened. "And before you go freshen up, I have something I want to show you if you can spare a couple more minutes. Now if you'll just close your eyes." He put his hands on her shoulders and gently guided her around the corner toward the library. "Okay, you can look now." She looked around the library until she saw it.

"*My desk!*" She ran over and began to run her hands over the smooth surfaces, examining its perfectly straight proportions closely. "Oh, it's so beautiful, Jed. But how did you ever get it back after Kate sold it?"

"I made you another one. That's why I was so busy that week before you suddenly had to take off for San Jose. I knew you were feeling blue about your mother and Leah being gone and I was trying to get it done for you. In fact, I'd driven over to deliver it that same afternoon when you told me about Leah and Gavin. But I was so stunned by the news that I totally forgot about the desk."

"Well, I absolutely love it! I can't wait to set it up and try it out."

"Sorry, but you'll have to wait." He glanced at his watch. "It's almost seven now, and they'll probably start looking for you soon."

"I'll be down in a few minutes." She lingered in the library for another moment as she looked into his face, still almost afraid to believe all that had just transpired. "Thanks, Jed—for everything."

He smiled down at her with warm, dark eyes. "Just make sure that I get the first dance tonight, okay?"

"You can count on it! Why don't you go ahead and let them know I'm coming, and I'll see you down there."

⌕

Maggie strolled through the crisp evening air toward the barn, allowing the coolness to wash over her and hopefully subdue the flush of excitement that was warmly painting her cheeks. As the full skirt of her copper silk dress blew gently in the breeze, she felt almost like Cinderella on her way to the grand ball—and tonight Jed would be her prince. She caught her breath at that thought, then warned herself not to elevate her expectations so high that disappointment would inevitably follow. Other than a first dance, no real promises had been made. Better to relax and enjoy, she reminded herself. Simply savor the moment.

A large, painted banner, that looked suspiciously like her son's hand, hung over the entrance proclaiming: 'Welcome Home, Maggie, Audrey, and Leah!' And inside the barn's interior was nearly unrecognizable with all the colorful decorations, tables, chairs, and people. From a makeshift stage of straw bales, a talented three-piece band of fiddle, guitar, and banjo played a folksy style of bluegrass music. Already, numerous couples had filled the hay-strewn dance floor. Maggie quickly spied Buckie with a big grin across his face as he whirled Kate, her long denim skirt swirling around her ankles; and there was Scott and Chloe, both happy and smiling for a change; and then of all things the sophisticated

Jordans from Seattle dancing right alongside Dolly and Jinx; but perhaps the most surprising couple on the floor was Cherise dancing with her own husband. Whoever would've believed that Greg Snider might actually be spotted dancing in Maggie's barn!

She greeted numerous other friends as she made her way to where her mother was seated with Elizabeth Rodgers and Abigail at what they good-naturedly called "the old crone's table." "This is absolutely wonderful," said Maggie. "Who in the world thought of all this?"

Audrey shrugged. "Don't look at me. It was already in the works when we got home yesterday. I haven't had to lift a finger."

"All your friends helped out," said Abigail. "Rosa and Chloe planned the refreshments. Scott and Jed hauled over the decorations." She lowered her voice. "I'm not supposed to tell, but Clyde footed the bill. I must add, although it makes no sense to me, that he was in quite a happy mood after getting a letter from that no-good nephew of his."

Maggie smiled to herself as she spotted Clyde over by the punchbowl, chatting congenially with old Cal from the hardware store—probably swapping hunting stories since elk season had already begun.

"And don't forget that Buckie found the band and Kate worked real hard all day just to rearrange all these decorations," added Elizabeth. The older woman had always taken somewhat of a protective, motherly role when it came to Kate.

"We just felt so bad that you all missed the Harvest Festival," said Abigail, then with a sly smile, "and frankly I think we just wanted another excuse to have a good time!"

Maggie felt a tap on her shoulder and turned to see Jed. His dark eyes glowed like warm coals as he smiled upon her. "Seems to me I have a dance or two coming."

She glanced back to the seated women. "If you ladies'll excuse me, I owe this gentleman a dance." Was it just her imagination, or did her mother wink at her?

The sturdy feel of his warm hand across the small of her back, the smell of sweet hay mixed with the spicy aroma of candles burning in carved pumpkins, the lilting sounds of fiddle and banjo, and the blur of color and movement as other dancers performed the two-step all around them—it was enough to make anyone lightheaded. They danced several unforgettable numbers together. And in between dances, they visited with friends at the heavily laden refreshment table, complete with an assortment of pies, cakes, and cookies. Then Jed abruptly excused himself and began making his way toward the stage of straw. He nodded to the musicians as he stepped up to the microphone and began to speak.

"Ladies and gentlemen, we promised to give our band a little break before the refreshments got too picked over. But first, why don't we give them a great, big hand in tribute to their fine music." He paused as the crowd clapped and cheered. And then Maggie noticed Spencer and Leah stepping up to the stage from the side. She had barely seen those two all evening, and there behind them came Daniel toting his bright blue guitar. That's when she noticed Spencer's drums all set up on the back of the stage. Were they going to perform—just the three of them? Now Jed was continuing, "And for your listening pleasure, I'd like to introduce another musical group that has agreed to play a special song for us tonight." He turned and looked at the kids. "Here we have Spencer Carpenter on drums; and this is Daniel Abernathy on lead guitar, also the creator of the song. And last but not least," he paused and put an arm around Leah's shoulders, "I'd like to introduce Miss Leah Hill. And I'd also like to take a moment to make a very important announcement. I am extremely proud to tell everyone that, as it turns out, Leah is related to me. She is, in fact, my very own daughter. We've been separated for far too long. But thank God, he has brought us back together." He turned and smiled warmly at Leah as people in the crowd passed surprised murmurs amongst themselves. Clearly the rumor hadn't had a chance to make the rounds yet. "And now these kids will play their latest song for you. In fact, it's so new they've only had one day to rehearse it—it's titled 'Harvest of Friends.'"

Jed stepped down from the stage to join Maggie with the rest of the spectators. She gave his elbow a squeeze and he slipped his arm snugly around her waist, and together they watched as the three teens began their song. To her pleased surprise, the music was somewhat quiet and subdued, especially compared to what she'd heard from them in the past. And the melody of the guitar playing over the soft beat of Spencer's drums was really quite pleasant. But it was the touching lyrics and the sweet sound of Leah's voice that actually brought tears to her eyes. She swallowed hard as the dark-haired girl sang a ballad of love and loss, of forgiveness and true friendship. And suddenly Maggie realized that she could learn a lot from these kids, and she recalled the verse about how a little child shall lead them. She glanced up at Jed—was he as moved as she? With satisfaction she noticed how his dark eyes were also misty as he watched his daughter in open admiration. Then the song ended and he turned and looked down on Maggie. His moist eyes glowed as the corners of his mouth turned up, sending an unexpected warm rush through her.

"Thanks for everything, Maggie," he said in a husky voice. "If it wasn't for you, I doubt that any of this would've ever happened."

Her eyes darted heavenward and then she smiled. "You know, I had a whole lot of help, Jed."

"I know." He nodded with a firm chin. "And I think that God has some even better things in store for us."

She laughed. "I think you're right!"